GOLDEN LOCKS AND RIDDLES

DREAMING PRINCESSES, BOOK 4

Books by C. Rae D'Arc

Dreaming Princesses

Dreaming Beauty
Fairest and the Frog
Little Red and the Lumpy Bed
Golden Locks and Riddles

Haunted Romance

Don't Date the Haunted
Don't Marry the Cursed
Don't Dance with Death

* * *

Oz's Haunting Survival Book
From Horror with Love

Dead and Back Again

Specter Inspector

Royal Families of Rezhina

King Rezhnum & Queen Venizhus Reo of Somnus

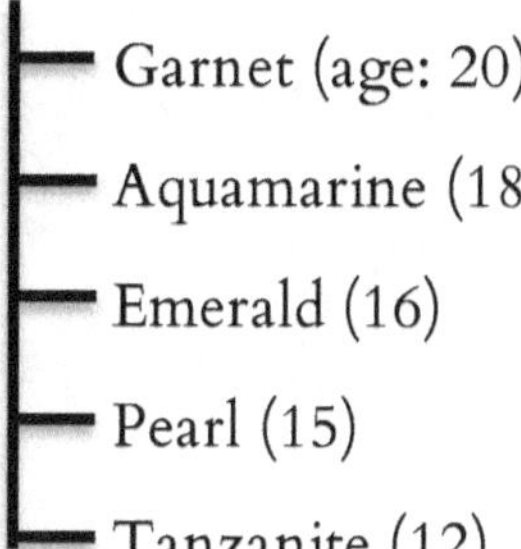

- Garnet (age: 20)
- Aquamarine (18)
- Emerald (16)
- Pearl (15)
- Tanzanite (12)

King Eric & Queen Candice Fashio of Ormio

- Diamond (18)
- Cephas (16)
- Peridot (15)
- Ruby (15)
- Opal (13)

King Leroy & Queen Rhiannon Zhenero of Huiess

- Amethyst (19)
- Sapphire (14)
- Topaz (13)

Golden Locks and Riddles

DREAMING PRINCESSES, BOOK 4

C. RAE D'ARC

ISBN: 978-1-961733-10-7 (paperback)
ASIN: B0DT5QYCT3 (eBook)

Cover design by: Karen Dimmick / ArcaneCovers.com

Published by Bursting Box Publishing
www.burstingboxpublishing.com
www.facebook.com/c.rae.darc
www.instagram.com/craedarc/

To the good men in the world
who support the women in their lives
(no matter how crazy they might seem).

Map of Rezhina Valley

and surrounding kingdoms

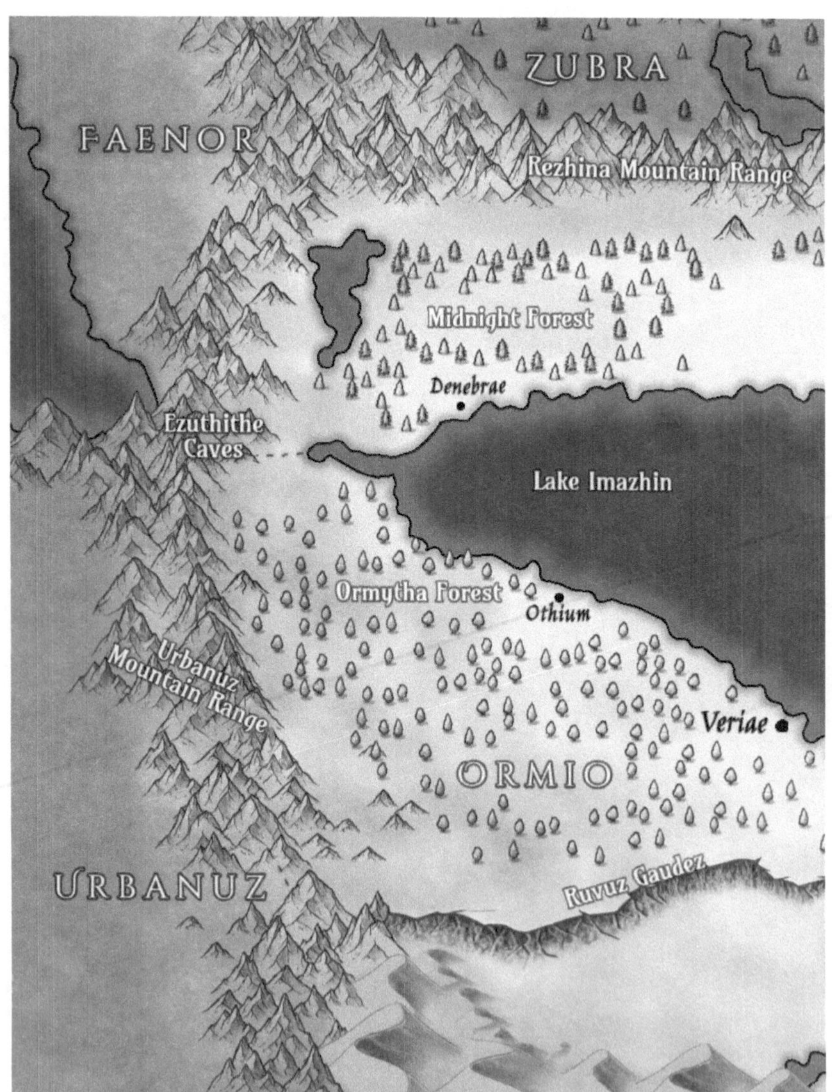

ULDRA
CHAFAN
Sophor Forest
SOMNUS
BRAEDER
Lithus
Somnus
Rehuiess
NOZISLE
HUIESS
Sesso Desert
Remizio
Levamen

Prologue

DIA

Spinning straw into gold had to be one of the most ridiculous scams I'd ever heard, but I needed Prince Stanford to choose me in this stupid competition to impress him. With most of the Somnus princesses under a poisoned sleep and my younger sisters under the same spell, I became desperate enough to accept Riddle Maker's scheme.

For the sake of the whole Rezhina Valley, I needed this trick to work. Who cared if I'd be miserable for the rest of my life? I'd learn to work through it. Anything to protect my people.

There was little for me to do while Riddle Maker swept the small bale of straw out of my cell—I mean, cellar—to exchange with the peddler for a similar sized ball of golden thread.

"Are you sure there's nothing I can do to help?" I asked.

"I got this." Riddle Maker gestured toward the small mat in the corner. "Go get your beauty sleep and rest your worries away. You'll pay me in full later unless you have an answer for my riddle."

I cringed, wishing I could answer his riddle.

Extra irritated, I folded my arms. "You assume I'd be comfortable falling asleep with a man in my room? Riddle Maker, just how many times have women fallen asleep with you present?"

He paused in his straw sweeping. Was he counting? Riddle Maker leaned to smirk at me over his shoulder. "Why, Princess Diamond. Are you saying this would be your first time?"

"Out." I jutted my finger at the hide-away entrance in the cellar, hoping my face wasn't as alarmed as my mind.

"Fine, fine," he said, raising his hands in surrender and stepping outside. "Sheesh. Princesses."

I waited until he was out of sight before curling onto the little mattress. It was hardly large enough for a hound. The decorators of my cell probably hadn't expected me to sleep that night. How could I sleep while spinning an entire bale of straw into gold?

The whole concept was absurd. I put my back to the stone wall and rested my head against the corner. Ten minutes later, Riddle Maker asked if I'd fallen asleep yet. I answered him with a wide-eyed glare, and he ducked back out.

Tired as I was, I barely heard the shuffling of Riddle Maker returning. At least, I assumed it was Riddle

Maker until a scratchy voice asked, "Did someone order some gold?"

I jolted awake as a short and cloaked figure stepped through the secret passageway. They reached under their cloak to pull out a large ball of glittering yellow thread. "Catch," they said, throwing the ball to me. It twirled through the air, catching the light from the dim firelights, trailing its unravelling end. I was never one for sports, and I fumbled as the ball bounced right off my chest and arms. It left a strange residue sticking to my arms and dress.

Riddle Maker shouted from the hide-away doorway, "Who are you? What are you doing here?"

My vision spun as I inhaled the scented residue and attempted to wipe it off. My balance tilted, and my eyelids drooped. What was happening to me?

Riddle Maker confronted the peddler, but they dodged and scampered away with a little girlish yelp. Despite my slumping body, my mind felt alert as I realized what had happened.

I'd been poisoned by Tanzi! Garnet had warned me! She came for me! I needed to…

Riddle Maker asked me something that became fog in my ears. He approached and picked up something from the ground… something shiny.

The fool! Hadn't he spotted the trap? He needed to chase that peddler! Instead, he spent the next second standing on wobbling feet before falling to his knees beside me. No! She was going to escape!

I urged my body to go—to stand—to move—any-thing! No response. It hurt too much to strain my eyes open. I closed them and leaned back into my corner.

"Hey, hey, Princess!" Riddle Maker's hand flopped on my knee. How dare he touch me so intimately?

I forced my eyes open to glare at Riddle Maker. Even glaring took too much energy. The subject of my glare lay on his side beside me, also struggling to keep his eyes open. "We need to stay—wake," he slurred. "Princess… Dia… Hear me?"

"Garnet…" I tried to say more, to tell him to warn her. My strength faded too quickly.

"Garnet? Of Somsss?"

I tried to nod. I thought I nodded. Didn't I nod? Or did I simply dream that I had?

"Right… Get her."

No! The fool! He'd bring her straight to this trap!

The more I struggled to stay awake, the more slippery my consciousness became. The blackness enveloped me.

I loved to dream. Dreams were my only escape from my future burdens of ruling a kingdom at war. So, as I fell endlessly into a dream, I welcomed it with open arms.

I fell asleep thinking golden thoughts, and I dreamed of gold. I splashed into a sea of thick metallic liquid and sank under the surface. It flowed around my fingers, through my blonde hair, and around my dress. Shining hues of orange and yellow filled my vision until I saw them, even when I closed my eyes. There was no swimming. Only drifting against the thick current that weighed heavier and heavier like the responsibilities of ruling a kingdom of worn people who warred with a hardened people.

My feet found the bottom of the golden sea. My legs slipped under me, and I landed on my rump on the sea floor. The golden sea drained into the edges of my consciousness, and my head broke through the surface. I kept my eyes closed, enjoying the sensation of the liquid easing down my shoulders, arms, then slowly disappearing as noises and shapes solidified around me.

I was seated with my usual plate of biscuits when the Somnus Princesses arrived for the Noz Isle Masquerade. They wore masks like the rest of us, but I easily recognized Garnet Reo, the Crown Princess of Somnus, and her four younger sisters. Many of us wore the same mask to these midnight gatherings, making friends recognizable despite the costumes and code names.

Garnet's dress and dragon mask matched her name, trimmed with gold and flowing with grandeur. A woman slid over to meet her, half-dressed for battle. Half-dressed, meaning her purple-dyed suit of armor was missing half of its pieces, revealing her wrists, elbows, and even shoulders. Much more appropriate for dancing and attracting attention than for fighting.

Her "helmet" was shaved to the pieces around her nose and eyes to create her purple masquerade mask.

That would be Amethyst Zhenero, Crown Princess of Huiess, moving with the nimble flow of a warrioress. She took Garnet by the hand and led her to the dance floor to meet some gentleman behind a black horse mask. They smiled and waved to me as they passed. I responded with the same, sitting alone at my table, content as a clam.

My mask mimicked a diamond ring, its oval cut covering my entire round face, mineral dust stuck behind jagged pieces of glass to appear bright and shimmering. My face was surrounded by a frame of tiny rounds of diamond-carved glass, all tied back with a thick golden ribbon that held up my updo.

On Noz Isle, at these midnight masquerades, classes didn't matter. Nationalities didn't matter. Not even time mattered as the music played. We danced until the night became as worn as our shoes. Or, at least, everyone else danced.

I snacked on biscuits beneath my mask, uncaring if the crumbs landed on my shimmering golden dress, if people saw me slouching in my seat, or even if they recognized me as Diamond Fashio, the Crown Princess of Ormio. I almost wished for a certain someone to recognize me.

Instead, Princess Emerald of Somnus pranced over to my table. Would she try convincing me to dance again? That young woman never knew when to quit.

She would dance all night and frequently ask me to join the floor. I always declined, happier at my table and watching everyone else exhaust themselves. I preferred to be a spectator in the sport of romance.

"Gold?" she asked.

"Flora," I answered, using her codename for the anonymous masquerades.

"Did you receive the invitations for my birthday ball next week?"

I smirked behind my mask. "My parents suspect a hidden agenda. Why else would a princess of Somnus invite every royal from both Ormio and Huiess?"

Emer laughed. "Of course, because how could we possibly be friends? According to them, we have had no opportunities to become truly acquainted, and with the war, we should naturally despise anyone from Huiess."

"Exactly," I said, rolling my eyes. "That invitation nearly blew our secret. We would need more than Phoenix's sleeping potions to bypass our night guards if my parents discovered these secret rendezvous with the Huiess princesses."

Emer pinched her lips in worry. "Please tell me that you can come. I want it to be exactly like the balls here, except with our parents."

I nodded. If our parents saw the possibility of the peace and friendships that we knew on Noz Isle, then maybe we could stop the war. "I'll do what I can to persuade my parents. Even if they deny us, my sisters and I are well-practiced at sneaking away to evening balls," I finished with a wink. We'd be there to celebrate her birthday, no matter what.

Emer left with a smile, letting me return to my people-watching. Indeed, I found people-watching highly entertaining and enjoyed the sonders that came with it. I quickly scanned the ballroom for my younger sisters.

My youngest sister, Opal, had found her best friend Topaz of Huiess. They could not be more different in appearance and circumstances, yet their friendship knew no boundaries. The two of them giggled as they crawled under a table for some "secret" meeting.

I found Dot dancing with a young man, grinning widely while Ruby stared from the sidelines. She tapped her foot, impatiently waiting for her turn to dance with the man. Why did my twin sisters always want the same thing at the same time?

I sympathized with Ruby, however, as my eyes found my man of mystery. As usual, he wore a jester's mask that covered all his forehead with white. Large diamond shapes pointed downward over his cheeks— one gold, one black. Thick ribbons curled around his mask, ending with little bells. Even if he had worn a different mask, I would have recognized him from his wavy black hair, shorter height (still tall compared to me), lean build and skin tone that didn't seem to fit perfectly with any of the kingdoms of Rezhina. He was a mix of all three, but he attended every event, suggesting that he lived nearby. Perhaps he was a native of Noz Isle?

That was my most solid guess. I watched as he danced with some unknown woman behind a mouse mask.

A chair rumbled against the floor beside me. I turned and found a new young man with blue-grey eyes, silver hair, and a strong jawline visible around his black horse mask. He was the one Ame had introduced to Garnet earlier.

"This," he asked, "is how Rezhina parties? Do you people ever sleep?"

If his hair color and words weren't enough to call him a foreigner, his accent was. His slight slurring of words reminded me of the traders from Urbanuz beyond the western mountains. I asked, "First time?"

"Yes," he said. "I hope it's fine that I join your observations? I'd feel foolish dancing out there while I barely have my feet beneath me. My legs are still wobbling from the trip over the lake."

I smiled. "I commend you for your wisdom. Most people make utter fools of themselves by trying to blend into the dancing before recognizing what the dances even are. Who invited you?"

"Er…" He shuffled on his seat. "They said that we cannot use our normal names here."

"This is true," I said. "Do you know their masquerade names?"

He shuffled again. "I forgot."

I laughed lightly to express my understanding. "Can you point me to them?"

"Oh, sure. One is… oh, where did she go? I just saw her…Oh! There!" He pointed at Ame.

Unable to suppress my surprise, I turned to the man and examined him closer. Ame had invited him? With his Urbanuz accent, this had to be Huiess's rumored visiting diplomat, Prince Stanford Muli.

I almost had to stop myself from laughing, wondering what he would say if I revealed myself. How would one casually introduce oneself as the heir of his neighbors? However, if he was at Noz Isle, that said something about his thoughts on the war. He enjoyed peace enough to visit this neutral ground for an event that embraced equality in all things.

Regaining my bearings, I said, "Ah, that would be Summer."

"Is not—oh, right, her nickname. You know her then?"

I grinned. "Well enough. Summer has attended these masquerades almost as long as I have. I would even consider Summer one of my closest friends. Then her younger sisters, Winter and Fire, are truly delightful to watch."

"Wherever they went," Stanford muttered, stretching his neck back and forth to find his escorts.

I pointed at the table where Opal and Topaz had hidden. "I saw Winter go under that table with Lucky. Fire is probably outside with Princess."

"Princess?" he asked.

I waved my hand lightly. "She might be the youngest one here. You cannot blame her for her lack of creativity."

My man of mystery danced close to our tables, catching my attention again. He held the hand of his current partner, despite the unnecessary connection to the dance.

He found his lover for the night then?

I turned my face away, ashamed of my own thoughts. No one should captivate my focus as much as he did. Those feelings were logically natural, but impractical. He always danced around with various women until focusing on one to pull away from the party. They always returned before the break of dawn, laughed over some joke, then went their separate ways. Whatever they shared together was a mystery. It embarrassed me how much I wanted to know what they did, how much I wanted to be the woman he chose...

"Excuse me." Stanford yanked me from my daydreams as he stood from his chair and gave me a nod. "I never got your name?"

"Gold," I said, giving my Noz Isle nickname.

"I appreciated your company, Gold, though it seems my escorts are summoning me. Thank you for the conversation and company. I appreciate that you're not the type to prattle on meaninglessly or to guilt me into asking you to dance."

"Is guilt the only reason you would dance with me?"

"What?"

"Sorry." I waved my hand to excuse him. We weren't acquainted enough for banter, but I imagined someday he could make a comfortable friend. Even if that happened, would he have the wit and humor to keep up with mine? Few men did. I liked to imagine impressing my mystery man with my ability to turn a phrase. He obviously appreciated lovely dancers, but I hoped he'd keep me for more than one outing as I'd prove my worth beyond my masked appearance.

The man was a puzzle, and I loved solving puzzles.

* * *

Beeping jarred me from sleep. I lay in bed, struggling to remember where and who I was. The dream had been so vivid, I still remembered it as reality broke through my consciousness.

I'd rather lose my sight or hearing than lose my memory. Fortunately, I knew exactly who and where I was. I was Diana Mason, native of the beautifully chaotic Las Vegas.

PART 1

"And then she lay down upon the bed of the Little, Small, Wee Bear; and that was neither too high at the head, nor at the foot, but just right. So she covered herself up comfortably, and lay there till she fell fast asleep."

- The Story of the Three Bears, by Robert Southey

EMER

For the second time that night and the fourth night in a row, Emer woke in a cold sweat. She sat up on the bench she pretended to call a bed and tried to reorient herself back into reality. Unable to see in the darkness of the state coach, she drew back a window curtain. Clouded moonlight created shadows from the surrounding bare trees.

"You too?" her younger sister whispered from the darkness. Pearl's blanket balled in her fists beneath her chin. She lay beside their older sister, Marin, on the stack of mattresses piled on the carriage floor. Their sleeping arrangements in the stately carriage became a bit cramped as Dot took the bench across from Emer's. They'd relocated their trunks of clothes and meager belongings to the roof every night to make room for the twelve duvets from Dot's previous sleeping arrangement. The mattresses had been miraculously preserved and Marin said they could use the fabric and padding for the impending winter.

"Huh?" Emer asked, keeping her voice down to let Marin and Dot sleep. She glanced left and right, up and down, through the window to make sure the monsters from her dreams were nowhere in sight.

Pearl shuffled uneasily with her blanket. "You also had a nightmare?"

"Yes." Emer released a slow breath, attempting to calm her heart. Staring outside to the Ormytha Forest did little to ease her nerves. Caden and the other men slept beside their fire pit under a cloth covering on the other side, out of sight. Instead, Emer saw only unfamiliar trees and dark mists. She wanted to close the curtain to hide from the outside but was too afraid of becoming blind in the shadows.

Pearl whispered, "Did yours also involve the mære?"

"Uh-huh," she mumbled. Ever since their first encounter with the mære, the monsters had plagued the edges of her dreams. Every night, they became more prominent. Their black scales glimmered from the shadows. Their finned manes and tails swept around corners. And their needle-like teeth… Emer shuddered.

"What did they do in your dream?" Pearl asked. "Did they kill you as they did in mine?"

"No," Emer said, thanking the goddesses. Watching Caden or one of her friends die at the hands of the monsters wasn't any better, but it seemed a bad omen if she and Pearl dreamed of the same death. "Can you ask Lucy to create some dim stars on our ceiling?"

16

"Yes, that would be nice. Lucy?" Pearl addressed her magic. "Could you appear as a soft and dim duo-decim constellation on the coach roof above us?"

Spots of light appeared to match Pearl's descriptions. Emer closed the curtain and lay on her back to stare at the twelve star lights above her. She could pick out the cluster that created the bright eye of the queen and the three stars in a row that resembled her staff. According to Huiessian legends, it was a sword, but Emer preferred the version of the staff as it pointed down toward the constellation of the kneeling knight.

"I miss the stars," a quiet voice said from the other bench. Dot.

"Sorry," Pearl breathed. "Did we wake you?"

"No," she said. "I had a bad dream."

"About the mære?" Emer asked.

"No. About Ruby."

Silence.

What could Emer say? *Sorry we couldn't save your twin in time?* Dot had said that Ruby chose to stay in her dreams, but that didn't make Emer feel any less guilty about failing to wake her.

"In Washington," Dot said, referring to the strange land of her dream, "we didn't see the stars much between the mountains, forests, and regular rain. But in Big Spring, Texas, with no mountains or forests… you could see from horizon to horizon. Every night, that big open sky was filled with stars. I didn't recognize any of them." Her voice choked at the end. Pearl

17

reached over to hold her hand, and Dot squeezed back.

"How about this?" Emer tried. "Caden said these permeating mists originate around Noz Isle and are part of Tanzi's curse on the land. That should mean that after her curse is removed, the mists should clear. Then we will have our own stars to enjoy again."

"Yes," Pearl added. "That will be nice, right? And until then, I can mimic our constellations with Lucy. Would you like that, Dot?"

Dot sniffled and mumbled, "Yes, thanks."

They whispered words of kindness and comfort to one another until Pearl and Dot found their sleep again. Emer lay awake, staring at Pearl's stars. Maybe her nightmares wouldn't return a third time in one night. There was a saying, a favorite of Opal's, "Third time's the charm."

Emer closed her eyes and tried to picture the youngest Ormio princess. According to Dot, Garnet had continued toward Veriae to warn the rest of the royal family. However, according to Caden's research, Veriae had been destroyed. Yet his notes also indicted there was a disturbance in Veriae similar to the briar of thorns that grew around Emer while she slept. Did that mean one of the Rezhina princesses lay sleeping there?

Emer fell asleep with a prayer to the goddesses that they wouldn't be too late again.

When Emer woke, it was blessedly to the morning light and without more nightmares. Marin and Pearl had already left the coach, and Dot lay with her back to Emer. Her shortness of breath and occasional sniffle suggested her wakefulness, though she remained unresponsive to Emer's soft queries.

Throwing on an overdress and wrapping Dot with her own warm blanket, she stepped out to give the Ormio princess some alone time. As soon as the latch closed behind her, she wondered if she'd made the right decision to leave her alone.

While Marin and Pearl had seemed happy to wake from their poisoned dreams, Emer considered Dot's experience closer to her own. She had woken as the first of her family, discovering that her parents and everyone she knew had died during her hundred-harvest absence, her sisters were missing, her beloved city was destroyed and abandoned, and her homeland had fallen entirely to Tanzi's rule.

On top of that, they'd failed to save Ruby. The twins had been together since birth, making Dot's loneliness all the more severe.

Finding Pearl at the fire pit, Emer sat on the side of her that wasn't occupied by the ever-present former Prince Mica of Zubra. Her sister's long black hair was braided back into a thick tail revealing her pale face, red lips, and deep brown eyes. Her pink gown was a hand-me-down that was ten sizes too large for her, yet by pinching the fabric up and back, she managed to show off her feminine curves.

She held hands with Mica, a man whose round eyes, face, and dimples made him look younger than his eighteen years. However, his premature balding reversed the appearance of youth.

"Pearl," Emer asked, "would you mind checking on Dot in the state coach? I think she needs some company after losing… so much." Even still, it was hard to speak aloud about the loss of Ruby. Pearl didn't seem to notice or mind as she readily agreed to help and returned to the coach. It was hard to remain sad around Pearl. Even before she gained the ability to control light, she had a brightness about her.

Footsteps across the fallen leaves announced the arrival of her older sister Marin with her husband, Ranae. Marin—officially Aquamarine—was a lean woman despite her rounded face, and she kept her long black hair braided up into two buns over her ears to hide them from the autumn's morning chill. Marin loved to dress for the occasion, whether it was hanging around the docks in a plain kirtle or dancing in an extravagant bliaut at a masquerade. With their limited supplies, she seemed dissatisfied with her simple turquoise gown as she lifted her hem to step over a log. Their limited shelters of a single tent and state coach separated Marin from sleeping beside her husband, but Emer was grateful for her mothering presence after her nightmares.

20

Ranae offered Marin a hand in assistance, and she took it with a smile. As the former Admiral of the Somnus Navy, Ranae was a tall man with his dark brown hair tied back into a low tail. Emer had a hard time imagining his large and muscular build as the little amphibian that Marin had dreamed him to be.

Emer's heart lightened to see the man behind them. Prince Caden Seaver of Uldra limped, using his sword sheath as a cane. He and the sheath were decorated in his kingdom's colors of white and green with gold trimmings. He was only two years older than Emer's sixteen harvests, though he kept a well-maintained beard around his angled jawline. When his sky-blue eyes met Emer's green, he smiled, sending Emer's heart into another leap.

Leo Bahr, the prince of the fallen kingdom of Braeder, brought up the rear with a wrapped dead goat. He was easily the largest in their group, built like a man who could wrestle a small bear and win. He wore his thick brown hair loose to his shoulders, adding to the mane of his full beard.

"But if you hurt yourself more," Leo was saying, "you'll never recover."

"I know," Caden grumbled. "But I can't stand by, useless."

"Useless?" Ranae scoffed. "Since when have brains been useless? I had several people on my ship who could barely hold a sword, but they had other necessary skills, such as navigating, cooking, or strategizing."

Caden frowned with defense. "I can do more than 'barely hold a sword.' I might not be a hunter like Leo, but I could hold my own in a battle. I was trained in duels before the ogres attacked Uldra. Then it was two years of battle training."

"That," Marin said, "was before you were tackled by an ogre, shot with an arrow, then bitten by a wolf. These last couple of weeks have been rough on your body."

The injured prince shrugged. "When adventure calls."

Emer could remain silent no longer. She stood and folded her arms at the man she loved. "No, Caden. You are hereby sentenced to a full moon cycle of coach riding."

Marin raised her eyebrows with both surprise and challenge. "If you want him to heal entirely, he needs at least two full moons."

"What?" Caden protested like she'd betrayed him. "What about Tucker? Only I can ride him, and with Princess Peridot, we have an extra person. Also, who knows what the moon looks like beyond this mist?"

"Last night was a full moon," Leo said, laying the dead goat on the ground and unwrapping it for cleaning. "Plus, if Dot has an influence over animals, she might convince your horse to be less of a mule."

Before Caden could argue more, Pearl exited the coach with Dot. Dot's eyes went directly to Leo, then dropped at the carcass. She waved her hands with quick gestures.

What was she saying? And to whom was she saying it?

When Dot finished with her hand signals, Leo picked up with curt movements. His signs weren't as fluid as Dot's, but he'd clearly been practicing sign language… sometime when no one had seen him.

Caden also noticed their movements and asked Emer's silent question. "What are you saying? You know you're not deaf anymore."

"What was that?" Leo shouted back.

Caden grunted. "I guess you've always been hard of hearing. Care to share your conversation with the rest of us?"

Without even pausing in his gestures to Dot, Leo growled, "No."

"Oh?" Caden asked, eyebrows high. "So, I assume you're signing sweet nothings to each other?"

Leo's neck and ears burned red as he glowered at Caden.

Dot cleared her throat. "No, we just have, um, things to discuss from our dreams. We can discuss it another time, Leo."

They each turned their own way, with Dot returning to the coach and Leo sheepishly continuing to clean the goat, ignoring Caden's probing questions.

Something was off between Dot and Leo. Not necessarily wrong, just… off.

Emer analyzed Leo, trying to spot the difference. After she'd woken, she'd been in love and then argumentative with Caden. Pearl remained in her state of young-love with Mica, doting on him as much as he doted on her.

Leo had woken Dot, but their relationship seemed… confused. They could speak a secret language of hand signs and—unlike Mica and Caden—had shared dreams before Dot woke. Yet they barely spoke. They hardly even looked in one another's directions since every glance or simple touch caused extreme blushing. The hunter prince hadn't been afraid to make his opinions known before. Now, he was as silent as Shinópu had been.

Emer released a heavy sigh from considering the Chafan Prince. Shinópu was gone. Dot had confirmed Leo's account of his death. The Shino of Texas had dreamed of Shinópu in Uldra while cleansing the capital of ogres. He'd died a hero. Yet, if their dreams were to be believed, he lived happily in Texas with Ruby.

Emer reflected on her time in England, wondering if she'd known she had a choice, would she have stayed in England?

Sweeping her gaze across her sisters and new friends, she reaffirmed her decision. What would have happened to Marin and Pearl if Emer and Caden hadn't been there when they woke? She was needed in Rezhina.

Chapter 2

EMER

"Caden?" Emer asked, sitting beside him at the smoking fire pit. "Do Dot and Leo seem… off?"

He rubbed the back of his neck nervously and retrieved his notes on Dot. Most of the charcoal words looked fresh.

He must have stayed up late again to add everything we witnessed after waking her.

"Oh!" Caden exclaimed. "Dot's magic involves animals, right? She told the animals to fight the mære, and they followed her commands. Were they signing to each other about the dead goat? She realizes that we need to eat something, right?"

Marin overheard from across the campsite and folded her arms. "Meat is not necessary for life."

Leo grumbled and shot scowls at everyone. "If you're all going to gossip about us anyway, yes, this dead goat was the topic of our last signing conversation. But I'm the best hunter in the group. What does she expect me to do? Not provide? I thought that was what she wanted. That was why I went to Texas…”

He drifted back into silence. Caden pestered him for more information until Leo glared at him and threateningly raised his blood-covered gutting knife.

While Emer understood Dot’s sorrow for the goat, it didn’t explain the shyness and lack of affections between Dot and Leo. But, based on Leo’s glares at Caden’s questions, if Emer wanted answers, they would need to come from Dot.

Over the last few days of traveling between Othium and Veriae, Dot had revealed little about her dreams of a strange land called the United States of America. According to her and Leo, it was an entire ocean away from England, where Emer, Marin, and Pearl had dreamed. While she’d lost her hearing, she’d also lost her mobility, cursed by a persistent pebble beneath her.

Between those two factors, she had admitted, “My dream was a lot less adventurous than yours. I was confined to bed and miserable almost the entire time. I’d rather not dwell on it. I miss Ruby.”

Emer had to agree. She’d preferred her own dreams of exploring the beauties of England with the Honorables Caden and Mica, even if she never felt anything more than wool and became numb at the end. Still, she sensed that Leo and Dot weren’t telling them everything. Did Dot have secrets? She could easily keep them with her new knowledge of sign language.

Leo had gained the knowledge too, but cracking information from him required a prybar.

Emer returned to the coach, but paused when she heard hushed voices behind the door. Their allies were too few to keep secrets from one another. Pressing her ear to the door, Emer picked out the voices of Dot and Pearl inside.

Dot groaned. "I need to find Dia. I can't stand the thought of her staying asleep forever like Ruby. I need her here. I need to talk to her."

"Dot," Pearl's sweet voice said. "You are not alone here. We will find Opal and Dia, though in the meantime, I always considered each of you as closely as my sisters. Surely, Emer will say the same. You also have Leo's support. I have not known him long, though his loyalty to you is undeniable. He was most eager to find you and Ruby."

"Yeah, but I can't talk to him about what to do when he's the problem."

"Problem?" Pearl asked. Emer leaned in closer. Was this the reason she and Leo acted oddly around one another?

"It's… I need to talk to Dia."

"Dot," Pearl said, and Emer imagined her taking Dot's hand for reassurance. "It is better not to wait to sort out your feelings."

Dot released a long breath and spoke extra quietly. "I…I feel a connection to animals now. I can sense what's in the surrounding woods, where they are, and what they want. I know Leo's a hunter—he was in the dream too, but seeing him with the goat…I couldn't sense the goat. It hurt more than I thought it would."

Pearl didn't respond right away, pondering the issue, then said, "I cannot say that I understand your experience. My magic is different. Though, perhaps you can discuss this with Marin. She abstains from eating meat and has fought to protect our environment since the first time we visited the butcher."

"Maybe," Dot said. "And there might be another matter I need to discuss with her. I'd rather talk to Dia about it, but Marin's the only one with the experience."

"What experience would that be?"

The coach creaked as Dot shifted weight. "In our dream, Leo and I were engaged."

Emer's jaw dropped. If she had been holding something, she would have dropped that too and spoiled her spying.

Pearl, however, innocent as she was, asked, "Engaged in what?"

"Marriage. I had a ring, and he was working for my—Ruby's dad in Texas as a way to provide for our future together."

Pearl squealed. "How exciting! Where do you want your wedding hosted? I suppose everything has changed, and you have not yet seen any venues. Oh, I see why you must speak with Marin and wake Dia. Naturally, you want their support and opinions."
28

"Pearl," Dot said. "It was only a dream. I have no ring."

"Oh. We can make you a new one."

"It's not that simple," Dot said, and Emer agreed. If Caden from England had proposed to her, she would have required it again from Caden of Uldra. Dot continued, "Other than signing, Leo has hardly spoken a full sentence to me since I woke. I think it's because he's equally unsure whether to continue our engagement."

Pearl hummed with thought. "Yes, he spoke little before waking you unless it was to demand his opinion be heard. Also, he was shaken by the sight of his brother."

"Chase? Chase is here too? In my dreams, he was in San Antonio."

"Here, he was presumed dead until last week when we caught him attacking us."

"Attacking?" Dot asked. "No, from the vague memories I have from Dorothy and everything Leo told me, Chase was a beloved younger brother. Maybe a little reckless at times, but he had a good heart."

"We cannot say why he attacked us," Pearl said. "Emer believes that the men from our dreams are not exactly the same as the men who wake us. Though it may explain Chase's differing characteristics, I beg to differ. Mica is equally sweet and wonderful regardless of his location. I believe Leo will be equally eager to provide for your future here."

"Maybe," Dot said. "Either way, I want to find Dia. We should help the others pack so we can leave right away."

The coach creaked as they stepped toward the door, and Emer hastened away, hoping not to look like an eavesdropper. Her hopes were dashed when Dot exited the coach and caught her with wide eyes and red cheeks. Pearl offered Dot a reassuring pat before skipping away to help Mica with packing.

"Forgive me," Emer said, pausing Dot from walking away. "I overheard your discussion with Pearl."

Dot's face cringed with unease. "How much?"

"Enough to agree with your decision to wait until we wake Dia to decide how to move forward with Leo."

Her face flushed.

"Even though Prince Leo has the memories of your Texan Leo—"

"Washington," Dot said. "We were Washingtonians in Texas. Sorry, that's not important. Please go on."

"Yes, well, they grew up in different situations. This Leo grew up as a prince to a kingdom that was attacked by ogres for several years before losing the war. His experiences made him the man he is, but—based on Caden and Mica's experiences—he loves you as much as he did in Texas. I may not be Dia, but until you can receive her advice, I suggest you and Leo take things easy. Consider your courtship at the beginning stages. Test your friendship and compatibility without expectations, then see where it takes you."

Dot nodded slowly. "I can do that."

"Also," Emer added, "I have a connection with plants, but I still eat fruits and vegetables. I need to ask the plants for permission before harvesting them, then I encourage them to grow to replace what I take. Perhaps you can become a vegetarian like Marin, but… I think there are ways to use our powers respectfully."

Dot nodded again. "Maybe. As much as I hated the death of that goat, the smell of cooking meat still tempts me." Her mouth twisted with a paradoxical grimace and grin. "Thanks for understanding. It seems the men aren't the only ones who changed a little."

"What do you mean?"

Dot nudged Emer with her elbow. "You. You were always trying too hard to act like a leader before. Now, you don't try. You just lead."

Emer smiled at the inferred compliment, but her insides squirmed. Was that how Dot had perceived her from before? As someone who tried too hard? And now, had Emer assumed a leadership position? She hadn't meant to seize control. She'd simply been the first to wake and gain experience with the ogres and Caden's research. Marin was the second to wake and the oldest princess in the group, but Emer found herself reluctant to let Marin make all the decisions. Marin wanted to be more conservative with their powers, and she wasn't as invested in helping Uldra in its war against the ogres.

The thought made Emer mentally cringe. Did that mean she was tainted with the same power-hungry trait as her sister Tanzi?

She forcibly swept those thoughts away and linked her arm through Dot's. "Come then. Shall we ensure the proper respect given for our goat?"

They were the last to join for breakfast, but there was plenty of space for them. Leo's troubled attitude had given him a wide berth, and Caden's overflowing research pages created an island around him. Emer smirked, picked up a few that he wasn't looking at, sat in their place, and spread her dress wide to create a table for his notes and her plate of food. She eyed Dot and Leo as they timidly spoke after swallowing and signed after taking bites.

Caden raised an eyebrow. "So, that's convenient. And speaking of convenient things inspired by dreams, I had an idea about improving your vine phone."

"Oh?" Emer asked. Her potted vine phone wrapped its two-hundred meter length back and forth across the length of the state coach. Its two speaker ends had served them well during the wolf attack, though its weight imbalanced the carriage.

"What if," Caden said, "you took two branches from the same tree, planted one in one area and another somewhere else. Could you connect them through

32

the roots, like when you connected with them to find Ruby?"

Emer reflected on the two times she connected so deeply with the plants that she mentally traveled through their roots, jumping between underground connections to sprout into the trees that recognized the odd wolf activity around Ruby. Except, she hadn't successfully located Dot because she had been in the city, disconnected from the forest.

"It works best," she said, "in the forest and places with many plants, but we could give it a try. Perhaps if I propagate a branch, it will connect best with its sibling."

Caden nodded and drew schematics in his notes' margins. "You'd need to do the planting to weave your magic through it, but once they're planted, any-one should be able to use them, right? Just like the vine phone?"

"Theoretically."

With everyone's breakfast finished, Emer helped Caden to pack up his notes and sat with him on the carriage while Dot convinced Tucker to allow Ranae and Marin to ride him instead.

On the road again, Caden and Emer picked up their conversation on ways to improve her vine phones.

"Actually," Mica pitched in, "Pearl and I have been talking about how to create a camera. We'd need a box with a pinhole and a mirror to start. The trickiest part will be finding the right material for printing the picture."

"Imagine how exciting it will be," Pearl said, grinning. "If we create pictures of us together, awake, and doing magic, how it may spread the word of our cause and stir the people into action."

"That's not a bad idea," Caden said, "but creating flyers requires a lot of paper." He gestured to his note-covered stacks.

Emer rolled her eyes. "Fine. I will ask the plants if they can help us to make paper."

Mica and Pearl grinned. "Actually, you'll need to be more specific about the photography paper. It will need a weaving of chemicals to accept an imprint of light, then dry to hold the imprint without gathering more when exposed to daylight."

Dot shook her head at the concept. "Is that how cameras worked? I had one on my phone, filling my gallery with pictures of birds, but I never printed any of them."

"That sounds complicated," Marin said. "I imagine the boat engine that we make will be far simpler."

Ranae grinned at his wife. "I cannot wait to sail the lake again." Then his face dampened. "If we can pass the mære."

As if the mere mention of the creatures passed a current through them, everyone shuddered, winced, or twitched. Caden made a second twitch toward the forest as an arrow slammed into one of the carriage horses.

The horse released a terrible cry as Leo shouted for everyone to "Take cover!"

Their party scattered off the pathway and into the trees.

Emer looked back at the direction of the shooter. "Trees, hide us!"

Branches lowered around them and thickened until a leafy wall separated them from the attacker, but not before Emer spotted him. A large young man dodged between the trees, barely visible in his green and brown patchwork clothing.

"It's that bowman," Caden grumbled while rubbing his left shoulder. He was still sore from the arrow that had pierced him there.

The young bowman loosed his arrow and had another one docked as Ranae shouted in pain.

Marin echoed Ranae's shout as his torso bled from a grazing.

"Admiral!" Emer shouted, jumping from the carriage and running to their aid. Caden called after her and limped to follow.

The bowman loosed his next arrow, and Emer barely had time to see it flying toward her.

Her vision was thrown upward as a body shoved her to the ground. An arm wrapped around her head, protecting her from the fall, as a masculine grunt sounded in her ear. As soon as she had her balance again, she sat up. Caden lay beside her, his right arm stretched against the ground as her temporary pillow, the other arm bleeding from a deep gash.

"Caden!"

She couldn't help him until they were out of the line of fire. Turning back to the bowman, she found him aiming a new arrow at her chest.

"Chase!"

The bowman jerked and turned his arrow on Leo. His hold quivered. "How do you know my name?"

Leo frowned. "You're my brother. Don't you recognize me?"

The bowman snarled. "I have no brothers. My family was slaughtered by ogres years ago. I serve none but the queen now, and you are all traitors to this kingdom."

"Chase," Leo said, "none of that's true. We fled to Uldra, but we survived. Mother and Father are alive, and they miss you. We all missed you. We thought you were dead."

"No, you're dead!"

Chase's arrow shook. He released it, but it flew wide and missed Leo. The young man fled as Leo called after him.

"Ranae," Marin cried. "How bad is it? Emer! We need some healing moss!"

Emer sat up to survey their situation. "Is anyone else hurt?"

"We're fine," Mica said, riding back with Pearl. He blinked hard and rubbed his eyes.

"Sorry," Pearl murmured. "I assumed that if he could not see us, then he could not attack us."

"Sure," Mica said. "It seemed to work, but you blinded me, too. Could you warn me next time you create a flash-bomb?"

"A what?"

"I'll explain later. Caden, why are you always the one bleeding?"

"Honestly, why is it always you?" Emer muttered in agreement before beginning her chant to grow healing moss.

"This horse needs medical aid," Dot said, unharnessing the first wounded warrior. "Oh no, does it hurt that much to walk?" She spoke quietly to ease the animal as Emer grew moss and Marin clarified water for cleaning the human and animal wounds. Leo kept watch in case his brother returned while Pearl grabbed rags from the coach to use as wraps and tourniquets.

They were nearly finished wrapping everyone when a thundering of hooves reached their ears.

Leo squinted in the distance. "Riders?"

"No," Dot said with a rising smile. "They're wild."

"Who?" Caden asked before a large herd of mixed horse breeds crashed through the trees.

"This horse is too injured to pull a coach and travel long hours with us, but I couldn't simply release it to the wild. Horses need herds for protection. Also, I wonder if any of the herd might be interested in joining us."

Marin beamed almost as brightly as Pearl. "Oh, Dot! What a wonderful idea!"

Dot pointed at three different horses; a smaller one and two sturdy types. "The smallest is ready for an adventure to meet new friends. She'll do well on the coach." Pointing at the other two, she said, "Those two are eager for a challenge and hope to learn new skills with capable masters. They'll do well with riders. Leo, did you want a horse?"

His neck shaded red. "Thanks. I've missed mine ever since Shinópu left."

Emer and Caden shared a sad look at the reminder of their lost friend. "We should continue onward," Emer said. "We cannot lose anyone else."

Chapter 3

OPAL

I would have done anything to fit in. Some people wanted to be the extremes, like the smartest or most beautiful. Not me. I wanted to be just right.

My sisters loved the spotlight. Dia wanted to be the cleverest and had no problem proving it to others. Ruby and Dot often argued over which of them was the prettiest. As twins, I thought it was a dumb argument and refused to offer any opinions on the matter. I didn't like choosing sides. I preferred sticking to the middle for balance.

As the youngest of my family, I despised people's habit to give me the smallest of anything. The smallest food portion, the littlest seat, the tiniest toys… etc. I didn't want the biggest of anything either. I just didn't want to be left with less simply because I was born a year later. As if I had asked for it.

Not that I would ever say anything to ask for more. That would be too embarrassing to request more than I was given. I preferred to wear my lucky bracelets, rings, necklaces, or hair accessories. Dia said that things couldn't be lucky, but ever since I started wearing my opal jewelry, people stopped giving me smaller portions. Coincidence? I thought not.

When I was poisoned, it had taken me completely by surprise. Mostly. I'd had a dreadful feeling all day, choosing to wear every single piece of lucky jewelry I owned. Maybe it was too much. My fingers stretched with my rings on every finger. There was no such thing as a quiet moment when wearing six bracelets on one arm and seven on the other. My neck weighed heavily with my bulk of necklaces, and my hair was a mess between my collection of lucky pins.

After the entire day of suffering from curious looks, I removed each piece and crawled tiredly into bed. I quickly realized my error of climbing onto Dia's mattress, but there was nothing wrong with her bed. In fact, it felt just right after sitting on a too hard chair while eating too cold porridge for dinner.

The only warning of poison was Garnet's presence at the Veriae fortress, alerting us of the state of Ruby and Dot. Then there was the nightmare.

There was no "drifting" off to sleep that night. As soon as I closed my eyes, sleep slammed into me, knocking me unconscious to the world while my dreams came alive. I lay on my back with no light to see.

Movement in the darkness caught my eye. How? There could only be shadows if there was light, yet somehow these shadows were extra dark.

The darkness shifted. Were there two shadow beings? Three? One towered over me like a giant bear, while another faced me at my own level. My breathing quickened as they loomed closer and closer. Desperate to keep them away, I began kicking, clawing, and screaming. The shadows growled like angry bears. The smaller one reached for me with a clawed hand of black scales. It grabbed my shoulder and shook me.

"Hey, are you sleeping?"

I woke up with a little scream, raising my face from my arms folded over a wooden table. Surprised by my odd clothing, I took a moment to analyze myself. I wore a yellow long-sleeve shirt made of the softest material, overlapping in the front with buttons. I also wore pants like the warriors of Huiess, except mine were blue. I shuffled a little, uncomfortable with the fabrics against my legs despite their incredible stretchy softness. A stiff indentation on my face indicated that I'd fallen asleep in the exact position to imprint my sleeve button on my cheek. Lucky me.

I surveyed my surroundings, finding myself in a massive outdoor pavilion, floored with smooth stone like hardened clay and lined with ten tables, connected to benches on each side. I sat at one of the tables with a broom leaning against the edge. Was I supposed to be sweeping?

A young man snickered as he drew back his hand from my shoulder. He'd been the one to grab me? He held one of his own brooms.

He was a handsome young man and was maybe two years older than my thirteen harvests. He stared at me with light brown eyes curtained by shaggy and thick brown hair. He wore a simple shirt over his muscled figure.

Normally, being caught sleeping in public would have embarrassed me to no end, especially to be caught by a handsome boy. For some reason, I didn't care one bit. Huh. Maybe because some back part of my brain recognized that I was still sleeping. This was a dream. A very, very realistic dream in an unfamiliar place with a handsome boy.

He blushed a little, as if embarrassed to be caught looking at me while I "woke." He flashed a nervous smile and waved in front of my face as if to test my vision.

"Earth to Oprah?"

"Who are Earth and Oprah?"

"Funny," he said without a hint of humor. "You keep spacing out like you don't know what we're doing or why we're doing it."

"What are we doing?" I asked.

"We're supposed to be cleaning the campsite."

"And why are we doing it?"

He frowned at me. "Because it needs to be clean before we go home for the weekend and our final group of campers next week. But yeah, it's a bit ridiculous. We're sweeping outside. What's the point? It'll only get dirty again with the next wind gust."

"Just my luck," I said. I was asleep, and this was a dream. I couldn't escape from chores even in my sleep?

"Oprah," he laughed. "I know we're just volunteers, and we're not getting paid, but this is—"

"Why do you keep calling me Oprah?"

His eyebrows meshed together. "Because that's your name?"

"No, it's Opal. What's yours?"

"Chase. We've known each other these past seven weeks, and you're only now learning my name?"

"You were calling me the wrong name," I shot back.

"Ah-uhh…" He stumbled on his words. "Did you hit your head or something? You're acting different."

"I feel different." Gone were my worries of acting just the right way and the pressure to say just the right words. I was dreaming. Dream Me had no inhibitions because dreams had no real consequences. I could do whatever I wanted, and I definitely did not want to sweep a pavilion. "Days are too short to waste. Come on, Chase. I never get to try sweets in my dreams, but I have the feeling this strange and vivid dream is different. I want to try everything."

He didn't move, but continued to stare dumbfounded at me. Real Me never would have been so bold to grab a man in Ormio, but Dream Me wanted to jolt Chase out of his stupor. Taking hold of his arm was enough to tell me that Chase was more than a handsome face. His solid arms verified his physique.

"Come on," I urged. "Is there a sweet shop nearby?"

"Ah-uh, hold on. We're in the middle of the woods. We can't just walk to the nearest IT'SUGAR."

"Fine, we'll take a horse. Let's go."

Chase laughed. "A horse? You're that desperate to skip out of sweeping?"

I pulled on his arm a little more.

"Fine," he relented. "We only had a couple more duties, and I've been wanting to visit Kilwins, anyway."

He led me through the pavilion and down a well-worn path to a paved place with rows upon rows of strange enclosed carriages. Chase stretched out his hand and clicked on a small device. A carriage responded with a beep and flashing red lights. How had that worked?

Leading me to the beeping, flashing carriage, I stepped up and peered into its interior through its massive and smooth windows. It wasn't the largest among the carriages, but had plenty of space for the two of us. There were three seats in the back, but Chase gestured for me to sit up front with him. Hopping inside, I marveled again at its leather materials, shapely seats, and… buttons? What did they all do?

44

While Real Me would have taken a few minutes to gather the courage to ask, Dream Me went ahead and pushed all of them. Real Me squirmed at my brazenness and was relieved when nothing happened. Dream Me was disappointed.

Chase motioned for me to buckle in, which seemed odd. I'd never known carriages that required restraints.

He inserted a key, and the carriage growled to life. Numbers and dials illuminated behind the wheel, and warm air rushed into the cabin from little vents. The carriage moved without horses or any visible help.

"Is this thing alive?" I asked.

"Barely," Chase muttered. "My parents gave it to me, knowing it was on its last leg. They expect me to run it to the ground."

I stared, a little horrified. Was that how he treated his beasts of burden? He checked a few indicators, pulled a lever, and flicked a switch. "Let's go."

He held two buttons, and the side windows lowered into the door itself, welcoming the cooler, shady air. He said something about "rolling the windows up when the air conditioning kicks in," but I was too busy examining all the little buttons and knobs. Was this an animal or machine? I analyzed his double-checking and almost nervous movements as he made the carriage move forward.

"Are you alright?" I asked. "You seem like you aren't sure what you're doing."

"I–um, don't have my official license yet. Only my permit."

He needed government permission to use one of these beastly carriages? Huh. "No time like the present to learn," I said. "Let's go!"

He gulped heavily, then rolled us away from the other resting carriages. His control with the carriage was jerky, like an untrained horse, lurching forward and stopping too quickly. Once we reached a highway, Chase was tenser than ever, checking the mirrors and twisting his neck to see behind us.

"Chase?"

"Sorry, this is only my fourth time on the freeway. I drove down here with my brother at the beginning of the summer, but long drives are different from city drives."

I stared out the window at the passing scene beyond the road, as the low forest gave way to a great city with buildings that stood tall against the skyline. I realized for the first time how flat this dream land was. The "mountains" we'd been camping in had been mere hills. We were surrounded by clear blue skies as far as the eye could see. We were also surrounded by hundreds of beastly carriages driving beside us and past us. I gaped as we passed a large green town sign. My neck could barely follow it as we zipped by.

"I've never gone this fast before!"

I stuck my head out the window and flinched into the wind. Chase laughed from the driver's seat. He might have said something, but I couldn't hear it over the rushing air. I sat back in my seat with my hair pushed back and my face stiff.

"What did you say?" I asked.

"What are you, a dog?" he laughed.

"What makes you say that?"

"You stuck your head out the window."

"And dogs do that?"

"Yeah, don't you—" He paused as someone moved into the lane in front of us, forcing Chase's attention back to the road. "Never mind."

Why did only dogs stick their heads out of windows? What were dogs doing inside carriages? In Ormio, dogs were never allowed in carriages, always left to run beside the horses. If Ruby had her way, she'd probably bring the dogs inside to play with them during the trip.

Then again, the carriages of Ormio never went this fast. The dogs wouldn't be able to keep up. I almost put my head outside again, but the window slid upward.

"The air conditioning's cool enough," Chase said as if in explanation, but his words still confused me. "We don't need the windows open anymore."

He drove us into the depths of the city with me craning my neck to find the tops of the buildings. We pulled into another area where more beastly carriages slept, and Chase put the creature to rest.

We stepped outside and any of my questions for clarification were lost. A road of black stretched before us, utilized by more speeding carriages. Turning back to the building beside us, I couldn't see the top without stepping away. With a break in the passing of carriages, I ran across the road.

"Oprah—uh, Opal!" Chase ran after me with much more caution. As soon as I was across, I wasn't sure which sight was more magnificent. The sheer height of the buildings, or the park that greeted me below. I counted the windows of the tallest building to estimate its height. I couldn't see all of them between the balconies, but there were at least twenty-five levels. I'd never known any buildings in all of Rezhina to be so tall!

I grinned at my luck to dream of such fantasies. Turning back to the park below, my view was largely blocked by trees. I needed to see more of it. A set of stone stairs led me down to a path between cultivated trees, ferns, and flowers. The path stretched beside a road of water. Large and brightly colored rafts floated down the dark green waters, hedged with manicured gardens.

"Wow," Chase said, stepping beside me. "So this is San Antonio's River Walk? No wonder people kept telling me to check it out."

Was that what this place was called?

Chase gestured down the walkway. "We can walk along the river for a few blocks before going back up to the main road for Kilwins."

Chapter 4

OPAL

The river walk was like no other walkway I'd ever seen. We crossed over the cultivated river with a little bridge made of some blue metal, then walked along, frequently meeting and passing others on their journeys. I waved to everyone, receiving confused looks between the occasional smile and return wave. Many of the leafy trees that we passed reminded me of home with their wide leaves and outreaching branches. A few trees, however, were completely bare trunks until they flowered at the top, high above our heads. Maybe that was to keep people from climbing them? I wanted to try it anyway, but my stomach gurgled with a reminder of our mission to Kilwins.

We continued along the river, passing under bridges, around gardens, and back up some stone stairs to the black road. We came out not far from where we started, but the buildings weren't as tall.

Chase stepped up to a pole on the street corner and pushed a button. I walked past him, and he grabbed me, holding me back. One of those beastly carriages turned by two seconds later. I may or may not have been right in its path if Chase hadn't stopped me.

"And that," he said, "is why we use crosswalks." He gestured to a little black box across the road with a red hand. What a morbid image of a bloody hand, telling us to "Stop, or else."

I stood and waited at the corner with Chase as fewer carriages roared past. A crowd began to gather around us as we waited together for the bloody hand to give us permission. On the opposite side of the street, a similar crowd gathered. The opposing stand-off reminded me of the border disputes with Huiess.

Real Me would have kept my thoughts to myself, but Dream Me wanted to act out a rare daydream to be like Ame. As soon as there was a break in the carriages passing, I bellowed at the other side, "You think you can cross to our side?"

"Opal, what—"

"You think you can just walk over here? You think you can cross to our side without us noticing? We see you!"

The people on the sidewalk behind me stared like I was a loon. Not that the other side would notice their subtle expressions. For all they knew, the people behind me stared at me as their leader. Indeed, the opposite side shuffled uneasily, glancing between themselves and muttering.

Looking behind myself for a cue, I read the building sign and continued, "We of the Chamber of
Commerce have gathered here today to take back our
street! The moment that bloody hand lets us go, we
are charging over there and coming for you!"

"Opal!" Chase half muttered and half laughed.

The bloody hand disappeared, changing to a white
image of a person walking. I marched forward at the
head of the people crossing and punched my fist into
the air. "Charge!"

More than a few people on the opposite side of the
street bolted in the other direction. Apparently, they'd
cross the street another way or another time.

Chase burst into laughter behind me. He was the
only one who didn't give me a wide space. I joined his
laughter when we reached the other side, linking my
arm through his for support.

He escorted me all the way to the sweet shop,
making the door ring with a little tune as he opened
it for me. He hadn't opened the carriage doors for me,
but now he smiled at me with good humor.

I skipped inside and breathed deeply to inhale the
scents of cooked butter and sugar. Then, I reached for
Chase for stability against the sensory overload. The
floor was decorated with little hexagons in a black and
white spotted pattern. The walls were likewise white,
but covered with fine black designs. Even the black
ceiling was carved with intricate swirls. The shop was
remarkably clean, though crowded with candies and

treats as if they had no worries about their food expiring within the week. Mirrors on one side made the store seem even larger as it extended down a hallway with small tables for dining.

The air was nice and cool inside. All sound echoed like a small cave as workers joked with customers, and buyers moaned with pleasure after every bite.

Needing a focus, I pressed my face against the glass blocking the sweets and might have drooled a little. I didn't know what I was looking at, but the little brown squares and glossy brown balls with sticks were beautifully designed. If they tasted like they smelled, they were surely divine.

"Opal," Chase laughed again. "You're not supposed to touch the glass."

Real Me would have withdrawn immediately with shame. Dream Me slid farther down the glass. "Good. That means no one else touches it, and it should be clean. I want one of everything."

Chase snorted. "That's a ton of food. I don't think even I could eat that much. How would you even pay for it?"

Hmm…money? "What if we share it?"

Chase scratched his chin in thought. "I guess. You really want to try one of everything?"

"Of course," I said. "How else am I to know if I like it or not? What's that brown stuff covering everything?"

Of the many things I'd done to earn confused stares, that question was the winner of perplexity.

52

"You mean chocolate?" he asked, dubious.

"Chalk…lit." I'd never heard of such a thing, but apparently it was a main ingredient in this dream world.

"Are you for real?" In response to my shrug, Chase gave the worker a determined order, "One of each of your most popular caramel apples, dipped pretzels, covered cookies, turtles, truffles, marshmallow things, and a quarter slice of fudge. And don't worry about paying, Opal. My treat."

"How lucky am I that you're so kind, Chase."

"If this is really your first time trying chocolate, you'll be paying me back with entertainment."

I wasn't sure what he meant by that. Was chocolate like alcohol and made people act differently?

Chase received a couple of boxes full of treats, then he gestured for us to sit at a table near the back of the store.

"Let's see, what to try first… Do you want to start small or big?"

Real Me would have wanted to start in the middle, but Dream Me spoke, "Big."

"Alright, caramelized apple it is."

He picked up one of the glossy balls with the stick. There was an apple hidden in there? There was no sight of it beneath the chalk-lit. And what was the other word he'd used? Carmle-ized?

With a bit of grunting and effort that showed off his nice arm muscles, Chase managed to cut the apple in half with a little white knife, proving that there was, in fact, an apple under the thick layers of gloss. He raised his half to me with an anticipating grin. "Bon appétit."

I had no idea what that meant, but the fruit was sticking to my fingers. I bit into its edge.

Sensory overload.

I didn't know such a thing was possible in the mouth. As my top teeth sank into the apple, its tangy tartness juiced. My bottom teeth worked harder against a shell that cracked and landed on my tongue. It was sweet and quickly softened, then left a bitter aftertaste. The next layer was like a thick honey, except buttery and salted. All three flavors together created a choir of harmonies.

The man across the table chuckled at my expression. "This really is your first time, isn't it?"

I was too busy chewing to answer, smashing the tart between the salt, the sweet, and the bitter. The rest of the bites became a balancing challenge. One bite had too much apple. The next had too much caramel. I planned my bites like a strategist to get it just right. I sadly finished, thinking that surely nothing else could be so wonderful.

To my utter delight, I was terribly wrong. Chase cut every piece in half to share. Real Me might have been too timid to eat this much in one sitting, but no such worries bogged down Dream Me. There was only a desire for more. No wonder he'd been surprised that I'd never tried chocolate. If we had something this delicious in Rezhina, we'd drown our foods in it too.

After the apple, pretzel, cookie, fudge, and something he called a marshmallow, I realized my mouth and stomach needed a break.

"This is," I moaned with both satisfaction and ache, "the best dream ever."

Chase chuckled. "Kind of feels like one, yeah?"

"Dia says it all the time, 'Life is short. Eat dessert first!' I've always been too nervous to try."

For some reason, Chase's face fell from my comment. "Yeah, life is short. Who knows what'll happen tomorrow?"

"Hey," I poked him. "That was supposed to be amusing. Most people chuckle when Dia says it. You became sadder."

His sad face gained a layer of confusion. "I thought everyone at camp knew."

"Knew what?"

"About my brother, Leo?"

"No, what about him?" I asked.

"You didn't hear about my brother's disappearance? And his fiancée? I swore I was the pity party of the camp."

"No. What happened?"

Chase exhaled heavily. "We don't really know anything. He came with me to Texas for a summer job. I heard Dorothy followed him and stayed at the homestead for a few days. Then, no one has heard from either of them for ten days. No one knows why or where they went. No notes, no bodies. Just—poof! Gone." He turned to me, shocking me with tears in his eyes. "Where did they go? What happened to them? Why did he leave me?"

"Why are you asking me?" I defended. "I don't know the answers. If you want to know something, then take the initiative to learn more about it."

"What—just drive four hours to Big Spring and look for clues around his workplace?"

"Sure, why not?"

Chase gaped at me. "Because that's insane. I barely have my intermediate driver's license, and we're only one week away from finishing our volunteer work at the camp. I can't just drive over there and ask questions like I'm some detective."

Even as he spoke, his eyes shifted through thoughts and plots. His tone drifted as he considered my suggestion.

"Why not?" I asked again. "I bet you know him better than any detective. Maybe he left a clue that only you'd catch."

"And we have a break this weekend as we're supposed to relax and prepare for our final week of volunteering…" His eyes gleamed with schemes, but with a blink, he frowned at me again. "But if anything goes wrong, it'll go very, very wrong."

Real Me didn't understand the possibly bad consequences, but Chase's serious face would have stopped me. Instead, Dream Me shook away the unknown consequences.

"Who cares?" I shrugged. "What's the worst that can happen? It's probably worth the risk, considering the best that can happen."

He stared at me like I was a puzzle to be sorted. "You really don't have a care in the world, do you?"

"I know," I said brightly. Dream Me kept surprising Real Me with my carefree attitude. Gone were my worries of upholding my family name, of acting as a princess should, and of what the future might bring. "It is rather liberating."

"It's a little scary," Chase said with a nervous laugh. "I have no idea what you're going to do next."

"What does it matter? This life is a dream, and at any moment, I'll wake up and nothing I do here will matter. I might eat until my stomach is stuffed, but when I wake, my stomach will be empty."

"What do you mean, you'll wake up?" he asked, his expression becoming confused.

"Exactly what I said. I'll wake up, return to Ormio and all the annoying little duties of a princess."

"Princess?" he guffawed. "What, like you're sleeping beauty or something? Is this some desperate ploy to make me kiss you?"

I jerked back, surprised. "What does kissing have to do with anything?"

He shrugged, cheeks adorably red. "That's how you wake a sleeping princess."

"Is it?" I asked. "What bizarre rules. Sure, shall we try it?"

I had never kissed anyone before, but all the worries and proprieties built around the concept were gone. Who cared? It was just lips touching.

I leaned over and puckered my lips at Chase, but he leaned back, suddenly terrified. "What? Right now, in a public shop? We barely know each other!"

"Sure. Who's going to stop us?" I asked, but Chase's expression didn't change. "Fine, then I'll kiss someone else."

I was in no hurry to end this dream, but maybe my stomach would stop aching if it did. I stood from the table and scanned the shop. A lone man stood nearby, watching as a worker scooped into deep buckets filled with something Chase had called ice cream. He stood with slumped shoulders and an empty stare. Maybe a little kiss would cheer him up.

I marched over, smiling, when he noticed my approach. He cleared his throat as if preparing to speak. I didn't give him the time.

Grabbing his face with my palms, I shoved my mouth against his. I didn't bother holding it or closing my eyes. Real Me would have been embarrassed beyond words from my actions. I'd never kissed anyone before, and now I'd just forced it on a complete stranger? In public? Dream Me didn't care even the slightest. Maybe because it really did feel like "lips touching" and nothing more. Apparently, kissing was horribly overrated.

Every eye and mouth in the shop gaped at me. I made my way back to Chase and huffed. "Well, that didn't work."

Chase sputtered between incredulous laughing and shocked coughing as he raised his hands to the strange man. "I'm so sorry—I don't know what's gotten into her. Come on, Opal, we should leave."

He rushed to pack the remaining treats in the box, then tugged on my arm to lead me outside. As soon as the door closed behind us, he burst into laughter.

"What was that? You really just kissed a stranger?" He hurried across the street, looking over his shoulder as if afraid someone would follow and restrain us.

I followed and shrugged. "You said a kiss would wake me."

"For real? You really think you're Sleeping Beauty?"

"I don't know who that is, but I'm sleeping and not ugly. This is all a dream. How else would I come to this place with its massive buildings, strange beastly carriages, and amazing flavors? I have absolutely no inhibitions like I do when I'm awake, so if you say a kiss will wake me, then that's what I'll do."

"But kissing a random stranger won't wake you. You need to love them. It's love that wakes the princess." We crossed to the other side, again to the pathway along the stream.

I frowned. "Says who? I'm not in love with any-one. How am I supposed to fall in love while stuck in a dream? Oh, I know!" I grabbed Chase's arm, finally jerking him to a stop. "I need to go to the most romantic places around! That's where I'll find my true love!"

"We can't just pick up and go."

"Why not? Your brother did. Come on!" I started to pull Chase forward again, but this time, he held back.

"What?"

"I said, come on! Like you said, one day we're here, then the next—poof! Then I say we live every moment as if it is our last."

He folded his arms and frowned at me. "If I'm going anywhere, it's to Big Spring to hunt for clues about my brother, and if I go, I can't take you with me."

"Why not?" I asked again, this time a little irked. Even if I wasn't interested in going to Big Spring, his sudden limitations on our travels annoyed me.

"I barely have my permit to drive." He paused to rub his palm over his forehead. "I'm supposed to drive with only immediate family members or someone over twenty-one. I already broke the law by driving you here because I figured it wasn't that far." His voice drifted and cheeks blushed like he wasn't telling me every reason. "But driving all the way to Big Spring is another story."

60

"That's a slandering rule," I said, pouting. "You're referring to that beastly carriage, right? Are they much different from driving horses?"

Chase frowned. "Okay, it was funny when you pretended not to know anything about reality when you ate all that chocolate and kissed a stranger, but this is different. You're talking about breaking the law."

"Who cares?" I burst. "I'm dreaming! Nothing I do matters! You already broke the law to bring me here, and you will again to take us back to camp. Unless you plan to leave me stranded here? Who cares about a little technicality at a time like this? I could slide down these stair banisters, climb that tree, or use the rocks to bury those plants, and what would—"

I paused as a collection of clicking sounds gathered from the flowerbed I recently indicated. Chase and I stared as the rocky stair walls crumbled and rolled out of their tight molding to pile atop the flowers.

Chase grabbed my arm, though I wasn't sure if he meant to pull me away from the incident or restrain me from running. Stuttering on his words, he pointed at the new pile of rocks. "What…what was that? How did that happen?"

I shrugged. "I simply said I could, and then they did."

Oh, slanders. I used words, and the rocks obeyed me. Of all the blasphemous words and slanders, did this dream give me the powers of the Words? Testing my theory, I called to the tree nearby, "Hey, would you mind giving us some more shade?"

The tree remained as it was.

"Try something with the rocks again," Chase urged.

I picked up a rock from the flowerbed. It was rough and bulky. Bouncing it in my hand, I said, "This rock will skip five times down this waterway." Then I chucked the rock that was shaped for sinking into the river. To both of our surprise, it bounced across the surface. Five times.

Again, Chase seemed lost for words as his eyes went from me, to the buried flowers, the sunken rock, then back to me. "Okay, that's unreal. Maybe…maybe there's some truth to what you're saying."

"Great! Then let's go on an adventure to find my true love and solve the mystery of your missing brother!"

He continued to eye me as if waiting for me to reveal a punch line. "This is really crazy. But let's do it."

Chapter 5

OPAL

Chase and I didn't run off to Big Spring right away. Apparently, he had "things to pack" first. We returned to the campgrounds that Chase called Government Canyon. He helped me to find my campsite with a fancy weather-proofing tent that rested in the middle of a rockbed. How strange. They made a permanent placement for temporary housing?

Chase shuffled in his steps as he said goodnight. "Running off to Big Spring is kind of crazy, so, um, sleep on it. If you still want to go tomorrow, then I'll bring you along, but of all the rash things we did today, we probably should think on this one."

I shrugged and went into my tent. With no fear of consequences, I doubted my decision would change.

I was in the middle of sorting through my clothes for sleeping-wear when a girl about my age entered the tent. She shrieked with embarrassment for catching me in my under-clothing. Real Me would have been mortified. Dream me didn't even twitch. She wasn't my sister, but maybe she was the owner of the second bedding in the tent. Based on her clothing, I guessed she wasn't a handmaiden.

Studying the other belongings labeled for "Alexa," I called her name and welcomed her inside. Even if she wasn't my handmaiden, I needed help to figure out which pieces of my odd clothing were meant for sleeping. There wasn't a single dress in my entire luggage. Alexa wore trousers like I did, so maybe that was simply the fashion of this dream. Alright then.

While looking over and deciding our outfits, Alexa prattled on and on. "I heard the craziest thing today—that you skipped out of cleaning to go off with Chase? Like, everyone knew you two left, so no cap. Spill the tea. What happened? Where did you go? What made you two go off like that? Were you like big yikes? Because, like, you shouldn't be. Things are only embarrassing if you let them be embarrassing— that's what my big sister always says. And Chase is fire, right? Did you two go on a date? What's he like? Please don't tell me he's all looks and no brain, because he's got the looks. He's only two years older than us, right? Where did you go—did he pay—was he extra sweet?"

Alexa finally paused, staring at me eagerly, as if she couldn't wait for my response. She was a complete stranger to me, but Chase had been too at the start of this dream. What would it hurt to talk about my day?

Unable to remember all of her questions, I answered her last set, "We went to Kilwins and had the most divine delicacies! Never. In. My. Life. Had I ever eaten anything so delicious with so many incredible flavors!" I told her all about the River Walk, Kilwins, and the treats. Apparently, only her own words fueled Alexa's energy, and she drifted off to sleep before I began my explanation of dreaming, kissing a stranger, and my plans to help Chase find his missing brother in the morning. Oh well.

The bed was oddly softer than the beds I knew at home, despite the rocks below the padding. The mix made me toss and turn uncomfortably.

When I finally found sleep, I found myself back in Ormio. Had I woken up? No, I couldn't remember how the day had begun or how I came to be standing in front of a tall woman with long black hair and a bright red dress. Garnet, the Crown Princess of Somnus.

Also, there was something familiar about the amount of luck charms I wore—even though I never wore all of my charms at once. Yet I had this one day, feeling the need for extra luck.

Right, this was Garnet's first night in Veriae. She had arrived earlier that day, meeting with Dia and Dad, then Dia had brought me to visit her quarters. My eldest sister stood beside me, looking almost as worn as Garnet.

She sighed with relief to see us and greeted us both with a hug that spoke of her exhaustion.

"Garnet," Dia asked, "what really happened? You said Emer's poison has spread? Where are Ruby and Dot?"

A sob broke from Garnet before she restrained her feelings again. Had I ever seen her so frayed? Whatever had happened to her since our last visit for Emer's birthday had truly taken a toll on her. She required a couple of deep breaths before speaking. "A protective curse surrounded Emer soon after everyone left, forcing everyone to abandon the castle. My parents warned my sisters and me to flee the city. We were prepared to sail to Lithus when our ship—even the great ship Liverthas—was sabotaged and sank."

Dia gasped. "You lost the Liverthas?"

I blinked in astonishment—the pride of the Somnus navy—king of the Imazhin Lake—, victor and peacemaker of many battles? Losing that could be a problem. Without that ship as a constant guard, our naval battles between Huiess could become more deadly.

Garnet nodded. "We had to flee to Lithus by land. There, Marin was attacked by Tanzi. Tanzi was the one who poisoned Emer."

"Tanzi?" I burst, disbelieving. "She's the youngest of us all!" She was a full year younger than I was. Sure, I'd seen Ruby and Dot put their minds to something and, with the support of adults, they accomplished incredible feats. But Tanzi? How could she come up with such schemes to poison her own sisters?

Garnet hung her head solemnly. "I found it hard to believe even as she drew a sword on me, then publicly accused me of performing *her* traitorous acts. Pearl and I escaped to Denebrae, where I left Pearl to petition Dot and Ruby for aid. We were too late to save Pearl from Tanzi. I swore to protect them. I hoped to protect them…" Her sobs returned with a vengeance, cracking her voice, and moaning her words. "I thought I could protect them."

Garnet fell to her seat and sobbed into her hands. Dia and I stared at the crown princess, shocked. If all she said was true, she truly had great cause to mourn. Removing one of my lucky bracelets, I offered it to Garnet. She seemed to need it more than I did.

"Here," I said, "this will bring you better fortune."

Garnet managed to laugh between her sobs. "Thank you. I could use all the good fortune in the world right now. I need your help." She finished by meeting us with her red and tear-stained eyes. "Regardless of the alternative routes we took, Tanzi still caught us. Your sisters, Ruby and Dot, are under the same poisonous sleep as Emer, Marin, and Pearl."

My sympathy for her tears became empathy. I wanted to doubt the news, call it a joke, or wish it away. The thought of Dot and Ruby lying incapacitated from poison devastated and terrified me. Would they wake? Were they doomed to sleep like Emer until we could find a cure or…? I hated to think of the alternative. If Tanzi targeted my sisters, would she target me too? I had thought we were friends…

Dia asked a bunch of questions about what Garnet knew of the poison. Dia's approach to handling bad news was always to learn more about it. She picked apart the details until it made sense in her head, as if understanding the reasons for bad situations could make them alright. Garnet explained the causes and curses of the poison, though it all went in and out of my mind in a haze. My approach to bad news was to hide away and pretend it never happened.

"Alright," Dia eventually asked, "how can we help? Other than ensuring your comfortable stay while in Veriae. Would you like me to remove or double the guards at your door?"

"Thank you," Garnet said, her relief evident through the lowering of her shoulders and small smile. "I appreciate the guards. Tanzi has followed me all the way from Lithus, and I fear… I fear her. She is more devious than I ever imagined and has stooped to unfathomable acts."

"How have you escaped?" I asked.

She paused to reflect, then shrugged with a pointed look at her new bracelet. "Luck? I was always with someone else when the attacks happened. At least until Dot was attacked. I was present when Dot fell into her poison trap, and Tanzi was gone. It would not surprise me if she laid her trap with Dot to make it appear as though I had poisoned her. Please, I assure you by the goddesses, I did not."

"We believe you," I said. While I'd known Tanzi to plan and tease with trickery, I'd never known Garnet to lie.

"If that's the case," Dia said, "I can double the guards by your door and add a few outside to keep you safe."

Garnet nodded with hopeful eyes. "Thank you. Perhaps you should sleep somewhere else, away from your usual quarters. Somewhere that Tanzi might not think to look for you. For that reason, I dare not stay long. Tanzi will look for me here, and I feel the need to alert Huiess of the situation."

Dia nodded. "Ame and her sisters should be in Remizio, entertaining their princely guest from Urbanuz."

Garnet's face wrinkled with a curious thought. "Maybe you should come with me. Remizio is the last place Tanzi or anyone would think to look for the princesses of Ormio."

Dia barked with a laugh. "Us in Remizio? Our kingdoms are at war."

"Ame may grant us sanctuary," Garnet said. "Perhaps now is the time for us to reveal our friendships to our parents. End the war and form alliances—especially with Urbanuz in attendance. If we can form a united front with all three of our kingdoms and a kingdom beyond the mountains, we may hold strong against any confusion caused by Tanzi's betrayal."

I had no idea what to think of Garnet's proposal. It sounded like a good idea, but I looked to Dia for her opinion. She stared Garnet hard in the eyes. "Ormio and Huiess aren't likely to suddenly play nice simply because their royal families became friends. I want peace for our kingdoms, but running to Remizio would be the plan of the desperate. I'll need to ponder and sleep on it. Opal, how about we stay together tonight?"

While the prospect of sharing a room with Dia excited me, I worried a little about Garnet's newfound paranoia. We should be safe within the fortress. Fleeing to Remizio was insane, though if Dia decided to follow Garnet's instructions, I would too. That was a worry for another night. For tonight, I'd enjoy a sleepover with my eldest sister, "As long as I can use my own bedding."

"Of course," Dia laughed. I wasn't as picky as Dot with my bedding, but I had my favorites, and none else would do.

Dia continued to talk with Garnet about options for securing the kingdoms. I lost track of the subjects as they referenced the prince from Urbanuz and methods to compel a treaty. Something about a political marriage. Politics.

I knew they could stay up all night talking, so I left early and relayed to the guards Dia's order to double their positions.

With such late notice, our biggest security measure was unpredictability. Before I'd left, Dia told me to arrange for our accommodations in the servant's hut near the hunting grounds on the far side of the fortress. She would join me "as soon as Garnet and I finish talking." Meaning I would be asleep before she came to bed. So much for the fun sleepover.

The servant's hut was a little house equipped for accommodating hunters during long stays in the fortress. The servants had already arranged for our stay, but our nighttime guard hadn't yet arrived. Alone in the little hut, I tested its amenities. I wanted everything to be just right.

Unfortunately, having my bedding and dinner delivered away from our usual dining hall put everything out of sorts. One chair was too tall, another was too short, but the last one was just right. My porridge was too bland, the guard's was too spicy, but Dia's was delicious.

"Third time's the charm."

I remembered crawling into the bed and snuggling for sleep. I was so tired, but every time I closed my eyes, shadows shifted to my sides and clawed hands crawled from the corners. I was surrounded by monsters that I couldn't see. Every time I tried to focus on one, it disappeared, only to reappear in the opposite corner. Whatever they were, they were everywhere, and they were growing stronger. It was as if they fed off my fear, solidifying as nightmares. They grew from the shadows until I awoke screaming in Texas.

Waking gave me no sense of security. Why was I back in this place? Why couldn't I wake to reality? And why was the world shaking around me?

"Oprah?" my tent-mate asked, groggy and blurry-eyed. "Oh! It's an earthquake! Quick, get down."

Get down?

She grabbed my arm and pulled me back down to my sleeping bag. We lay in our tent, trembling as much as the ground until the shaking stopped. My tent-mate yawned.

"It musta been a big one. Usually, the little quakes of Karnes don't reach past Floresville. I bet most people slept through it. Anyway, good night, Oprah."

I stared at her, confused and terrified. Slanders with sleep! Even if I went back to bed, I doubted that I'd be able to find sleep again after my nightmare and the ground shaking.

Chapter 6

OPAL

I followed my talkative tent-mate to the indoor gallery hall for breakfast in the morning. This building had massive windows to create the same appearance of being outdoors as the pavilion, but was enclosed with controlled cooling and even running water into a basin. Wooden panels and floors made an impressive scene of cleanliness. Someone swept this room, for sure.

My tent-mate talked with everyone, asking if they felt the earthquake, seeming somehow proud that she hadn't slept through it like the others had. I hadn't returned to sleep after the nightmares and earthquake, but was eager for a day of adventures. After filling a plate with a "continental breakfast," I found and joined Chase at a table.

"Are we still going to Big Spring today?"

He jammed a finger to his lips, shushing me. "You didn't tell anyone, did you?"

I shook my head.

"Good. I'll bring you along, just to keep you from blabbing about it to the camp directors. If you're up for it. We have the weekend off, and lots of people are leaving to explore the area. And it's only four hours to Big Spring, so we should be able to drive there and back before anyone misses us."

"Sounds good to me," I said around stuffing my face with the sweetest of breads and jams.

Chase frowned at me as if to doubt my sanity. I was too busy enjoying my breakfast to argue. Chase encouraged me to grab an extra bagel and water bottle for the road trip. I added a muffin to my stash.

We headed to his beastly carriage again and buckled in, but this time, as Chase awoke the creature again, he asked if I wanted "tunes."

Music instantly surrounded us. I braced myself against the armrests, ready to bolt, but in which direction? The music was all around us, yet there wasn't a single singer or drummer in sight.

And those drums! Deep and alternating, their simple rhythm seemed to guide the rest of the chaos. Voices sang in jumbled unison, "Perfect!" with criers, cheerers, and clappers in the background. After another, "Perfect!" it continued with, "Oooh, I'm sorry, but I'm not perfect!" then the song simplified to a hum and simple tune.

Chase turned a knob, and the sounds quieted. "Sorry, do you not like Strangels?"

"What are strangels?" I asked, hoping he didn't refer to the horse disease of strangles.

"You've never heard of them? They're a music group. Their name is like a combination of strange and angels."

I stared at my surroundings of the beastly carriage, finding the source of the music from the walls itself. "How is the music coming from the walls?"

"Uhh…" Chase slurred, then swore with an unfamiliar word. "Will I need to explain everything to you? There's kind of a lot going on when it comes to radio, so… can I just call it magic like your weird stone trick yesterday?"

"I guess that's fine. Dreams rarely make scientific sense. Now, are we going to find your brother or not?"

"Right. Let's go."

We left the campgrounds as we had the day before, but this time we drove farther from the city. Despite the incredible speeds of the ride, the trip dragged. I asked Chase about what he knew of his brother's disappearance, but he didn't really have anything new to add. In turn, he asked me about the life outside of this dream. Were dream characters allowed to know?

I waved away that worry and told him about my life as a princess; helping with dinner parties with my sisters, sharing the leftovers with the needy at the temple, and about my favorite hobby of pottery sculpting. Despite my many attempts, I'd never completed any projects. My pots always turned out too round or too thin, too tall or too short. I could never make one just right.

Maybe it was because I could never wear my lucky rings or bracelets while sculpting.

I told Chase in detail of my favorite pieces of jewelry, with their charms for luck. He didn't seem terribly interested, but neither did he seem bored, so I asked him more about his brother.

He told me about Leo, how he was a few years older and had recently proposed to his girlfriend. Since she was about Chase's age, they planned to have a two-year-long engagement. That seemed like an eternity to me. Chase described their relationship with conflicting emotions and expressions, at some points seeming wistful, and at other times mocking.

"I mean," he scoffed, "who gets married when they're eighteen these days? Like they're in love, and it's that easy?"

"Are you jealous?"

"Of my brother? No, ew! Just because Dot's my age doesn't mean I'm jealous of my brother for having her."

"Dot? I have a sister named Dot. I didn't think it was a common name."

"It's a nickname."

"For Peridot?"

"Dorothy."

"Oh." Not the same. Either way, "I didn't mean that you were jealous of Dot, but jealous of their situation. You want to fall in love and marry young?"

His mouth wiggled with indecision and reluctance to answer. With a quick glance at me, he said, "Not really. Part of me thinks it'd be nice to fall in love and be done with it. Skip the drama, and never know the pain of heartbreaks. Another part of me knows that's not realistic and kind of looks forward to the adventure of making mistakes."

I tilted my head at him. "You can be very wise sometimes."

He cracked a crooked smile. "It's been known to happen. Even a broken watch is correct twice a day."

The watches I knew were the night guards of the fortresses. How could they be broken and still be right twice a day? I asked, "What's a watch?"

Chase blinked and swore again, but muttered excuses rather than explained.

We reached the town of Big Spring, but the farm where Leo had worked was still a half hour away. We stopped for lunch at a restaurant, walking in to stretch our legs and sit in a booth with different seats than the car's. Again, I was tempted to try everything on the menu, but Chase convinced me to limit myself to a single appetizer of nachos, a burrito entrée, a Cola drink, and a sopapillas dessert. I hadn't the faintest idea what any of those were. Real Me wouldn't have dared to try anything so exotic, but Dream Me was eager to find other flavors like chocolate.

First came the drink. I stared at it for a moment, confused by its soiled color and bubbles.

Chase urged me, "Just close your eyes and try it."

I did and flinched back as it stung my tongue. The bubbles hissed and popped in my mouth and down my throat as I swallowed. The underlying flavor, though, was worthy of another sip. Chase laughed and suggested that I let the drink sit for a bit to calm down the carbonation—or the bubbles and sting.

My first plate was nachos, which Chase explained as corn chips, fried and salted, then covered with melted cheese. The salt was unmistakable, and the crunch was down-right delightful. My next bite included a heavy helping of cheese. How could a cheese appear so creamy while tasting so spicy?

Then came the burrito. It was almost as large as my forearm! Simply cutting into the log revealed smells to rival the nachos. How did anyone taste the food beyond the spice? And—oh, how I wanted to taste the food with its juicy meat, soaked beans, and layered cheese. I only managed to eat half of the burrito as Chase ate his tacos—a meal within a large folded chip. Our waiter visited to refill my drink and left a note on our table as we ate dessert.

I leaned back in my seat to stretch my stomach, grateful that my dad wasn't around to scold me for doing so. With a groan, I rolled myself from the chair.

"Alright, I'm officially full. Time to find clues about your brother."

"Opal, we need to pay for our food."

"I don't have any money."

Chase's jaw bounced and stuttered. "No money at all? Then why did you order all of that? I can't afford it either! Not after Kilwins, and I need to plan for gas money."

I shrugged. "Then let's run. What are they going to do? Make us vomit for a refund?"

"Opal, that's stealing!" he hissed under his breath.

Again, Real Me wouldn't have even considered the option, too concerned about consequences. Except this was a dream without consequences. I grinned and pulled Chase by the hand to run out a side door. In the rush, Real Me squirmed with both terror, shame, and elation.

Chase sputtered the beginning of a hundred worries without finishing any of them as he ran behind me. As soon as we were outside, he took the lead and pulled me around parked cars and building corners. There may have been shouting from the restaurant, but no one ran after us. Winding our way to an alley, Chase stopped to lean his back to the wall and catch his breath.

Checking that we hadn't been followed, he began to laugh. "That...was...insane! I've never dined and dashed before."

"Neither have I," I said, grinning. I'd never done any of that before. I'd been too worried about what people thought, too afraid of the consequences. Now, I felt no guilt, no restraints, and no inhibitions holding me back. This was my dream. I could do whatever I wanted.

As if to prove it, I swore with exhilaration, "Words, this is the definition of freedom!"

"I think you mean anarchy." Chase chuckled nervously.

But he said nothing about my language. No judgment or reprimand. No consequences. The one and only other time I'd sworn by our gods, I'd been forced to eat soap after. I'd felt too guilty to even be tempted by the thought of a repeat.

Chase didn't seem to have the same exhilaration as he shook, presumably with nerves, while heading back to our vehicle, starting it, and speeding away from the restaurant. Once we were clear of the town, he managed to laugh and shake his head with disbelief. The thrill waned as we drove down the long road to the place where his brother was last seen.

Chapter 7

OPAL

As Chase's magical map announced, "Your destination is on the right," he eased the vehicle to the side, but stopped before the turnoff.

"What are you doing?" I asked. "The house is pretty far back into the property. Did you want to walk?"

"Are you sure we should do this?"

"You probably should have asked that before driving four hours. Come on, don't you want to find out what happened to your brother?"

Nervously tapping his hand against the steering wheel, Chase wiggled his jaw back and forth like he chewed on my words. With a little huff, he took his foot off the pedal to roll into the private road. He went so slowly, I was tempted to jump out of the car and jog up the driveway.

Slanders, why not?

Clicking off my seatbelt and opening my car door nearly sent Chase into a panic.

"What are you doing? I thought you didn't want to walk—you don't jump out of moving vehicles!"

I rolled my eyes. "I've jumped off of carriages going faster than this." Before he could retort, I hopped out, shut the door, and walked beside the car.

Chase finished the drive up to the house, then sat in the car for a few more seconds, double checking the address and wiping his hands on his pants.

I opened my door to check on him. "Are you nervous?" I teased. "Come on, let's go talk to them."

As soon as he unbuckled his seatbelt, I skipped up to the doorway, then knocked. A dog barked twice from the back side of the house. No one answered in the time it took for Chase to join me at the doorstep. He pushed a button that made an absolutely cheerful ding-dong sound.

"Ooh!" I reached over to push the button, too. I pushed it again and again with a fit of giggles until Chase pulled my arm away.

"Opal! You're only supposed to push it once," he said between gritted teeth and a suppressed grin.

"Hello?" a voice called from around the house. A dog bounded toward us before I could react. Luckily, the dog was well trained and didn't jump, but sniffed our shoes, pants, and hands until I pulled mine away. Next, a young woman appeared from the corner of the house with her arm linked around a young man's.

"Ruby!" I shouted and ran at my sister.

She stumbled and reacted with extra surprise when I wrapped my arms around her.

"Uh-um," she stuttered, "it's Biddy. Who are you?"

"What?" I pulled back, but her eyes didn't meet mine. In fact, her green-brown eyes were slightly clouded.

"Slanders," I swore. "You're blind?"

She winced. Unlike everyone else I'd spoken to, she recognized "Slanders" as a curse word.

"Who are you?" she repeated.

"Ruby, it's me, Opal."

"Opal?" Ruby gaped. "You're here too? Crap, please don't tell me you're engaged to Shino."

The young man chuckled, "No," even as she tightened her grip on his arm.

"No," I laughed. "But if you're worried, I can try my true-love's kiss thing on him just to confirm he's not the one."

Ruby scoffed and muttered, "That would be just my karma."

"Who's Karma?" I asked. "Don't you mean 'luck?' And who's the mister? You two seem attached."

Ruby blushed and frowned at me. "Is that really you, Opal? Sure, you sound like her, but you don't act like her. My younger sister never swore or spoke so… boldly."

"It's all a dream, right?" I spread my arms and face to the sky. "Nothing we do matters here."

"No," Ruby said, surprisingly stern. "These people are real. Shino is real. Mom and Dad are real. They're here—I can have Rayban fetch them."

A small terror built in the depths of my chest. No, I didn't want to see Mom and Dad. What would they think of me and the way I acted here?

No, it couldn't be the real Mom and Dad, just as this wasn't the real Ruby. This was nothing but a dream. Besides, she called herself Biddy.

Before I could announce another glorious proclamation, Chase burst. "Where's Leo?"

Both Ruby and Shino twitched.

"You knew Leo?" Ruby asked.

"He's my brother. What do you mean 'knew?' He disappeared from this farm, but I refuse to believe he's dead."

Ruby smiled sadly. "No, I don't believe he is either. He went to Ormio with Dot. But I recall him talking about you. Chase, right?"

"Right." Chase said, eyes widening with interest. "What do you mean he 'went to Ormio?' Isn't that where you're trying to go?" he asked me. I nodded and stayed silent for Ruby's answer. Had Leo gone to Ormio with Dot? How? Had Dot taken him with her, or had he simply woken up? A deep piece of me panicked with the idea that the people in this dream were part of my subconscious mind, pulling them from real people that I didn't know I knew. That would make them real people in real life.

84

No, even if they were real people from Ormio, they wouldn't know my actions here in this dream. They weren't sharing it with me. I was free to act however I wanted. How else would I feel this carefree of consequences?

Though it could be sweet to befriend Chase more fully in real life.

Ruby reached to her empty side and Shino automatically took her arm as an escort. There was something in Shino's eyes that said his actions came from true kinship to Ruby rather than an obligation to serve.

Ruby said, "We can take our conversation to the porch, and I can show you the room where they disappeared. Opal may see the inside, but, unfortunately, Chase will need to see the room from the outside. Shino and Chase aren't allowed inside. House rules."

I scoffed. "That's dumb."

Ruby threw me a closed-eyed glare as we walked around the house. "That's offensive, Opal. Really, you weren't like this in Ormio. Has Chase been a bad influence on you?"

Chase scoffed. "Other way around, really."

"Ah, come on," I said, grabbing his arm the way Ruby held Shino. "You can't tell me that you haven't had any fun."

"It's been… enlightening."

I stuck my tongue out at him, then skipped ahead. We stepped up to a wooden porch lined with benches and tables. When seated, Ruby asked Shino, "Can you point them to the window where Dot stayed?"

As if it was hard to guess between the three windows, one leading to a dining room, another beside the door to a lounge room, and the farthest window on the right was to a dark room. I could barely make out the shapes of a bed and dresser inside.

Shino pointed to the bedroom. "Biddy's twin slept in that room. Mr. Bahr was allowed to see her, and they disappeared."

Ruby slid him a smile. "Your English improves every day." Then, to my surprise, Ruby spoke a stuttered phrase in another language. Shino laughed and responded fluidly.

"Words," I swore, "what was that?"

"Nihongo–er, Japanese. Shino's language. I'm not as fluent as Shino's English, but I'm learning."

Huh. With all of our surrounding kingdoms speaking the same language, I'd never thought to learn another one. Sure, the accents shifted drastically between kingdoms, and the Huiess slang seemed like another language sometimes, but only the dwarves spoke their old languages, and rarely at that.

Chase frowned with defiance. "What do you mean, they disappeared?"

"Just that," Ruby said. "I was in the room as their chaperone. Dot had been bed-ridden since the first day she arrived, and Leo had been a real grump about not being able to see her, so we made an exception to our rule about no workers in the house. Since I'm blind and Dot was deaf, Leo helped as our translator. Dot and I came to a truce about me staying here while she planned to return to Ormio. Then, she and Leo shared a conversation, and the two of them went quiet. I heard them signing with each other, then nothing. No creaks from Dot moving on the bed, no footsteps, no opening of the window—nothing. I would have hit one of them when waving my stick around looking for them. Even when I asked Rayban to locate them, he simply sat there, like he couldn't sense them anymore. They were gone."

Chase's frown remained, but less in defiance and more in confusion. "But how?"

Ruby shrugged. "I don't know. As far as I knew, Dot didn't know how to leave, but maybe they signed some pass code or did something together. I'm just as confused as anyone else that she managed to take Leo with her. Then again, this is Dot we're talking about. You know how she always gets what she wants."

Chase asked a bunch more questions, though evaded the one I wanted to ask.

"Did they kiss?" To Ruby's confused expression, I explained, "That's how Chase says you wake a sleeping princess. But it hasn't worked for me."

Ruby drew back with surprise. "You kissed someone? Who? When?"

I shrugged. "Someone who looked like he needed something sweet in his life. He was in a sweet shop after all."

Ruby's cheeks blushed. "Opal! These people are real! You can't toy with people like that!"

I folded my arms. "As if you've never done anything crazy. You and Dot were always throwing yourselves out there, even in reality."

"This is my reality, Opal. I made the mistake of kissing someone without permission and have regretted it ever since."

"Then have you kissed the man sitting next to you?"

I thought she'd been red before, but now her face shaded to match her name. "Shino and I haven't kissed. He respects me, and… I'm learning to respect myself too. Holding hands is enough with Shino."

I stared at my sister. Dream Ruby was like a different person. Where I'd lost my inhibitions, she'd seemed to gain more. Or was it something else that she'd gained?

Eh, that was too much thinking for Dream Me. I let Chase lead the rest of the visit as he asked questions about his brother, where he worked, and how he spent most of his time. Ruby led us to a little cabin on the farm where Leo had lived. Chase searched high and low and all around for any sort of clue but stepped out disappointed.

The other workers were finishing up, and Ruby invited me to stay to meet Mom and Dad. I wanted to leave all the more, embarrassed by the thought of my parents meeting Dream Me, but Chase was adamant about staying longer to study Leo's disappearance. When Mom came home from the grocery store with enough food to feed an army and Dad didn't recognize me, I allowed them to convince me to linger. I was grateful for the confirmation that they were dream-versions of my parents as Mom cooked and Dad sat to eat with commoners. Real Mom and Dad never did that. We shared dinner with Ruby and the farmers and talked until it was too late to drive back to San Antonio.

Mom and Dad were sympathetic to Chase's plight and let him stay in Leo's old room with Shino while I was bunked in the guest bedroom with Mom—where Dot had stayed and disappeared.

I didn't sleep well that night, maybe catching a few hours between my restless nightmares of shadow monsters, but I gave up with the early rise of the summer sun.

Chase slept in while the rest of us ate an early breakfast. Dad went out to join the field workers while Mom and Ruby cleaned the dishes. Chase came by for food a little later, then we wandered around the farmhouse looking for clues. We searched until lunch to no avail, leaving Chase discouraged, but resolved that he wouldn't find answers. Unsatisfied, we prepared to leave after lunch.

"I still can't believe it," Chase said, shaking his head and buckling himself into the driver's seat. "How does someone just disappear? Especially someone like my brother. He's a big guy."

"Hey," I said, resting a hand on his shoulder. "Life is too short to waste on questions no one can answer."

Chase scoffed. "Life is too short. Ain't that the truth. We never know if one day—poof—we might be gone too."

"Poof," I said, "and I wake up in Ormio like Dot did."

Chase frowned. "Is that what you want? To poof away and return to all those worries you told me about? Your sister chose to stay."

"One sister," I clarified. "I have three sisters and a brother. Ruby stayed, but Dot returned." Still, I considered his words. Did I really want to wake up and return to Real Me with all those worries and consequences? Dream Me was having fun, going on adventures, exploring this world of leisure camping, towering cities, and endless farmlands.

Chase continued, "How do you expect to fall in love if all you want to do is leave that person behind?"

I rubbed my forehead. "Why do I need to fall in love again?"

"It's part of the rule. It's not just the kiss that wakes the princess. It's true love."

"Right, right. What a slanderous rule."

"Don't you want someone to care about you? Don't you want your prince charming to know you better than anyone and be your best friend?"

"What are you talking about?"

"Love, Chika. Do you need me to spell it out for you? L-O—"

"I know how to spell. Stop being ridiculous. I know all about love, how it can strike you like a lightning bolt the first time you meet, or see their smile, or share a kiss. It hasn't struck me yet, but that's why I need to keep exploring until I meet him. Then, we'll kiss, and I'll wake up."

"You say that like it's all so simple. But I've heard that love takes time."

"Isn't it simple? You were the one to say kissing is how to wake a sleeping princess. Besides, since this is all a dream, what'll happen when I wake up? I'll leave all of this behind and never see my newfound 'love' again, anyway. Nope, I hope to kiss a stranger and be done with it."

Chase shook his head and muttered, "That is so messed up. Did you have to do it in front of everyone in that sweet shop?"

"If I'm willing to do it in private, then it shouldn't matter who's watching. Isn't that a definition of integrity? That you don't act differently when you're alone—or think you're alone. If you don't want to be caught doing something, then you probably shouldn't be doing it."

That small piece of Real Me in the back of my mind screamed that I'd be ashamed of myself if anyone saw me in this dream. Ruby had seen me. Mom and Dad had seen me. True, they didn't act like Real Ruby or Real Mom and Dad… but if this was truly a dream, wouldn't they act exactly like I'd expect them to? Were people able to grow and change in dreams as Biddy, Mom, and Dad had?

And if this wasn't a dream… Real Me blushed shamefully with the thought, and Dream Me shook my head to clear it away. Of course, this incredible and incredibly strange world was a dream. I needed it to be a dream without any real consequences.

"That's really what you think?" Chase asked. "That everything you do in private, you'd be willing to do in public?"

"Who cares who's watching?" I shrugged.

"Use the toilet?" he challenged.

Another shrug. "It's only natural. Everyone poops, and if others want to smell it, that's their issue."

Chase laughed. "You're crazy, you know that?"

"Only when I'm dreaming."

Chapter 8

EMER

Their travels between Othium and Veriae were a reverse version of their travels between Lithus and Somnus. Instead of leaving the capitol with its higher density of abandoned buildings, they went toward it. Instead of waking each day to clearer skies as the mist thinned, it thickened.

There were also several other differences to Emer's perspective. First of all, her sisters Marin and Pearl accompanied her with Dot. Instead of traveling over roads broken by coniferous plants, they traveled wide of the lake on paths barely distinguishable between the overgrown deciduous Ormytha Forest.

Though the terrain was difficult on the state coach, Emer cleared their pathway of plants, and Dot's ability to connect with the animals helped the horses to pull along. They stopped more often as Dot voiced their needs for nourishment or rest, and soon they were all as spoiled as Caden's horse, Tucker.

Pearl was also eager to use her ability to help Mica create a camera. Anytime they paused to let the horses rest, Pearl and Mica explored the abandoned houses for bits and pieces to create their "light reflecting box." They managed to find a small wooden box, a broken piece of mirror that was large enough for their needs, and a cap to fit around a glass bottle bottom for the lens.

"It's rudimentary at best," Mica said, "but I think we have a good start."

As they neared the city, the mist grew thicker. Veriae was the closest port town to Noz Isle, making the mists thick enough that their visibility shortened to a kilometer even on the outskirts of the great city. Caden theorized that the mists were created in part for the mære and to increase people's fears of them.

He rambled aloud, "Queen Tanzanite was too young to be respected as a queen. She needed to earn the people's loyalty, but not out of love. It makes sense that she chose to rule with fear. I don't know how she created or recruited the mære, but ordering them to attack Veriae made a statement of her power."

Emer listened and occasionally offered her thoughts as he continued to theorize and take notes.

Searching for Opal proved more difficult because of the mists and the city's destruction. Pearl attempted to send Lucy into the air to search from above, but the magic ball of light returned without direction.

"Probably because of the mist," Mica said. "Can we try the plants?"

Emer shook her head. "The seeds have scattered through the rubble, but there are gaps where the plants do not connect. I cannot map the city between the gaps."

"So," Caden slurred and rubbed the back of his neck, "it's the old-fashioned way. We split into pairs and search every block for some unnatural phenomena."

"Can my animals help?" Dot asked.

Caden answered with a thoughtful look. "I don't know. Can they?"

Dot shuffled. "I don't know, but I can ask. What exactly are we looking for?"

"Unnatural phenomena," Caden said. "Like a thicket of thorns."

"Or a whirlpool in the middle of the city," Marin said.

"Or impenetrable darkness," Pearl added.

"Or," Leo finished, "the largest pack of wolves and ravens you've ever seen concentrated on one spot."

Dot blinked wide eyes. "Oh. Yes, I remember Garnet mentioned you were each surrounded by curses, and a pack of wolves dragged me away from Ruby. They surrounded us and guarded us for an entire century?"

Leo smirked. "Why else did you think a hundred animals lay in wait for you to wake?"

She shuffled as if she wanted to nudge him playfully, but held back. "I had just woken from a stranger-than-life dream to find you in real life, my hometown destroyed, nightmarish monsters attacking, and my poisoned friends awake—with magical powers, no less. Being surrounded by animals seemed like the most natural part."

Leo chuckled and didn't refrain from passing a friendly nudge, reddening Dot's face faster than a hot pepper.

"Alright," Dot said, shaking her muscles loose like she was about to jump into a winter lake. "How do I do this? I just think really hard to send a message to the animals?"

Caden leafed through his satchel to find the right page of notes, then read, "The magic of the princesses seems to respond to verbal commands. If the magical element is capable of performing the task given, it does so. Emer has grown more capable as she experiments, talking to plants and giving them various commands to test their limits and her own understanding. While her magic was slow to begin, she can now grow a me-ter diameter of healing moss from plain soil within thirty seconds."

Dot raised her eyebrows and mouth corners at Emer, who had shrunk into herself at the focused attention.

Is she impressed or simply amused at Caden's meticu-lous research regarding me? He even penned me as "Emer," but still refers to Dot as "Princess Peridot."

"That makes sense," Dot said. "In Ormio, we honor the Words. In the beginning, Words created our world. Naturally, our magic powers are merely abilities to serve the Words."

"Merely," Marin scoffed.

Emer moaned. They'd stepped into the largest religious debate between the beliefs of Ormio and Somnus.

"Your Words," Marin said, "are the words spoken by the goddesses. There is nothing 'mere' about the goddesses. They had the powers to create this world."

Caden chuckled. "Then there's nothing 'mere' about you princesses. You all have the same powers."

Turning sharply, Marin accused Caden, "Are you saying that our magics are in similitude of the god-desses? Careful how you answer, scholar, for your words may be blasphemous."

Caden immediately raised his hands in surrender.

"Plead the fifth," Leo laughed. "Oh, wait. You were British. Just kidding, you're screwed."

"We have the right to remain silent when being arrested," Caden muttered.

"Please," Pearl whimpered, "we do not need to fight."

Emer rolled her eyes and stood between her older sister and Caden. "Accept it, Marin. We have magic to change the world. Maybe they are the same powers that created the world, but what does it matter if our world was created by goddesses, Words, or stars as the Huiessians believe? What matters is, for whatever reason, we have powers to influence the world around us, but what is new about that? We were born princesses. We have always had the power to change the world."

"Actually," Mica said, "you don't need to be princesses to change the world."

"What do you mean?" Dot asked.

He shrugged. "Pearl wasn't a princess in England, but she changed my world. I'm pretty sure she changes the world of everyone she meets simply by being who she is."

Pearl glowed from the inside out as she beamed at Mica.

Dot nodded. "Wise words."

Leo shielded his eyes from Pearl's brightness. "I'm already hard of hearing. Are you trying to make us all partially blind too?"

"Oh! Pardon me," Pearl said. "I may hide behind the coach until I can control my happiness. Mica, if you would like to join me, I have some fruit for you."

"Ooh! Fruit!" He eagerly took her hand and let her pull him around the coach as Pearl's glow intensified.

Dot furrowed her brow. "Fruit?"

"You don't want to know," Caden said, hiding his forehead into his palm.

Marin's eyes widened with inferences, then she marched toward the coach. "Pearl! Remember what I said at the masquerades? Stay on the dance floor!"

Ranae laughed, ignoring Leo and Dot's confused looks.

"Sooo," Caden slurred and gestured to Dot, "are you going to try talking to the animals?"

"Right." Dot twitched, snapping back to attention. She stepped away from the group to face the city. "Animals of Veriae, all who can hear my voice—am I doing this right?"

Leo shrugged. "We won't know until you try."

"Right," she said with another twitch. "Um, come here?"

"With confidence," Emer said. "If plants can recognize my doubt in their capabilities, then the animals can, too."

"Right," Dot said, then jumped back in surprise. "Oh! You're already here?" A variety of rodents scampered to her feet, then looked up to Dot with anticipation. "I wonder," Dot pondered, then gestured quickly with her hands.

The rodents scattered like a firework in every direction.

"That worked?" Emer asked. "What did you say to them?"

"I told them to search the city for a sleeping person. They may not recognize strange phenomena as we might, but they should be able to sniff out a resting human."

"They understood your signs?" Marin asked, walking back to them. "That clears the misunderstanding of us acting as goddesses or Words."

Dot shrugged. "A single sign can be used in countless ways by varying movement, expression, or other classifiers. ASL isn't a word-for-word translation, but it is a language and living form of communication."

"In fact," Caden whispered to Emer, "that might make you more powerful than Words."

Beshrews, he was right. Emer blinked at the unraveling implications. Hoping to contain her spiritual questions, she smirked back. "That can stay between us, you blaspheming scholar."

Rather than wait for the rodents to return with their findings, Dot wanted to push into the city. Emer never would have thought that rolling a state coach through a wild forest would be easier than the city, but with the rubble of fallen buildings and broken roads, they were forced to take off-beaten paths. Accustomed to his agile horse, Caden grumbled to guide the carriage through the carnage.

"Come on," Caden chided the horses at a particularly broken crossing. "You've been over rougher patches than this."

The four horses snorted and backed away.

Dot laughed. "They argue that those other patches were on cleared tracks. They're not mountain goats to hop around precarious rocks, especially while towing a bulky carriage."

Caden blinked wide eyes at her, then relented with a huff. "Fine. We'll go around. Again."

Eventually, they made it to the city center, and the main fortress—even the royal seat—came into view.

It had everything Emer expected of a castle: high walls, turrets, towers, a center keep, battlements, and a gatehouse. Except it was made entirely of wood. Thick wooden logs stacked atop one another, interlocked at corners and edges for stability. They had coated the wood with plaster to make it impervious to fire, bugs, and weathering, ensuring its sustainability after these many harvests of abandon.

"It still stands," Dot said, dismounting her horse, awed. After withstanding years of war against Huiess, hundreds of raids, and dozens of sieges, the castle remained standing.

Yes, to Emer's amazement, the wooden castle of Veriae still stood. At least half of it did.

Dot fell to her knees and cried. With her face shifting between smiles and despair, Emer wasn't sure whether her tears were joyful or miserable. Maybe it was both? Joy at seeing the foundations of her home still standing, but despair to see it in ruins and with half the glory of its former days. Leo knelt beside her and awkwardly rested a hand on her shoulder.

As if sensing her sorrow, a rat ran up to her knee. Dot cleared her tears to stare at the little creature.

"They found her!"

"They did?"

"At least they found a small-ish sleeping human with golden curls. Opal would fit that description."

Leo frowned. "What are the odds that it's someone other than your sister?"

"Either way," Caden said, "we should say hello. We might need to leave the horses if we want to go quickly."

"I have a feeling it's Opal," Dot said, finding her feet and running after the rat. "Let's go!"

Marin and Pearl decided to stay with the horses and prepare camp while Leo dashed after Dot.

Emer followed with Caden limping behind, helping him around broken road sections, over fallen walls, and up a hill of rubble. The rat had directed them to the far side of the castle, beyond the hunting grounds, to a small servant's hut at the edge of the fortress. Emer stopped as soon as her eyes landed on the strange phenomena that marked the resting place of a princess.

Stone spikes.

Thousands of them rose from the ground. Some went as tall as her hip, and others were as large as she was. Every centimeter between them was covered with smaller spikes…thorns…needles.

"Emer?"

Caden's voice shook her, and she took a gasp of air, unaware that she'd stopped breathing. His smile flipped into a frown as he followed her eyes to the spikes.

"Oh," he said. "I believe the thorns surrounding your place were far more frightening."

She took another conscious breath. "If you say so."

"Don't worry," he said. "We'll find a way through. We'll save her."

EMER

They returned to the coach and discussed methods of reaching Opal with everyone.

Emer offered, "I could grow a tree and vine again to swing across as we did with Marin's whirlpool."

"Correction, if I may," Caden said, "as *I* did. You didn't make it and nearly drowned. Landing on one of those spikes would be equally life-threatening."

Marin offered to splash water on the spikes to attempt eroding them, but Caden theorized that if they stood a hundred years through weathering, then they probably wouldn't wash away quickly. Leo suggested digging, though Emer imagined that would be as effective as Charlotte's efforts to chop down her thicket of thorns. Did they have that time to spare? What if they were too late, as they had been with Ruby?

Emer shook her head, unwilling to let that thought take root. Yet it lingered.

That night, sleep evaded Emer. She tossed and turned on her coach bench, rearranging her blankets, fluffing her pillow, and even tried counting sheep. Her mind was too anxious about Opal and the sight of all those stone spikes stabbing into the sky. How would they pass them? What would they find when they managed to cross?

When she finally found sleep, it wasn't for long. The spikes invaded her dreams. She found herself in the middle of that forest of giant stalagmites, calling out for Caden, hearing him calling for her, but never finding one another. A shadow curved around the spikes in front of her, but before she could hope that she'd found Caden, a watery growl drowned her hopes. The mære wandered through the spikes with her. Had it seen her? Were there others? She woke with a start as shadows surrounded her with angry growls.

Based on the shuffling from Marin, Pearl, and Dot, she guessed that they likewise struggled to sleep. They whispered to each other, voicing their fears and worries, offering consolation, and sharing their wishes of hope. Sometimes, one of them managed to fall asleep, but quickly stirred awake again with frightened breathing.

Eventually, the sun gathered enough courage to poke its face over the mountains and through the fog, and the princesses prepared for the day with simple clothing, fit for hard work. However they planned to cross the spikes, and whatever happened, they braced themselves and each other for the worst.

The men joined them at the fire pit for breakfast and more discussion about how to cross the spikes. The ideas became more ridiculous with each suggestion.

"What if—"

"Please, stop," Caden cut off Mica. "You haven't even seen the area. Maybe you should hold off from suggesting another hot-air balloon idea which we have no materials or knowledge to make. At least until after you've seen what we're facing."

Mica pouted, causing Pearl to ask for his crazy ideas, anyway. They conspired together while Emer took Caden's hand for comfort.

"Are you alright? Mica only means to help."

"I know," he grumbled and leaned into Emer's touch. "I'm just tired and tired of feeling lost without a solution."

"Maybe we need to visit the site again. Let everyone see the obstacle we must cross so that we may cross it together."

Caden eyed her. "You seemed a little shaken by the sight of those spikes. Are you sure you want to go back?"

No. But, "We need to save Opal. I cannot bear the thought of losing another friend."

Caden nodded, and the group decided to leave the coach and horses with the protection of some mean-spirited llamas and hawks summoned by Dot.

"If we can't reach Opal on horseback," Dot said, "we should let the horses rest and protect our camp."

Addressing the horses and their protectors, she said, "If anyone other than us comes near, I give you permission to chase them out."

One of the llamas demonstrated her distaste for others with a spit wad to the ground. Dot grinned back. "Excellent. Let's go."

They walked along the route they took the day before, though stepped more carefully without the rush of following a rat. When they arrived, Pearl gasped and Marin said a simple and understanding, "Oh."

Emer asked the question that burned through her mind all night and morning, "How do we reach her?"

Caden took her hand with a reassuring squeeze. "We'll find a way."

"Er," Mica wavered, "you didn't mention that they moved."

Emer frowned and—despite her natural response to look away from the frightening sight—studied the spikes.

The spikes… rippled.

Before Emer could panic about the needle-like spikes coming to life, unnatural screams with an undertone of horses whinnying filled the air.

She clapped her hands over her ears and joined the screams with her own.

Figures of black smoke exploded from the depth of the spikes, fleeing in every direction. Each smokey figure was headed with the face of a black scaled horse, screaming like it was drowning. Mære.

"Devils of—" Caden cut his own curse short as he scrambled back.

There were dozens of them, all fleeing from Opal's location. Seeing Emer and her friends, several of the mære turned their focus from fleeing to chasing.

"Run!" Caden panicked, grabbing Emer's hand and pulling them away.

"What's happening?" Dot shouted. "Are those the creatures that destroyed Veriae?"

Leo nodded and grabbed her around the waist to lift her as he ran. Pearl screamed from behind as a mære closed around her. Mica stood beside her with his sword drawn. The terror in his eyes and shaking hands warned Emer of their helpless situation.

"Caden!" she called. They needed to help them, but how? Caden had to have an idea, right? They couldn't let her sister and his best friend fall prey to those monsters. But they were too far away. Their weapons and magics were useless against the mære. But they needed to do something!

Emer watched in horror as one of the mære swept down on Pearl, its mouth gaping with its needles of teeth, arms stretching for her with pointed claws. Pearl cried for Lucy to shine her light through the shadowy creatures, but it had no effect.

Mica threw his arms around Pearl and ducked them into a crouch. A pathetic defense against the monsters. All it meant was he'd die first.

The ground quaked beneath Emer's feet as the mære loomed over her younger sister. It jolted to a stop, then suddenly puffed into smoke. In its place stood a massive spike of earth.

"What the dev—" Caden began, but was interrupted as the rocks beneath their feet trembled.

Other mære came for Emer and her friends, but the ground rose up with great spikes to impale several of the monsters. Emer stared as the stabbed creatures puffed away.

Shocked as she was, she didn't notice the dirt beneath her rising with a sharp point.

"Emer!" Caden shouted and pulled her to the side as spikes rose all around them. Emer yelped as shouts and screams sounded from her sisters and friends.

"Marin!" Pearl's voice shouted from behind the forest of dirt spikes. Emer grabbed onto the nearest spike that was already taller than she was. Rising above the growing forest of spikes, the mære screeched. The remaining monsters moved as smoke, fleeing from the area.

Emer watched the skies for the fleeing mære, but instead saw a figure in browns and greens launch itself over the ground, toward Opal. Had that been Leo's brother? What was he doing there? He'd been carrying a long and straight branch. Had he used it to vault over the spikes? How did he know where (or if) he could land safely? More importantly, what would he do if he landed on the other side? What would he do to Opal? If he was working for Tanzi, Emer feared the worst.

She didn't have time to ponder further as the spikes rumbled and grew, blocking her view of her friends. Thankfully, Caden was close enough, standing with his back against a spike nearby. A new spike grew between them, and he jumped to Emer's, landing beside her. He wrapped an arm around her, hugging both of them securely against their spike. She could no longer tell if the spikes grew taller or if the bottom sank lower. Either way, they were stuck in a valley between widening spikes.

Emer closed her eyes and prayed for the ground to stop shaking.

Instead, it grew worse.

The rocky spike that she and Caden clung desperately onto began to grow its own little spikes up its sides. Like an evergreen branch, it grew needles poking from its base, pricking Emer's hands, arms, and chest. She yelped back as her memories flashed.

Pricking her finger on the spindle. Falling into a dream. Feeling wool, only wool, nothing but wool, until a poisonous numbness that grew from her finger with a painful prick, swallowing her hand, her arm, half of her body, then…

"Emer!" Caden shouted beside her, pulling her back to the present. "Climb up!"

He gestured upward, holding onto one of the lower needles that was thick enough to support her weight.

Gritting her teeth, she lifted herself onto the horizontal spikes and started to climb upward toward clearer space. Her dress caught on one of the spikes, and she tugged it free with a wretched rip. Unfortunately, looking back and down gave her another reason to panic. Caden wasn't following.

"Caden?" She found him far below. Analyzing his footing, she found him stuck with one foot completely trapped by the ground. He twisted his body to avoid the new spikes, but they kept growing, and his awkward positioning trapped him below. He gave her a sad and regretful smile until a spike poked into his leg.

"Caden!" Emer cried as he shouted in pain. What could she do? Grab his sword and hack at the spikes? They were strong enough to support her weight. Breaking them wouldn't be easy, but she had to try.

She started to climb down, and Caden's face shifted to horror. "What are you doing? Go up!"

"Give me your sword," she said, slipping below another spike to lower herself.

"No, Emer! You need to climb higher! Leave me!"

"As if I could," she muttered, looking for the clearest path to him. There were too many spikes. They were too thick. They blocked her path downward and began to cover the path she'd taken upward.

"Emer?" Marin called from above. "Prince Seaver? Do you see them?"

"No," Ranae said.

At least Marin and Ranae sounded safe. Emer closed her eyes with relief, then forced them open to survey Caden's situation again. She hated the sight of the spikes and focused on Caden. She loved him. She was glad for her decision to remain with him even if it killed her.

As if he knew her thoughts, he gave her a small smile. "I love you."

"I love you, too."

The ground stopped. Like a tensed muscle, the dirt relaxed and settled with a shifting of sand.

"Wha—"

Before Caden could finish his question, the spikes jolted and collapsed like a sandcastle in a wave. Emer fell a few inches, landing with a poof on the sand. Caden became half buried, but at least it was in sand instead of solid spikes.

Emer's relief was short-lived as her sisters and friends screamed, falling several feet from the sudden disappearance of the spikes.

Dot landed on her rump, followed by Leo, who turned his fall into a crouch and roll. Mica landed hard on his side with Pearl across his stomach. Marin and Ranae fell the farthest from the height of a castle wall. Emer winced as bone snapped.

"Marin!" Pearl called and ran to their older sister. Ranae had managed to land at an angle like a long jumper, but groaned in his struggles toward Marin.

"Ow-ow-ow!" Marin cried, holding her right leg. Emer wasn't sure whether to go help her sister or to help dig out Caden. Marin had Pearl, Mica, and Ranae instantly at her side as Leo and Dot went to help scoop the sand around Caden.

In her indecision, Emer looked to the house in the middle of the field of sand. What had happened? She'd seen Chase go toward Opal. If the spikes were a cause of Opal's curse, he'd obviously done something to her to return the ground to normal. Reflecting on Ruby's wolves and how they'd abandoned her after her death, Emer cringed.

Needing answers, she dropped to her knees to help dig out Caden. "After the mære fled," she said, "I saw someone soar over the spikes toward the center. It looked like your brother." She gestured to Leo, and he immediately stilled. Then he stood and dashed toward the house.

"Leo!" Caden and Dot called. He gave them no heed. He ran toward the house, calling his brother's name. Caden scrambled all the more to dig himself free. They managed to free his right foot, but his left was injured from the wolf bite and spike. He grit his teeth and squeezed his eyes as he grabbed his leg to pull it from the sand.

Mica jogged over from Marin, asking, "Do we have two lame now?"

Caden turned away with an irritated blush. "We need to get to Princess Opal. Leo might need our help."

Chapter 10

OPAL

Driving back to San Antonio with Chase, I spotted a fascinating machine on the side of the road. It was like a giant white watermill, except there were people sitting in the slots! I had no idea how long we'd been driving, but I was done with sitting. I wanted to stand and stretch. I wanted to explore. The day wasn't over yet, and I wasn't ready to return to the place of chores.

"What is that machine, Chase?"

"The Ferris wheel? Looks like a pop-up carnival."

"It looks like fun. Can we stop to go closer?"

Chase glanced at the numbers that counted the time passing. "Yeah, I guess we have time."

He directed the vehicle off the freeway and we found our way to the carnival. The nearest parking spot left us with a long walk to the front.

Chase grinned as we neared the park. "I haven't been to one of these since I was a kid."

"Adults say that we still are kids," I said. "Which gives us all the more reasons to enjoy this while it lasts.

114

Come on!" I grabbed his hand and started running. He laughed, matching my pace.

As we neared the carnival, paradoxical scents and sounds grew. My nose tingled with sweet candies, salty butter, and filthy manure, while my ears rumbled between screams, laughter, music, and machinery.

We waited in line at a booth, but as soon as we reached the counter, I realized the entertainment wasn't free.

"I don't have any money," I said.

The man in the booth raised his eyebrow. "Then wha'd ya'll come here fer? Lookin' fer work?"

Working hadn't been my choice, but this lively place interested me. I wanted to learn more about it. "Yes," I said. "May I ride the Ferris wheel after an hour of work?"

Chase groaned, and the man scoffed. "Huh, we can always use extra workers, but aren'cha a bit underage? How d'ya like to watch over the Wheel O' Chance?"

Chase's eyes narrowed. "What's the Wheel of Chance?"

"Ah, don' look at me like that. It's just handin' out prizes. Customers pay a ticket to spin the wheel, and ya give 'em the reward."

"Sounds simple enough," I said. "Sure!"

"Opal," Chase hissed under his breath. "This is a carnival. There's always a catch."

The man in the booth laughed and led us into the park. Various smells teased my nose. We passed a red and yellow stand with an overpowering scent of butter and a petting zoo with simple farm animals. Kids squealed inside like they'd never seen a pig or sheep before.

My temporary employer gestured for me to follow him behind a red booth decorated with large question marks. A woman sat in a chair. Her long blonde hair reminded me of Emer, except it was combed in a way to make her head two times larger. She also wore a surprising amount of color on her lips, cheeks, and eyes.

"Darla," the man said, "you get an hour break. This little missy's gonna cover fer ya."

Darla raised a shapely eyebrow at me. "How old is she—no, don't tell me. I'd rather plead ignorance if the cops show up."

The man chuckled. "It's only an hour. Enjoy your break."

Darla smirked at me and stood from her chair. "Don't have too much fun, now."

She left with a laugh.

Chase groaned. "I can't believe you're doing this. What are the prizes? Ten new tickets, fifty new tickets, a chocolate, a sticker, or… it looks like the tiny slice of 'grand prize' is a thousand tickets."

"If ya'd rather do somethin' else," the man said, "the manure pits are always lookin' fer more workers if ya'd rather earn yer keep there."

Chase grimaced, and I nudged him for encouragement. "See? This isn't so bad."

"Right? Now, little missy, all ya gotta do is take their ticket, then spin the wheel. But don'cha go cheatin' or whatnot. We got a hidden camera, so don'cha try nothin.'"

He left us alone, and Chase leaned against the booth siding.

"You're seriously going to do this?"

"Why not?" I asked. "It's better than working the manure pits."

The Wheel of Chance wasn't a high-ticket item with long lines, so I stood up front, mimicking the traveling showmen of Ormio to encourage people to visit our booth.

After several straggling customers, a group of boys about my age walked by. One carried a cotton candy and stuffed toy, another had a bag of popcorn, and the third walked empty-handed. He complained, "Ya'll have tons of tickets left. Just a few more tries, and I'll win that BMX bike, I promise."

"Are you looking for more tickets?" I called to them. "Spin the Wheel of Chance to win a thousand!"

The boy came closer to study the wheel. "The grand prize looks impossible to get, but even if I just win the ten extra tickets, I bet that'll be enough to let me win that bike."

I took his ticket and let him spin the wheel. After playing with the wheel many times, I knew the size of the grand prize slice wasn't the only trick against him. The wheel was weighted, so the most common prizes were a sticker, plastic ring, or piece of chocolate. Even though I was new to chocolate, I'd sampled one to know that I'd had better.

The boy and his friends cheered for the grand prize, but as expected, the marker ended on the chocolate.

I wished him better luck next time and handed the downcast boy his winning chocolate. His friends nudged him.

"Dude! José got a kiss from a girl!"

José went beet red. "What? No! It's a chocolate! It's not the same thing!"

Chase said a kiss would wake me. I wasn't terribly eager to leave this dream, but I had no plans to stay like Ruby.

I leaned forward and puckered my lips. "Did you want a real kiss?"

José went impossibly redder while his friends burst into bigger laughs.

"Yeah," one of the friends laughed. "I'll take a kiss."

Dream Me: Sure, why not?

Real Me: Because we don't kiss strangers! It's shameful and rude to play with hearts like that!

Dream Me: What shame? I feel no shame, and these are only dreams. I want to wake up, don't I?

"Alright," I said, and faced him with my puckering.

118

Chase groaned and slid his hand down his face. "Opal, that's not how it works."

"How will I know if I don't try?" I asked.

The group of boys entered a teasing banter between betting, daring, and name calling. I waited patiently as the only other potential customers who came up to the Wheel of Chance appeared to be friends of José's group. Eventually, one of José's friends was shoved my way with five other young boys cheering, "Kiss her! Kiss her! Kiss her!"

He squeezed his eyes shut and bent toward me in an awkward bow. I pressed my lips to his before he could "chicken out." He pulled back almost immediately, making a fuss of spitting and wiping his mouth.

His friends laughed. "I think he enjoyed it!"

Well, I hadn't. I pouted my lips to the side. "You call that a kiss? Did anyone else want to try? I'm a princess waiting for true love's kiss to wake me, you know."

Chase grumbled something unintelligible as his jaw hardened, and he took over the Wheel of Chance for me.

The boys either didn't hear or believe me as they returned to their squabble of dares. A new boy stepped forward. Kiss, dares, name calling, squabble, repeat. Kiss after kiss, I quickly lost the thrill of the experience. His kiss was too hard. His kiss was too fast. His kiss was too slow. His kiss was too soft.

"I feel like I'm watching a train wreck," Chase muttered from the wheel, taking care of actual customers. "I don't want to watch, but I can't stop."

Darla returned, walking with no hurry to retake her post.

I stood and waved goodbye to the group. "Sorry, boys. Looks like none of you are my True Love."

Darla smirked at me. "If ya'll paid anything for that lip action, the carnival ain't got anything to do with it, ya'll hear? While they ain't strictly illegal, we ain't dealing with the liabilities of kissing booths."

I raised empty hands in surrender. "No money, no tickets. Only disappointing kisses were exchanged."

"Ain't that life." Darla laughed and handed Chase and me a small roll of tickets. "Thanks for the break. Don't have too much fun."

I grabbed Chase by the arm and tugged him into the middle of the carnival. We had enough tickets to ride the Farris wheel and a few others. What to do first?

Screams caught my attention as a machine spun people through the air like they were ants on a staff twirled by a giant. Real Me would have been terrified senseless at the speed. They nearly hung upside-down at some points!

"That one," I said, pointing at the twirling giant arm.

Chase shrugged. "I haven't eaten anything in hours, so at least I won't puke."

120

We stepped up to wait in line, but it didn't move fast enough. I tried skipping ahead to the front, but Chase pulled me back. Dear Mud, I found your stick.

When it finally came time to mount the machine, I was surprised by the strange seats. They were stiff and confining with the thickest seatbelt. I decided never to complain about the car seatbelts again, as I was restrained on both shoulders with enough padding to block my view of Chase beside me.

"Are you ready?" he shouted over the hum of the resting machine.

"Maybe?" I said. I had no idea what to expect.

Once everyone was seated, the machine raised us from the floor. I kicked my feet as they dangled in the air like a barstool. Then, the machine tilted, pulling my feet to the side—not like a barstool. The spinning was slow at first, but it quickly gained speed, twisting us forward and back, up and down, this way and that. The air rushed around me like when I'd stuck my head through the car window, but I also flopped around like I was on a bucking racehorse. Or, at least, what I imagined it would be like to be on a bucking racehorse. Real Me was too timid to ride faster than a canter.

My head continued to spin after the ride ended and we walked off of the stage. My hands shook with excitement.

"That," I said, "was. Amazing! What should we do next?"

Chase gave me a bewildered grin. "Bumper cars? I haven't done those since learning to drive. Maybe I'll be better at it now."

He led me to a large area with a smooth ground. While waiting in line, I watched and listened to Chase's explanation of the ride. We each had our own little vehicles to drive around the smooth arena. With no defined roads or lines to follow, the vehicles drove aimlessly. In fact, the entire purpose of these "bumper cars" was to intentionally run into other vehicles. How bizarre. What kind of masochist created this?

Entering the arena, I picked a yellow car close to Chase's green car.

"You wouldn't let me drive your friend's vehicle, but I can drive this?"

"This only has one speed. Press the pedal with your feet to brake, and turn the wheel to change directions."

Interesting, like tapping a horse's sides and steering with a ship's wheel. I could do that. But what was the point of driving into other people?

As soon as our vehicles growled with power, however, Dream Me came unleashed. I could ram into as many people as hard as I wanted, and what would it matter? I ran into strangers, jolted from the impact, laughed with them, then turned around to ram someone else.

After three minutes of bumping into strangers, I spotted Chase's green car across the arena and aimed for him. Cars zoomed around me, narrowly passing. I grinned with anticipation as Chase noticed me coming. His eyes panicked as he realized the inevitable bump that would throw us against our seatbelts.

The growls died as every vehicle in the arena suddenly went to sleep again. My face fell as my ram turned into a drifting nudge.

Dissatisfied, I unbuckled myself and tripped over my car in my hurry. Chase was barely standing from his car as I ran into him, smashing him with a hug. He grabbed his car to keep us both from falling.

"Got you!" I laughed, pretending my "bump" into him had been on purpose. "Can we do that again?"

"Don't you want to try the Ferris wheel? We only have a few tickets left."

Unfortunately, he was right. I grabbed Chase by the arm and headed toward the giant white watermill of the sky.

We waited in the longest line yet to enter the Ferris wheel. He glanced at his wristband and frowned. "The line's extra long because everyone wants to be on the Ferris wheel during the sunset. We'll need to drive back after this if we don't want to get into trouble."

"Shh," I said, putting my finger over his lips. "Don't ruin the fun of the moment."

Finally, we made it up to the giant machine, and a worker helped us into the bucket seat. We slowly went higher as they loaded each seat, until we were at

the top, staring west as the sun lowered over a mountainless landscape. I'd never seen anything like it. The
sky was still blue despite the long shadows.

Chase stretched his arm against the back of our seat
to angle toward the view—toward me. Real Me might
have become shy of his near cuddle until I caught sight
of the seat below ours. The couple inside were wrapped
in each other's arms in a messy embrace.

Following my gaze, Chase grunted. "You kissed
all those boys. Was it worth it?"

I shrugged. "None of them sent me home, and
their kisses were awkward, so not really. But I wouldn't
have known if I hadn't tried."

He frowned and pointedly looked away from me
and the vigorous couple below us.

"Hey." I nudged him. "Did I do something wrong?
You were the one who said a kiss will wake me."

"How could you do that?" Chase asked. "Kisses are
supposed to be special—to mean something."

"I might kiss every man I ever meet, and what does
it matter if I never see them again?"

"What about everyone else?" Chase asked. "You
do these things without a care about how they affect
you, but you have no idea how they affect others."

I scoffed. "I'm fairly certain that those boys were
hardly affected."

Chase ground his teeth and looked over the fairgrounds. "I know at least one person was affected."

"Who?" I asked, mildly curious. Maybe True Love's Kiss needed a primer test kiss? I prodded, but Chase refused to answer.

We spent three rounds in silence, staring at the sunset, ignoring the lip-locked couple in the neighboring seat, and struggling for words.

Chapter 11

OPAL

Little was said as Chase and I returned to the vehicle, and none of it was worth remembering. We were both tired and left slightly dissatisfied with our adventures. He didn't have any clues to bring his brother back to him, and I didn't feel any closer to waking up.

For one who was sleeping, I was incredibly tired. Running on a scattering of two hours of sleep for the past two days wasn't enough to energize Dream Me. I dreaded closing my eyes, though, seeing shadows of misty monsters creeping from the edges of my vision, hearing snarls in the distance. I stared out the window at the darkening sky, letting my mind drift between memories and dreams.

I thought of Ruby and the differences between Real Ruby and Dream Ruby. Like Dream Me, Dream Ruby had gained a sense of confidence, though she seemed surprised—almost mortified—by my own confidence. She seemed comfortable in her simple dress that showed her arms and lower legs, and I wondered

126

what my other sisters would say about the fashion sense.

Imagining Dia in her shimmering gown with her diamond mask and Dot in sage green with her bird mask, I inserted Dream Me with my stretchy blue leggings and simple cropped shirt.

"Do you like my outfit?" I asked my sisters. Shadows growled from the corners.

"What?" Chase asked. "Are you sleep talking?"

"No!" I jerked awake, stretching my eyes and willing them to stay open. Slanders, I couldn't let them close.

"When was the last time you slept?"

I yawned. "I managed to catch at least a wink or two last night. I think…"

"Only a wink or two? Why?"

"I can't sleep. Every time I try, I have nightmares. It's like they're waiting for me to close my eyes, to crawl into my brain and eat me alive."

Chase gaped at me. "Opal, that's not healthy. You need to sleep."

"I can't. The monsters are waiting for me."

"They won't get you. They're just dreams."

"So are you," I mumbled. I wasn't sure if he heard me. A little louder, I asked, "Will you protect me from the monsters?"

"Uhh, how?"

"Just… keep watch," I said, eyes already closed, my mind already drifting back to Ormio. Maybe I could catch some sleep before the monsters came again.

Leaning against Chase, I was reminded of a song from home about a person's love compared to a tree.

If I was a bird, I'd nest in your arms,
I'd make a home, you'd keep me from harm.
If I was a rabbit, I'd huddle in your wake,
You're there to ground me when the world shakes.
If I was a fox, I'd burrow at your feet,
You keep me cool, away from the heat.

If I was the sun, I'd feed your growth,
I'll raise you upward, this is my oath.
If I was the wind, I'd brush by your side,
You caress my aura with a tender glide.
If I was the snow, I'd fall in your arms,
Even as I have fallen for your charms.

If I was a lass, I'd lie in your shade,
I'd ponder the beautiful life we have made,
And compose a song of my wish to be near you,
Forever and always, may our journey continue.

According to the numbers on the vehicle's dashboard, one half hour passed before I woke up with a start, terrified of the shadow monsters reaching for me with their claws. A hand clasped around mine, but it didn't have claws. Chase sat beside me, watching me with red ears. More accurately, I'd fallen onto him while sleeping, using his leg as a pillow. I stared up at him.

"I feel like I should be horribly embarrassed," I said.

"You're not?" he asked, his ears burning brighter.

"No," I said, snuggling against him. "I feel comfortable."

Chase didn't speak as he took a few deep breaths. Was he calming himself? From what? It didn't seem to be working as his ears continued to burn like a blacksmith's blade before quenching its heat.

"Um, Opal, it's kind of hard to drive with you leaning against me. I'm still new to this, remember? We made it back to San Antonio. I just need to fill the car with gas and park at the campground entrance. Then you can sleep more comfortably in your bed. Can you stay awake until then?"

"Alright," I said, sitting up.

Chase stopped to feed his beastly carriage, relieved that we'd made the whole trip without "being pulled over." Whatever that meant.

"I hope Leo's employer doesn't call my parents to tell them of our visit."

"Why?" I asked. "We didn't cause any trouble."

"Yeah, I guess so. Maybe you're right. It'll be better if I tell them the truth right away than for them to find out later, right?"

"No fear!" I cheered.

"How do I tell them?"

"Good news," I offered. "You fed your vehicle recently. Bad news; you needed to fill it twice."

Chase smirked until it turned into a laugh. "Why does everything seem so easy with you? You really don't have a care in the world."

"Not in this world." I grinned.

* * *

I spent the evening attempting to stay awake, failing, then waking suddenly from nightmares of growling shadows. I didn't see Chase again until dinner at the indoor gallery hall. He walked with hunched shoulders and shifty eyes, like he expected everyone was gossiping about him. At least my tentmate squealed with excitement and quick whispers to the nearest ear when he beelined to me and nodded to the side.

"Can we talk?"

I had looked forward to the provided meal, but Chase's attitude worried me. I followed him away from the other volunteers to the outside patio. He leaned against the metallic railing and looked out at the wilderness of short trees.

With a heavy sigh, he said, "I told my parents about our trip, and… even though I'm glad I told the truth, they weren't happy with me. They ordered me to come home immediately and had me expelled from the camp."

"Slanders, that's awful. But why only you? I went with you, but no one's making me leave."

Chase turned back to give me a half smile. "I didn't tell them about you going with me. Remember, an unsupervised road trip is one thing, but driving with a minor is illegal."

"Oh." I wasn't sure what to say. A weird part of me wanted to go with Chase. I didn't care to stay with the camp, and he was my friend. An even weirder part of my insides literally ached with the thought of never seeing him again.

Unfortunately, the monsters I wished to never see again crept from the shadows of the building.

"Oh, Words." When I turned to stare at them directly, they disappeared, but I could sense them. "The monsters of my dreams… they followed me into *this* dream. We can't stay here."

Chase frowned and looked around us. "Monsters? Do you want to go back inside?"

"No. They hide around corners and in the shadows. I need a wide-open space. Somewhere they cannot sneak up to me."

There was a small open area before me, but it was too close to these monsters. I remembered driving around an open area near the parking lot. I ran for it.

"Opal! Where are you going?"

I ran into the field with Chase running after, calling me back.

Without shadows or corners to hide behind, I spotted three monsters following. One was massive, like the largest bear breed, another was tall like my parents, and the third was only as big as me. I had thought of them as bears from their growls, size, and monstrosity. Now that I saw them in the light, they were more like the shadows of wingless dragons, sometimes galloping or running on their hind feet with shark tails slashing behind.

The monsters were faster than Chase and easily outpaced him, passing him without sparing even a second glance. Chase likewise didn't seem to notice the shadowed monsters.

"Help me!" I called back to Chase. I wasn't sure what the young man could do against them, but I felt too vulnerable to fight them by myself. Desperate, I cried, "Stop them! Don't let them reach me!"

Chase stopped at the edge of the field, confused. His confusion switched into fear as the entire field shook beneath us. Was this an earthquake? The rocks and sand rippled outward from me, then burst into the air. The rocks became spikes, stabbing into the shadow monsters. They evaporated into ash with ear-piercing cries like horses drowning.

"What was that?" Chase cried from the edge of the field, behind the spikes of rock. "Opal, are you okay in there?"

"I'm fine," I called back. "I think the soil destroyed the monsters. Thank you," I added softly. "Can you go back to being smooth or do I need to—" There was no need to finish as the spears flattened. I found Chase twenty meters away, gaping.

"Is it…is it safe?" he asked.

"It helped me," I said with a shrug. I walked over to him, and he ran to meet me.

Scanning the circular field, he asked, "What was that? How did that happen? Why did the ground act that way? Is it like the stones at the river?"

"I asked it to protect me," I said simply.

"And it obeyed? Or is this area magical? Hey, ground, make me a snowman with rocks."

The dirt did nothing.

"A snowman?" I asked. "Out of rocks? Could you show me?"

With my words, the ground trembled again until it formed a little ball before us. A slightly larger ball lifted it, then a third and bigger ball carried the other two into the air. Three round stones lined down the middle ball, and a face of stones with a spear-like nose grew on the top ball. I laughed at its simple smile. Like sculpting with my mind and words, it was just as I had pictured it.

Chase gaped again, then turned to me. "It listens to you. Opal, this is insane! How did you do that?"

"It is insane, isn't it?" I said more than asked. "I'm going insane. I lost all sense of consequences, started seeing things that weren't there, and now…"

Chase shook his head with wonderment. "Then I must be going insane too, because I saw that. I didn't see any monsters, but what you've done with the earth… It's like you're an Earth bender!" Whatever that was. He paused to grin at me. Not just any grin. Not a playful grin or a teasing grin, but one of open admiration. "Opal, you're amazing, you know that?"

"Chase," I groaned. "No, you weren't supposed to like me. I'm going to wake up and disappear like Leo. Even though I've lost every worry in the world, I… I don't want to hurt you, too."

"Then don't. Stay. Stop this craziness of trying to wake up by kissing every man you meet. Just… stay here."

Like Ruby? Who chose to be blind and live on a farm rather than to wake up and return home?

"Oh, Chase," I whispered, "when you say that, I want to kiss you."

"I want to kiss you," he confessed quietly. "But after watching you kiss all those boys, I can't. Because I want it to mean something. You've kissed everyone else like you're purchasing lottery tickets, hoping one of them is the golden number to wake you up. I don't want to be another lottery ticket. I want to be that car that you save up for, working hard day after day for months—maybe even a year—to buy. That way, when you get it, you know you've earned it, and you'll treat it right because… you'll love it."

I listened and wished to understand. Real Me understood exactly what he meant but Dream Me was less sure.

Quietly, I said, "If that's what a real kiss is supposed to feel like, then I haven't really kissed anybody."

"You've kissed lots of people."

"But none with feeling," I said. "If that's what it means to kiss, then the only person I can imagine kissing for real is you."

He groaned and slid his hands down his face. "You're not making this easy."

"Making what easy?"

"Not kissing you. I want to, but—"

"But what?" I demanded. "I have no sense of consequences. What would you do if you lost yours?"

The next sound out of my mouth was a yelp as he yanked me to him and collided our lips together.

It didn't matter if I kissed every person on the planet. Kissing Chase was like kissing no one else. He wasn't too soft or too hard, too timid or too bold, too fast or too slow. His kiss was… just right.

Chapter 12

OPAL

When Opal woke in her kingdom, her homeland, her fortress of a wooden castle, a sudden flush of embarrassment surged through her.

She stared up at Chase Bahr, completely, absolutely, and thoroughly mortified to find him in reality.

"Oh. My. Word." With stiff arms, she pushed herself up and looked around. "This is unreal, right? This is still a dream. I have to be dreaming. You cannot be real, and you cannot be here. And this place… is like home, but is not."

"Opal?" Chase asked. "Do you know who I am?"

"Chase?" She trembled with terror. "But you cannot be. You cannot be real—it was all a dream, only a dream, where nothing mattered."

"Is that what you think?" he asked, his voice pained. "The dreams were so real. I tried to ignore them, but I couldn't. The queen's gonna kill me, but everything's been so confusing. My brother's alive, and he says my parents are alive—"

"Leo?" Opal shuffled to the edge of her bed. Why did she feel so sore and stiff? How long had she been sleeping? "Your brother is here? He truly made it to Ormio? Is Dot here? What about Ruby?"

Anxious for answers, she pushed herself from the bed, but her body lacked the strength to stand properly. She began to crumple to the ground, but Chase caught her, lifting her back to sit her on the edge of the bed again. The security of his arms felt so familiar, so… right.

"Slanders," she cursed. Twice in ten minutes. That was more than Real Opal had cussed in her whole life, but the moment felt appropriate. Shame of herself and actions terrorized her. "You had the dreams too? You know everything that I did? Every perfectly foolish and wholly embarrassing act?"

He chuckled. "Yeah, it was a little embarrassing, but also inspiring. I wished I could be more like you, more carefree and open to new experiences. You gave me the courage to go against the queen's wishes; to kiss you instead of kill you."

"Kill me?"

"It's what Queen Tanzanite demands."

"Queen—" Opal sputtered "—Tanzi? What happened? Where is everyone? How long was I sleeping?"

"Chase!" a deep voice roared from outside.

"Uh oh." Chase cringed.

"What is it?"

"It's Leo. Things are, um, different here. He and I haven't exactly been on speaking terms for the past three years, and, um, this might be awkward."

More awkward than waking up and discovering that her hopeful boyfriend had witnessed every embarrassing moment of her dream? It was supposed to be a dream that no one else knew about! If she'd known those moments would follow her into reality, she would have acted normally, like a good little princess.

But what had Chase said? That she'd inspired him?

Heavy footsteps pounded into the house. The deep voice called for Chase again, then came up the stairs. Chase wiggled nervously and darted his eyes between the door, the window, and Opal. She grabbed the cuff of his sleeve, willing him to stay. Her weak hold seemed to calm him as his twitching lessened.

A large man appeared in the doorway. He was a mirror of Chase, eschewed only by his size and age. His likeness confirmed his identity. This was Leo, Chase's older brother, the man who disappeared with Dot.

He stared at Chase for a long second before turning his eyes on Opal. "Thank the devils you're alive. What are you doing here?" he asked Chase with a cautious glare.

"I, uh, I don't really know."

Leo took a massive and threatening step closer. "Back away from her."

"I mean her no harm," Chase said.

"Is that so?" Leo challenged. "What about Ruby? Why were you there when she died?"

"Ruby what?"

Leo paid Opal no heed as he bore down on his younger brother. "Why did you attack Princess Emerald and Prince Caden? Why have you hunted us and served our enemy?"

"She isn't the enemy!" Chase said, stepping away from Opal to meet his brother's challenge. "Queen Tanzanite saved me! She gave me a home away from the ogres and raised me like a son! I thought you were dead!"

"And when you found out that I wasn't?" Leo shouted to match his brother's volume. "Even after you saw me, you came back and attacked again! And again! Why didn't you come home? We thought you were dead!"

Opal wasn't sure who threw the first punch or dropped the first tear, but the skirmish was over before she could call it to stop. The brothers ended up in a gripping bear-hug, crying into each other's shoulders.

Confused and unsure where she fit into the situation, she sat back on the bed and waited for the men to overcome their feelings. Eventually, they raised their heads from each other's shoulders to press their foreheads together.

Chase was the first to turn his sobs into words. "I'm glad you're here. I don't know what to do. Queen

Tanzanite demanded that I kill Opal, but I couldn't do it. I *won't* do it, but she'll punish me severely."

"Join the club." Leo chuckled. "Literally. Join us. Fight by my side again, Brother, and we'll fight her together."

Chase stared at his brother with glistening eyes. Looking back to Opal, he asked his brother, "You'll help me to protect her?"

Leo chuckled and made a strange gesture with his hands.

Chase answered automatically with his own gesture before both brothers' eyes grew wide.

"You know ASL?" Leo asked while Chase said, "You know about Texas!"

Leo laughed and slugged Chase on the shoulder. "Your signing is terrible."

The only part that made sense to Opal was the confirmation that Leo knew about the dreams. Lost in her worries, she didn't even hear the thudding of footsteps as multiple people entered the house and came up the stairs.

"Oh, Slanders," she cursed yet again. "Does everyone know about what happened in Texas?"

Even as she spoke, another man stepped into the room. Opal didn't recognize him, but she squealed with excitement for the two women who followed.

"Dot! Pearl!"

"Opal!" Her sister and friend rushed into the room to wrap their arms around her. She hugged them back as tightly as she could with her limited strength.

"Garnet said you were poisoned!"

"Yeah," Dot half laughed, half sobbed around her neck. "It's been going around."

Pearl giggled and stepped back to let Opal broaden her focus. Emer stood at the doorway, grinning and shouting reports to someone below. There wasn't enough room for everyone, as the voices below sounded like Marin and Ranae.

The first stranger who had entered the room glared at Chase. Despite his neatly trimmed black beard, the man was a mess of injuries, with an arm in a sling and ankle bleeding through its wrap. When Chase noticed the glare, he answered with a timid, "It won't happen again?"

"It better not," the man growled.

"Caden," Leo chided, "he wants to protect Opal. He's turning his back on Queen Tanzanite to join us."

"And you trust that?" The man named Caden scowled. "For all we know, he's in league with the usurper and the mære."

"But the ground saved us," the second stranger in the room said. He was a little stockier and lingered around Pearl like her shadow. "The spikes killed a mære that attacked me and Pearl!"

"Or," Caden noted, "simply made it disappear."

"Killed," Chase said. Everyone turned to him, suddenly curious about what he knew of the mysterious mære. He clamped his mouth shut. "Sorry, I shouldn't have said anything."

"Yes, you should have," Leo rumbled. "You know how to kill those monsters?"

"What monsters?" Opal asked, remembering the black shadows of her dreams.

"Mære," Dot said, almost in a whisper. "They… they destroyed Veriae after we were poisoned. The only part that remained protected was this little servant's hut because of your curse."

Opal gaped, wishing to disbelieve, but somehow knew the truth. Taking a guess, she asked, "The shadow monsters from my dream? They're real?"

Chase's eyebrows lifted. "You saw the mære in Texas? I guess that explains why no one else saw them. They can invade dreams. They're my high—er, Queen Tanzanite's creations, slaves, and pets. They serve her and her alone, and I was sworn to secrecy that I'd never reveal their weakness."

"They actually have a weakness?" The man near Pearl asked eagerly.

Caden shrugged. "The queen ordered you to kill Princess Opal, and you woke her instead. I'm fairly certain you already betrayed her. Based on her history, she's not one to forgive and forget. Help us fight her and her nightmares, and we'll do our best to remove her influence and keep you safe."
142

"I don't need your protection," Chase sneered.

Caden smirked back. "Yep, you're unquestionably Leo's brother. Maybe if you don't tell us directly, but give us clues, then you won't break your oath of secrecy."

Chase worked his jaw in thought, then hung his head and sighed heavily. "They're the spawn of nightmares. How would you kill a nightmare?"

"Positive thoughts?" Pearl offered.

"Waking up?" Emer tried.

Dot said, "Pray the Words to bless your sleep before going to bed."

"Or surrounding yourself with charms," Opal added. She glanced around for her dream sifter, but found more dust than decoration in her surroundings. No wonder she had nightmares with these accommodations.

Chase slid his hand down his face. "Fine. That was a bad clue. What are nightmares?"

"Bad dreams," Pearl said.

"The mind's projection of fears," Emer said.

Caden paused in his note taking to say, "Intangible."

Chase pointed at Emer and Caden. "Right. They're not physical. They're fears. Your fears feed them, and intangible concepts don't hurt them."

Leo grumbled. "Neither do tangible weapons. Do you know how many arrows I've lost trying to shoot those things?"

"They can be killed," Chase affirmed, then smirked at his brother. "You lost arrows from attacking the mære?" Before Leo could retort, Chase half shrugged and continued, "Not that I'm entirely surprised. You've all had nightmares of them the last few days, haven't you?"

Opal nodded, surprised that her friends all joined her. They all had nightmares about the shadow monsters, too?

Chase continued, "That's because Queen Tanzanite wants you to fear them. She needs the people to fear them, because, ah…"

"Our fears feed them," Caden echoed. "We can't hurt them as long as we fear them. Of course! That's why Queen Tanzanite had the creatures attack Veriae. She doesn't rule by fear because she simply chooses to. She rules by fear because it's necessary for her mære. What better way to create fear of a creature than to destroy a capital and leave mysterious rumors about the attack?"

Dot fingered her chin in thought. "That's why some of the animals were able to fight them, while others had no effect. Because they were scared."

Leo's face burned red. "I'm not afraid of the mære. There must be more to it than that. I've shot more than a few arrows at them, and they've all slipped through like smoke."

Chase tilted his head at his older brother with a teasing smirk. "You can't hit the mære because you're afraid of them."

Leo sputtered to argue, but Dot spoke for him. "Who isn't? You said it yourself. We've all had nightmares involving those monsters. How could we not be afraid of them?"

"What I don't understand," Caden said, "is how the stone spikes killed one. It was controlled by Opal, but she gained a fear of the mære in her dreams—which fascinates me, by the way. Were the mære in Texas or—"

"Caden," Emer cut him off. "One topic at a time, Love."

Opal blinked in surprise at Emer's term of endearment. There was also an obvious connection between Pearl and the man behind her. Even her sister Dot seemed partial to Chase's brother. Ruby had said they met and fell in love during their dreams. Had the same happened to Emer and Pearl?

Chase stepped closer to Opal to slide his hand around hers, reminding her that she also gained a boyfriend from her dreams. "You were marvelous with those rock spikes, and you didn't even know it." Addressing everyone again, he said, "The mære are shadows. Intangible, right? The more tangible the weapon, the greater the effect."

"Ah," Pearl added. "That explains why my light had no effect."

Caden nodded. "And why they left us alone when we hid in the Ezuthithe Caves."

Dot gasped with a sudden epiphany. "I need honey badgers! They're the most fearless animals and can face down bears and lions. They're fierce and difficult to catch with skin that's incredibly thick and loose, making them formidable foes. Yes, I like this plan."

She grinned, and Leo cracked a smile as he chuckled at her excitement. "You seem extra excited to add to our odd parade of animals."

Opal stared at the interactions of those around her, attempting to wrap her head around the conversations. Veriae was destroyed? The shadow monsters were real? Her sister and friends were awake and in love? Exactly how much had changed while she was asleep?

Chapter 13

EMER

Emer listened and helped Caden to take notes as Opal sat on the edge of her bed and explained the events leading up to her poisoning. She explained Garnet's arrival with the news of Ruby and Dot's poisoning, the distrust, and the plans for Dia to secure an alliance with Urbanuz. Dot sat beside her younger sister to wrap her in a side hug while Caden gave a brief rundown of Opal's hundred-harvest slumber and the last few weeks.

While Caden seemed eager to ask questions through the evening, stomachs growled and eyes grew tired.

Emer and her sisters gasped to hear that Garnet had planned to escape to Remizio with Opal and Dia. She was right to think that no one would expect the Ormio princesses to seek refuge in the capital of their enemy's kingdom.

Caden finished his record and nodded. "Then we continue into Huiess. We should pack and head out as soon as possible."

Everyone agreed, eager to leave the little servant's hut. Chase offered to help Opal stand and walk outside.

Pearl skipped beside her friend. "Tell us about your dream! We want to hear all about it!"

Opal cringed and shot a fearful look at Chase. "Don't you dare say a word."

He raised his hand in defense. "I wasn't going to."

"Wait—what happened?" Emer asked, all the more curious.

Dot rested a gentle hand on her sister's arm. "Were you as miserable as I was?"

"Miserable?" Opal repeated. "No. Ruby told me a little about what you went through in Texas with Leo."

Dot's gentle hold became an eager grip. "You saw Ruby?" Everyone gathered closer to hear.

Opal squirmed. "Yes, but she called herself Biddy. She said you came to visit and then disappeared, taking Chase's brother with you."

"But she's well and happy?" Dot turned surprised eyes on Leo. "I didn't leave you behind?"

"Yeah," Chase said, folding his arms at his brother. "You left *me* behind. I was so angry at you for disappearing like that."

Pearl nodded. "It makes sense. Mica said that Emer and Caden had disappeared together. You come here, becoming one with your other self."

Leo asked, "Did you see Shino too? Was he okay?"
148

Opal blinked in surprise. "You know Shino? Yes, he was fine. Better than fine by the looks of his attachment to Biddy. I think they were in love. Slanders," she swore, causing Dot to flinch back with surprise. Opal buried her face into her hands. "It all happened. It really happened. This is the worst nightmare ever."

"Hey." Chase slid his hand across her shoulders. "We've all done things we're not proud of." His downcast eyes flickered to Leo, implying a second meaning to his words.

Emer burst, "What happened?" Dot and Leo's silence about their dream was frustrating enough. She'd hoped to learn more, as Opal had shared similar interactions with Ruby and Shinópu. If they also refused to share their tales, Emer was sure she'd explode.

"If you don't mind," Caden said, stepping in with his notes, "could you answer some questions to verify consistencies? Every poisoned princess gained a magic and suffered a loss. Based on the actions of the stone spikes surrounding you while you slept, I assume your magic is through rocks. If you can tell us anything else about your dream, could you tell us what loss you suffered? This is for research."

Opal swallowed and turned wide eyes on Chase. "Is that why I acted that way? Why I did all those things?"

"Hey," Chase said, leaning close to cradle her under his arm, "I liked you all the more for it. You made my life an adventure. Irresponsible and hazardous, yes, but an adventure."

Opal pinched back her smile, seeming to gain just enough courage to tell Caden, "I lost my inhibitions."

Silence.

Everyone stopped and stared as Emer took a moment to consider what that would be like. No wonder Opal didn't want to talk about it. Emer imagined that her dream with Caden would have gone entirely differently if she'd lost her inhibitions instead of her sense of touch.

Marin, of all people, softly cursed.

Ranae raised his eyebrows at her, looking almost as impressed as he was surprised. "The only other time I heard you swear was while we were sailing."

Marin's cheeks reddened. "I was a proper sailor on that boat. Though, can you imagine how bad I might have been if I had lost my inhibitions? I shudder to think."

Caden paused in his notes to tap his chin in thought. "It isn't one of the five senses, but I guess it's a common thing to lose when dreaming, similar to Marin's loss of teeth. People do things in their dreams that they'd never do in real life."

"Yeah," Chase said. "It could have been a lot worse, but on that note, please don't ask us more about what happened."

"Then," Caden asked, "what's next? Do we have any clues about where to find Princesses Garnet and

Diamond in Remizio? As Huiess's capitol, I expect it would take a while to search the whole city."

Opal asked, "Did Dia, Garnet, and Ame make the treaty with Urbanuz's prince?"

Everyone answered her with expressions of either blank stares or curiosity.

Marin spoke first. "What is this about a treaty with Urbanuz? I remember Prince Stanford Muli of Urbanuz was visiting Huiess, was he not?"

"Oh, I guess you were all poisoned before the treaty was discussed, but if a hundred years have passed, don't you know what happened?"

Emer scoffed. "Queen Tanzi happened."

"Speaking of Queen Tanzanite," Chase muttered, then drifted with doubt and regret from speaking.

Leo nudged his brother. "If it's something she wouldn't want you to tell us, that's exactly why you should tell us. What about her should we know?"

Chase cleared his throat. "She knows about you all. And I mean about *all* of you. She has a magic mirror that can show and identify people as they are in the moment. Oh!" He snapped his fingers at Leo. "Like a satellite camera feed! You know what I'm talking about?"

Leo nodded. "That's problematic. How long until she learns about you switching sides?"

Chase cringed. "She could know already. Thankfully, she's dividing her army, so only her mære are coming after you."

Mica guffawed. "*Only* her mære? As if they weren't bad enough?"

Chase continued, "She's drafting an army among the citizens to fight the ogres up north."

Caden pulled up short, Emer frowned, Mica's eyebrows went high, and Leo barked, "What?"

"She's…" Caden blinked. "She's helping us to defeat the ogres?"

Chase shrugged. "She had an agreement with them to leave them alone as long as they stayed out of the Rezhina Valley. They broke their side of the treaty, so she's breaking hers to take up arms against them. I told you, she's not all that bad—"

"What's her agenda?" Leo growled.

If Chase knew, he didn't say as he ducked his head. Opal touched his arm with a little smile. "Hey. No matter what has happened and will happen, thank you for being here."

He smiled back, but their private moment was broken as they returned to their abandoned carriage and horses at the main keep of the fortress. True to the rest of Veriae, the once-great wooden fortress lay in rubble and decay with only a few of its walls still standing. The sight of it sent Opal into a burst of tears, only to be soothed by Dot and Chase.

Dot hugged her younger sister from behind. "I know. So much has been lost, but we're here. Together. I'm so glad you woke up, Opal, and returned to us. I'll do whatever it takes to make this our home again."

Caden, as usual, pampered his horse with apologies and treats, while everyone else considered rearrangements for traveling with two more people. Dot recruited another wild horse for Chase and Opal to ride as they picked their way through the rubble of the city. They talked little as they focused on their footing through the wreckage and debris, eventually finding the outskirts of Veriae near sunset.

Sitting atop the coach with Caden, Emer studied his map of the valley. "We have a long road ahead of us to Remizio. Perhaps we should set up camp before leaving the city?"

"Maybe," Caden said. "Maybe Dot can ask the animals if there's an abandoned house that can make a good den for tonight. I'd rather not sleep in our usual open-ended tent in these temperatures. If it's this cold already, I expect it to drop below freezing tonight."

To Emer's surprise, Chase spoke, "There's a home that's still intact." Leo gave him an askance look, and his younger brother shrugged. "I've stayed there a few times when Queen Tanzanite sent me this way."

Caden gestured for him to lead the way, and they followed Chase to a farther side of the city.

"See the biggest pile?" Chase said, pointing at a particularly large mound of fallen logs. "I cleaned out a room underneath. People still avoid the city for its proximity to the island, mists, and legends of Opal's curse, but when the queen sent me off the island for missions, I frequently stayed here."

The others nodded, and Emer parked the coach. The temperatures had dropped with the sun, and she shivered with the oncoming night chill. Marin pulled out every blanket and deconstructed duvet from their carriage to pass around the group. The duvets made for stiff and awkward blankets, but they had little else to work with.

Caden and Mica wore their riding gloves as they collected firewood, though Leo and Chase denied the chill.

Chase bent on all fours to climb through a burrow between the splintered logs.

Ranae rubbed his recent arrow wound and pointed at the entrance. "That looks like a trap. Are we sure he changed to our side?"

Leo growled. "I'll go next." He bent down and wiggled his massive figure through the hole. A few seconds later, he called back. "It's safe, just dark."

"Perhaps I can help," Pearl said. "Lucy? Please light the inside of the den before us."

Light burst from the cracks and slivers of the den, and Chase swore.

Leo laughed from within. "You'll get used to it."

Opal went in next, saying, "I want to see."

As if unwilling to let anything happen without him present, Caden followed with Emer behind. Once inside, Emer found herself in a wooden igloo large enough to stand. Most of the mound was held up by three walls remaining from one of the house rooms. Another hole, angled from the top, would let smoke out without letting rain in (supposing it ever rained harder than the constant mists anymore). Pearl's lights speckled the walls and ceiling like a net, eliminating shadows.

A draft blew in through the bottom hole, and Opal shivered. "It's a bit chilly still."

Caden shrugged. "It's better than being in the open. The women may stay in the coach, though this should be big enough for the men."

Pearl crawled through and dusted off her knees. "Except it is a bit crowded already with the four of us. I may volunteer to sleep outside—"

"Nah-ah," Mica said. "I know you love to help others, but there are limits."

Opal leaned over to Emer and whispered, "It's about time someone stopped her. I've always admired Pearl's charitable heart, but sometimes she took it too far."

Pearl pouted her big eyes at Mica. "Then what should we do? While this room may be large enough for all of us to stand inside, it is too small for all ten of us to lie down with proper space."

Eying Pearl's lights, Opal folded her arms. "I… you say I can influence the rocks to move?"

Caden grinned. "Is it time to experiment? Devils, I don't have my notes. Emer, can you—"

"Perhaps," Emer said, wrapping her arms around his like a restraint, "this time you can just observe and enjoy the magic."

"How do I do it?" Opal asked.

"Speak words to them," Dot said.

Pearl added, "I named mine Lucy."

"I don't think I could name every stone." Opal shuffled and scanned the dirt below them. "Um, rocks? Are you listening?"

"Give them direction," Emer said, "and show confidence in their capabilities."

Opal grumbled. "I'm the one lacking confidence, not the rocks."

Dot pitched in, "Command them like a trained hound. If you don't play the part as their master, they won't respect you."

Opal guffawed, "Their master? Rocks and stones are older than any animal. I'd sooner treat them like an elderly sage than a pet."

Marin tapped her finger to her chin. "That might be wise. While water wants to flow, change forms, and fill its measure, rocks only grow more sturdy and stuck in their ways over time. You may need to be more persuasive than the rest of us to influence your element."

Pearl whispered Lucy into her palm and demonstrated to Opal how to speak. "I treat Lucy as one of my friends, though I must be specific with my requests

156

or she might not perform the way I expect. Now, you try."

Opal shuffled again. "What if I make a mistake?"

Chase gently took her hand. "Who cares?"

Opal's chest swelled as she accepted his hand. She clearly gained confidence from him, or at least a stronger will to fight her worries.

Dot's head tilted, noticing the change in her younger sister.

"Try this," Emer said. "Repeat after me; rocks and soil from beneath my feet, roll and pile yourselves up between the cracks of logs and branches of this room."

Opal echoed her words, adding, "I will consider myself incredibly lucky if you could."

As she spoke, the ground trembled. Emer held tighter to Caden, and he held her back, widening his stance to support them both. A sound like shifting sand and rolling pebbles echoed around their hut, starting from the floor and rising.

Emer needed to shout over the rumbling, "Create solid walls around us, leaving the top hatch and entrance open."

Opal's mouth moved, though Emer couldn't hear her. Apparently, it didn't matter, because the rocks did.

Gaps between the logs were filled with larger rocks, pebbles, then fine dirt settled in until no gaps remained all the way to the top. The rumbling lessened to pebbles rolling, sand shifting, then finally solidifying into silence. Everyone looked about themselves, amazed by the solid hut that had been built around them.

Opal turned an accomplished smile at Chase. "Is that better?"

"Better?" He laughed, then grabbed her face and pulled her into a kiss… that held… and lingered.

Dot blushed with wide eyes at her younger sister, and Pearl whispered to Mica, "Is that still a prune?" Leo cleared his throat with more volume than usual.

Opal giggled and broke away.

Chase grinned. "Who cares who's watching, right?"

Opal winced above her smile. "Oh, I cannot believe I once said that. But if this is the result, then I'm not sorry."

PART 2

Chapter 14

DIA

I'd rather lose my sight or hearing than lose my memory. Didn't I say that before? Fortunately, I knew exactly who and where I was. I was Diana Mason, native of the beautifully chaotic Las Vegas. Right. I did say that earlier. Why did I feel the need to remind myself?

I rubbed my eyes clear of any residual sensations of sleep and groaned to myself. I'd drifted off to daydreams about my night's dream. Again. How embarrassing.

"Dee-ya?"

I winced as the cashier of The Cheesecake Factory mispronounced my name. I was Dia, like "dye-ah." But hearing "dee-ya" was better than announcing my full name of "Diana" to strangers who didn't need to know me that well.

Dia as in Diana Mason from Las Vegas. Not Diamond Fashio of Ormio as my dreams called me.

I grabbed my order of a whole peanut butter chocolate cheesecake without bothering to correct the cashier. They didn't need to know my correct name pronunciation. Just like they didn't need to know that I planned to eat this whole cake by myself. I'd probably ration it over four meals. Maybe three. Maybe I'd share a slice with my adopted parents if they were lucky.

I was celebrating my new job, after all. It seemed that my interview last week with Brian Wilburn, owner of The Golden Pawn, had gone well. I'd start on Monday. One step toward saving up for Stanford University student housing and toward becoming a food scientist. Because I was *not* a princess of an unknown land, and I needed a job like a normal person.

Typically, I let the weirdness of dreams fade away with my morning routine, but the vividness and odd connections between my last couple of dreams were too memorable.

The first dream had been about attending a ball where everyone wore the most elaborate masks. I'd been a princess wearing a flashy golden gown, eating delicate appetizers, listening to foreign music while watching strange dances. Women I'd never seen before approached me like we were friends. Even more disconcerting were the young women I called sisters. I didn't have sisters. At least, that I knew of. I'd been adopted. It was possible…

I shook my head to clear it of the ridiculousness. I didn't need dreams messing with my real life.

Except flashes of last night's dream crept into my mind again.

There was no use taking the dream to heart or trying to make sense of it. What made sense of me walking through a large fortress made of wood? It was like nothing I'd ever seen before; like a castle, but made of logs and solidified with some kind of fire-resistant coating. I had walked through the strange fortress as if I knew exactly what lay behind each door and around each corner. It had felt like home.

The weirdest part of all was running into a man I called Dad. Despite the kingly robes and crown on his head, he looked like me with incredibly blond hair, dark green eyes, but stood a whole head taller than my five feet and two inches. He looked nothing like my adoptive dad, Steve, who was two inches shorter than I was and had dark brown hair with eyes and complexion to match. I looked slightly more related to my adoptive mom, Cherie, with her dirty-blonde hair, light brown eyes, but hers had a hint of blue, unlike mine which had a hint of green.

In my dream, my "dad" had given me a battle report against some kingdom called Huiess, then said that Princess Garnet had arrived with news about my younger sisters. I followed my kingly dad to another wooden room to meet with a tall, but drained, woman. She looked so tired, like all she wanted was a nap, but if she dared to close her eyes, the world would fall apart in a blink.

With a blink of my own, I easily recalled the dream. The details had been more vivid than a typical dream, and writing them down after waking had helped to solidify my memories. Finding a seat on the Paradise bus and hugging my cheesecake on my lap, I closed my eyes and reimagined my dream.

"King Fashio," Princess Garnet had bowed. "I fear that I come bearing grave news."

Dad gestured for her to continue. "If the Crown Princess of Somnus came herself, unattended, to bear this news, then it must be important."

"It is," she said. "I came to warn you and your family that my youngest sister, Tanzanite, has begun a coup. She has poisoned all of my sisters, causing them to become ill and unable to wake."

"I'm sorry to hear that," Dad said. His frown begged the question, "What does this have to do with us?"

"King Fashio," Garnet continued, "I met with Princesses Ruby and Peridot while fleeing my kingdom. They were hospitable and empathetic to my plight. Unfortunately, Tanzanite followed me and passed her poisonous revolution to your twin daughters. They were poisoned and will not wake."

"Ruby and Dot?" I burst, earning a scolding look from my dad.

"You say," Dad asked, "that your youngest sister is the cause of this poisonous revolution? Where are Ruby and Peridot now?"

Uh oh. The skepticism in his voice didn't bode well for Garnet.

Garnet clasped her hands and dared to look my dad in the eyes. "Ruby was caught in a cabin in the Ormytha Forest. She is surrounded and guarded by wolves. Dot-er-Peridot was poisoned at an inn in Othium, now protected by swarms of birds. I do not understand the reasoning for the animals surrounding them, though they should be safe from further intrusion."

"So you say," Dad grumbled. "You have no other witnesses?"

"None with me, your highness."

"In that case," he said, "I'm inclined to disbelieve your story. For all we know, you are an impersonator playing a wretched prank. Be gone with you, or I shall call the guards."

"Wait," I said. "I can confirm this is Garnet, Crown Princess of Somnus."

"Oh?" Dad asked, raising a high eyebrow. "How would you know? You've sailed across the lake a total of four times."

"I, uh…" I wasn't one to stutter. I usually prided myself on my articulate vernacular. However, what could I say? "Unbeknownst to you, I met with Garnet and the other princesses of Rezhina Valley—including our enemies of Huiess—every weekend for the last couple of years. I would recognize one of my best friends by her mere speech patterns."

Instead, I fumbled and said, "Intuition. Besides, what is the worst that could happen if we give her board at least until we confirm her words?"

"The worst?" Dad asked. "She could be a Huiessian spy. Or she could be the culprit of this so-called 'poisonous revolution.'"

"Unlikely," I said. Again, I couldn't say, "I know Garnet and can vouch for her integrity." Instead, I said, "Another worst-case scenario is that she speaks the truth, and Ruby and Dot are factually endangered. Even if her situation is a lie, I believe this is the Crown Princess of Somnus, and if we turn her away, it may spur a war with the valley's neutral kingdom."

Dad grunted, then turned back to Garnet. "Fine. We will provide you sanctuary until we can confirm the status of Ruby and Peridot. You will be confined to quarters until then."

"Your Highness is more than generous," Garnet said with a humble bow. She passed a look to me that asked me to come visit her later. I planned to, if anything, to apologize for not having a better confirmation of her identity. Also, I wanted to know the full story that brought her to Veriae.

Obeying my wish to know what happened next, my dream skipped ahead in time.

I went down to Garnet's quarters with a young girl in tow. She was like a little version of me with a less pronounced forehead and bigger eyes with more green than brown. Her blonde hair had just enough red highlights to shimmer nicely in the firelight, and she decorated herself with opals everywhere; rings, bracelets, necklaces, earrings, anklets, and even hair combs. To my real-life mind, she looked like a jewelry store had thrown up on her. Maybe that was why I called her Opal in my dream. Maybe her physical likeness to me was why I called her sister.

I hadn't brought up her abnormal amount of jewelry during lunch, worried about her answer. As we walked alone together to meet Garnet, I asked, "You usually only wear two or three of your charms at a time. Is today special?"

"No," she said, then shrugged. "Maybe. I don't know. I've had a bad feeling all day and hoped to feel better by wearing all of my charms."

"Are they working?" I asked. I didn't believe in luck, but Opal swore by it. I hoped that maybe if she wore all her charms and they had no effect, maybe she would finally rid herself of the superstitions.

My little sister frowned at her bracelets and rings. "A little. Nothing bad has happened so far."

She hadn't been there for Garnet's first report. I murmured, "The day isn't over yet."

Two knights stood outside the room of the Crown Princess of Somnus. A simple wave was enough to let us inside for a private conversation. As the Crown Princess of Ormio, the only people who could question my demands were my parents.

I asked for a full update concerning her kingdom and my sisters. Even though I trusted Garnet, the news of Tanzanite crippling their family and superior navy was difficult to believe. I remained slightly suspicious simply because I refused to make any ruling without proof. Still, Garnet was one of my best friends. She and Ame understood me the best, and I knew their hearts as well as they knew mine. The three of us were heirs to our kingdoms, meaning only they understood my burdens, obligations, and expectations.

Opal thoughtfully offered one of her lucky bracelets to help calm our friend. I wanted to help too, though felt clueless how. I could solve numbers, not people. I honed into my training when lords expressed concerns, and I listened. What could I do to help her? Guests usually wanted fewer guards, though Garnet's fear suggested the opposite.

My youngest sister also seemed a bit disheartened by the news. What could I do to secure her safety and happiness? Hoping it was the right decision, I said, "Alright. How can we help? Other than ensuring your comfortable stay while in Veriae. Would you like me to remove or double the guards at your door?"

Garnet's thanks and Opal's smile let me breathe with relief. Right move.

We made quick plans, but I guffawed at Garnet's suggestion that Opal and I flee with her to Remizio. We would be as sheep among a pack of wolves. Except Garnet made some good points. Maybe it was time we came clean to our parents about our secret friendships. Maybe with the presence of all three crown princesses and the Prince of Urbanuz, we could make a difference. I needed to analyze the various possibilities.

"Let me ponder and sleep on it," I said. "Opal, how about we stay together tonight?" As an extra measure of security, I considered another location with sleeping and nighttime accommodations that would also be empty and unexpected of us. Ah, the servant's hut in the hunting grounds would do.

Confirming with Opal, I relayed our plans to a guard outside to double their stations and prepare the servant's hut for Opal and me to spend the night. Our appetite suffered from the bad news, so I made a request for a light dinner to be sent to the hut.

With eyes drooping over her tired smile, Garnet said, "With the state of affairs in Somnus, now, more than ever, we need allies."

I nodded. "I saw Prince Stanford Muli of Urbanuz at the last masquerade. I thought it odd that he's staying in Huiess since the direct route between their kingdoms goes through Ormio. An alliance with Urbanuz would change the war's dynamics. How would you suggest we gain their favor?"

Garnet lifted her shoulders with a tired shrug. "Marriage is the most common way."

I pulled a face, and she laughed.

"Come now, I saw you two talking at the last masquerade. He seemed to be a genuine gentleman. You could do far worse."

"So could he," I said, striking a flirtatious pose, knowing that I looked ridiculous. Garnet laughed again, and I joined her, feeling victorious for lightening the mood. Why couldn't every conversation with lords and ladies be this easy?

Garnet continued, "If marriage is out of the question, you can discuss a treaty with your resources, skills, or both. However, if Prince Muli is already in Huiess, waiting for him to pass through Ormio for his return trip home may be too late to secure your own alliance. Perhaps you should write to him, requesting his presence."

"I planned to," I said. "My only other option would be to travel to Huiess and talk with him personally, and that's not likely. Only if the situation becomes truly as dire as you paint it will we flee to Remizio for help."

Opal excused herself with a yawn, but I stayed to chat with my friend. I really didn't mean to stay long. Except the longer we talked, the more topics we found to discuss. Eventually, Garnet yawned and found comfort in her bed, and I decided to do the same. I stopped by my bedchamber to change into my sleeping gown and brush my hair before heading to the servant's hut across the fortress. I found it quiet and dark. Lighting a candle, I made my way to the bedroom and found my youngest sister in the wrong bed.

"Opal," I moaned and nudged her shoulder. "That's my bed. We didn't have your special mattress carried all the way over here just for you to sleep in mine."

She didn't stir.

Too tired to be nice, I rocked her shoulder. "Come on—"

She moved too easily without waking. Grabbing my candle, I shone the light on her face. Her golden curls streamed across her face, probably tickling her like mad, yet her eyes remained closed.

"Opal! Get up! Opal? Opal!" I yanked off the blankets and pulled my youngest sister from the bed. Words, she was too small, too young—too young to die.

No, she was breathing. Barely, but it was enough to say she was alive.

The grounds-keepers heard my cries and came to help. I ordered them to locate Garnet and bring her to me. She was found in her room with the guards, confirming her alibi. When she arrived at the hut, she analyzed the tampered porridge and my bedding to confirm Tanzi's work. Tanzi had meant to poison both of us, but Opal's choice to sample every porridge and sleep in my bed had saved me from poisoning.

My friend offered a sleeping drought to Opal, "To stave off the poison. However, I should warn you that soon after I deliver this, we may need to run."

Indeed, the ground rumbled and transformed as we abandoned the little hut with Opal sleeping inside.

How could this happen? If I wasn't safe in the strongest fortress of Ormio, was anywhere safe?

Those drifting thoughts were the last to float through my mind before my alarm woke me.

Normally, I gave myself ten minutes of snoozing, but that morning, with my dream so vivid in my brain, I grabbed a notebook and made an entry, recording everything I remembered.

Chapter 15

DIA

I dreamed of being a princess in the wooden castle again. If I thought the last dream of Garnet's arrival and news had been depressing, the mood this time was far more somber. Mom cried on Dad's shoulders as he took deep breaths and sniffled back his feelings. My shocking news about Opal's poisoning had been confirmed by the apothecary.

A young man stood with us in a room of wooden walls and thick tapestries as insulation. He was yellow-blond like Dad, but with light brown eyes. His overall appearance was similar to mine, supposing I spent more time in the courtyard training with swords instead of training my mind to budget and balance a whole kingdom.

I had a brother? He was two years younger than I was, but already past my height. Sometimes being short was annoying.

"Diamond, Cephas," the king said, beckoning us closer. My name was Diana, not Diamond, but my dream-self approached him like the name was only natural. The King of Ormio spoke. "In light of these disastrous events, there is an urgency to rally our supporters and collect allies. The situation is far from ideal, but Prince Muli is in the valley. Diamond, I know you were never one for romance, but we've forwarded a letter asking for arrangements."

My eyes widened. They couldn't possibly —

"Aligning with Urbanuz will strengthen our kingdom against traitors. His visitation to Remizio has allowed the Crown Princess of Huiess to bewitch him, but you must earn his favor for Ormio."

Did they factually —

"Win his heart if you must. However you wish to settle the marriage, it is your duty to secure our kingdom against our enemies."

Duty. I'd never cared for romance, hating the social games, the gossip, and the expectations. I'd always expected an arranged marriage for the sake of my kingdom, but to be thrown into it so suddenly with stakes higher than ever? My stomach clenched hard enough to raise its contents.

But emotions didn't matter. My opinions didn't matter. What mattered was protecting my kingdom. To do that, I needed to protect myself from the traitor and secure alliances, which were conveniently gathering in Remizio.

My dream shifted until I sat in a fancy carriage with my brother beside me and Garnet across from me, all of us hiding beneath hooded cloaks. We bounced and rocked back and forth as horses pulled us in a gallop.

"Alright," Cephas said, leaning away from the window. "We made it out of the city. Are you finally going to tell me where we're going?"

"Remizio."

"The capital of Huiess?" he asked, mimicking my incredulousness from the night before.

"What other Remizio would there be? Yes, I'm aware of the possible dangers, but we aren't safe in Veriae either. Remizio's the last place anyone would think to look for us."

"Surely, and for good reason," he guffawed. "No one would expect to find the Crown Princess and the Prince of Ormio in the heart of enemy territory. Have you lost your mind? That might explain why you snuck her out of the castle." He gestured to Garnet. "Who's to say she won't turn on us, too?"

"For the last time," I said through gritted teeth, "she's not our enemy. I trust Garnet. And you better leave that attitude behind because we're going to Remizio, where, despite whatever you might think, Ame, Sapphire, and Toto are my friends."

Cephas raised his eyebrows high. "Ame? As in Crown Princess Amethyst of Huiess? You call her Ame? And who, by the Words, is Toto?"

"Watch your language," I scolded, then clarified, "Topaz. We all call her Toto, alright?"

"All?" he echoed. "Who is 'we all?'"

"All of us," Garnet said, backing my statement. "At least, all the Princesses of Rezhina. We have all become friendly acquaintances during the midnight masquerades on Noz Isle."

I hadn't planned on telling my brother about the masquerades, but I supposed he knew the worst secret about our forbidden friendships. Still, I anticipated an onslaught of questions from him that would last the entire ride to Remizio.

* * *

I woke up in my parents' Nevada townhouse with a frustrating sensation. Again, I remembered every detail like it was more a memory than a dream. I knew the scenes would roll through my mind again and again until I wrote them down. I was collecting quite the story in my dream journal notebook. The strangest part was my building desire to know what would happen next. I tried finishing the stories in my head, but then the dream would continue the next night and reveal something completely different. New characters were introduced like old friends I never knew, and I went to places I'd never imagined.

My brother and I (goodness gracious, I didn't have any brothers, but I mentally referred to Cephas as my brother) were on our way to Remizio in Huiess. I tried looking up the locations online only to find places in

Vietnam. Maybe I didn't spell them right, but I doubted I'd find anything, even with the correct spelling.

My snooze alarm went off again, and I cursed. I was late. Again. With these dreams overpowering my mind for the first ten minutes of every morning, I needed to set my alarm clock earlier. Of course, because life was ironic, I figured the moment I started anticipating these vivid dreams, they'd probably stop. Strange how that possibility saddened me.

I dressed quickly and put my long blonde hair up in a quick ponytail. It was still wet from my shower, but I didn't have time for anything else. With a jellied bagel in my mouth, I hopped onto my enlarged bike and headed to work. "Get a bike," they said. "It'll be fun," they said. "You'll lose weight," they said. Screw them. I'd need a second shower with a gallon of Dr. Pepper after pedaling for two miles through the Las Vegas suburb streets that were far too hot and far too noisy from the nearby airport.

For the early hour, the summer sun hadn't baked away the morning chill yet. I appreciated the cool air as I panted and my legs ached with each downward push. Knowing that my ride home in the late afternoon would be in the triple digits, I made plans to take the bus home.

Some of my high school friends had gone off to universities, colleges, and tech schools. My grades and test scores had granted me a half-scholarship at Stanford University, but I didn't have enough money for

177

a car, let alone California housing. So, in the meantime, I worked and pedaled across Interstate 215,
dreaming of walking to a nutrition class on Stanford
campus with ABCD: Another Beautiful California
Day.

After an excessive amount of pedaling, I bent over
to catch my breath while locking my bike to a lamp-
post on the backside of The Golden Pawn shop. As it
was only my second day of work, I didn't have a key
yet for the building, leaving me to walk around to the
front. Most of the warehouse-style box building was
built of concrete painted white to ward off the hot Vegas sun, except a giant golden chess pawn outlined the
matching store door. A weak but cheery little bell announced my entrance.

Smells of dust and rust greeted me before the employee called "Welcome!" from behind the counter.
He was maybe a year or two older than I was, with
dusty black hair that could be called silver in the right
lighting. He was a pretty-boy type with blue-gray
eyes and a narrow jawline. He even dressed the part
with designer jeans and a black T-shirt featuring a top
40 band beneath a rolled-up button-up that hung
open and loose like a jacket.

"Hey," I said. "Did I make it before the first customer?"

"Oh, you're the new girl. Diana?"

Girl? I was old enough to work in a pawnshop.
Barely, but still. Since his friendly smile showed no

derogatory intent in his words, I focused on the more important correction. "Just Dia. I'll go clock in and be right back."

"Sure thing," he said, waving me to the back office. I returned shortly, struggling to tie a worn apron around my generous hips.

The young man was still grinning. "I'm Stan, by the way. I've been here since the beginning of the summer, so the only training I'm qualified to give you is the basics, but the boss wanted me to get you started. Someone else will be in later to correct anything I say. Are you familiar with the inventory?"

"Sort of," I said. "I've walked around the store a few times to get a feel of the layout and inventory."

Stan shrugged. "It wouldn't hurt to do it again. In fact, it's helpful to go around every day, so you'll recognize what's new. On my first day, Brian had me walk around the shop like a shopper. Supposing you had all the money in the world, what items would interest you? Go on, pick some things out. If a customer comes in, I'll help them, but you'll probably want to watch the transaction for a prime example of elite sales marketing and phenomenal customer service." He winked at me to show his tease.

Maybe it was from my recent bike ride, but my blood rose easily to my face from his flirtations. Guys didn't flirt with me. I'd once heard that eighty percent of the men dated twenty percent of the women, and if it was true, I wasn't part of the twenty percent. As much as I wanted to blame my extra weight, I'd seen other girls my size or larger have dates and boyfriends. I understood chemistry and physics, how greater masses had greater gravitational pulls, but that didn't work for me.

No matter. I didn't need a man to make me happy, just cheesecake.

I walked around the store, mentally cataloging the items, their categories of shelving, and their price points. Almost every counter was a glass showcase for unique jewelry or accessories. Another counter displayed fancy cameras and lenses. Even with our distance from the strip and any drive-thru chapels, there were plenty of engagement rings. The walls were decorated with shelves of collectable toys or posters. The Golden Pawn wasn't the famous pawnshop seen on TV or part of the network of pawnshops around Vegas, so we didn't have the greatest collection of historical pieces or inventory options, but what we had was unique.

The bell rang with an incoming customer, and I joined Stan behind the counter to watch as he refused to buy a chunky golden ring that the customer swore was real. Apparently, he'd bought it from someone at a gas station who "needed quick cash to get to the next town."

"Sorry, pal," Stan said, "but you were conned. That ring is 24-karat plastic. It's a common con, actually. See, we have a whole necklace of those rings." Stan reached back to a cheap golden chain with a collection of massive rings hanging at the bottom. "Sorry, but we don't buy and sell fake gold here."

The customer swore a handful of special words and stormed out, leaving his fake ring to "add to your collection."

Stan suffered through the whole ordeal with shrugs and a patient smile. After the customer left, he turned to me with another shrug. "Yeah, that'll happen. You'll learn not to take it personally."

"How did you know it was fake?" I asked.

"You get a feel for things after a while of working here, but there are plenty of ways to test gold. The most obvious way is its weight," he said, tossing the ring in his hand. "This little piece might even float in water, then its plating would tarnish with discoloration. You can also test it with vinegar, but that can damage any stones. If it's new, it should have an engraving with its karat, but since gold is so soft, that can wear away. If it's old or used, you'll be able to see any plating rubbed away from the edges. Then, if the customer is being stubborn about it, we have some nitric acid to test the purity."

He pulled up a little box from a cabinet under the register with small bottles and a flat stone. "By rubbing the jewelry on this," he said, indicating the stone, "we can test it with varying levels of nitric acid. If the rubbing disappears with this stuff—" he held up a bottle labeled with a "12" "—then the gold is less than twelve karats or fifty percent gold."

"Interesting," I said, looking through the bottles. There were a few for testing silver as well. "It looks like the twenty-four bottle isn't used much."

Stan smirked. "Twenty-four karat gold isn't meant for everyday wear, so it's not common. Plus, it's super expensive, so it's more often made in coins for investors. Here, give it a try. Test a couple of pieces in the case."

He opened the glass case and raised a thick necklace chain. Rubbing it against the stone until a smudged line of gold remained, I squeezed a drop of ten nitric acid over the line. It passed, but failed the twelve. We were halfway through a third piece when a gruff voice spoke from the back door.

"What are you doing?" I hadn't heard him enter the back storage or pass through the curtain. His matured face looked a few years older than Stan and me, with his full wavy black hair and a trimmed goatee to emphasize his Latino features. He didn't have a pretty-boy smile like Stan and was on the smaller side for a man, but his light brown eyes were the type that surely left heartbeats skipping. None of that really fazed me, but I flustered all the same to look professional.

Stan simply grinned and gestured to our mess of jewelry and acidic nitrate. "We're becoming acquainted with the products. Dia here's learning which pieces have higher purity levels of gold."
182

The man frowned. "You could tell that much from their prices. Don't damage them. Be sure to put them all back exactly as they were."

"Yessir," Stan said with a mocking salute. The man rolled his eyes and stepped into the office.

"Who's that?" I asked after the door clicked shut.

"Oh, that was Mr. Rindlisbacher. He's our top sales rep, and if Brian ever promotes someone to Assistant Manager, we all expect it'll be him. He's got the closing shift today and will finish your training."

"Lucky me," I muttered. I'd been having fun with Stan. I didn't imagine Mr. Rin—whatever his name was—enjoying science experiments with nitric acid and gold.

The man returned from the office, his jaw clenched and tight. "You're the new employee?"

I reached my hand forward to share a formal pump with the aspiring assistant manager. "I'm Dia Mason."

"Dia?" he asked, raising a dubious eyebrow. "What's that short for?"

As if he was one to judge names? "Diana, if you must know." My annoying dreams from the nights before whispered that it was short for Diamond. Annoying dreams. "What was your name again?"

"Rindlisbacher."

"Riddles-er—come again?" I stumbled.

"Rind-lis-bach-er," he said slowly, like I was a child. I might be new and fresh out of high school, but that didn't make me dumb.

I faked innocence with a light smile. "Is that your first name, or would that be Rumpelstiltskin?" Goodness gracious, did I just sass the boss's favorite employee on my second day of work? Please, don't fire me. Please, don't fire me.

He met my subtle sass with narrowed eyes and an I'm-so-much-better-than-you smirk. With the tiniest glance at my "fluffy" figure, he must have decided I wasn't worth his attention, as he quickly turned away. "They're both German-based, so do whatever you gotta do to remember my name. Stan, were you heading to the bank soon?"

"Yeah. We're low on fives 'cause I couldn't use the hundred from last night's deposit, so—"

"I'll take the deposit," the man said. "Do we need any other change?"

Stan's eyebrows went high, but he otherwise acted normally as he opened the register and discussed their shortage of five-dollar bills and pennies. The unnerving man took the large bills and deposit bag, then left without a word.

"Huh," Stan said, as soon as the back door closed. "Usually the person who opens the store takes the deposit and extra change. He must have really wanted to go. Or he didn't want to be left alone with you."

"Me?" I asked. "How am I the problem?"

"I don't know," Stan said, rubbing his smooth jaw. "But I've never seen him act like—hello! Can we help you find anything?"

184

A customer walked in, halting our conversation and returning us to business. Stan helped the customer while I carefully replaced every golden piece of jewelry back in the case exactly as it was. No, that was a lie. I moved a few around for better display and presentation. The customer left us with a small baseball card collection and eighty dollars in his pocket. Stan joined me at the case to verify and compliment my work when Mr. Rindlisbacher returned.

"Ah," Stan said, smiling at his entrance. "Am I good to go now?"

The man clenched his jaw and glanced at me. "Yes, you can leave. No use having three of us here if there aren't any customers."

"Thanks. Check out what Dia did to the display! I don't know how she did it, but it looks cleaner and more organized now."

His eyes narrowed on me. "She changed the display?"

"For the better. Hey, Dia, I'll see you tomorrow? Same time, same place?" He winked as if we were meeting for a party, not for work.

I smiled back and waved. "See ya, Stan."

Stan left with a smirk to me before leaving me alone with the other man. I tried to hold my smile as my eyes shifted to my other co-worker. Only two more hours of my shift.

Working his jaw, Mr. Rindlisbacher approached me at the jewelry display case. I held my breath as he studied my minor changes. He grunted with a bounce of his eyebrows, as if he wasn't surprised to be impressed.

"It looks good. Here." He tossed a thin binder onto the case. "Thankfully, Brian wrote down everything a new employee needs to learn. There's a checklist and instructions."

I opened the binder and leafed through the pages. Sure, it wasn't as thick as a novel, but a million times less exciting. I looked up to ask where he'd like me to start, but he was already busy with his own tasks on the register.

I sniffed back my retort. Little did he know that I was a quick learner. I was a third of the way through the list when he finally spoke to me again.

"We're slow today. There's no need for two of us here. You can go home an hour early and finish the list tomorrow with Stan."

I struggled not to shuffle uncomfortably. It helped when I realized that he had a similar struggle.

"At least it's mutual," I murmured.

"What was that?" he asked.

"Our discomfort," I said. "I'm sorry if I offended you. I really don't want—"

"I don't work well with women."

That was not what I'd expected. His coldness toward me wasn't because of something I'd said or done, but because he was sexist?

"Oh?" I asked. "Why is that? Do you think we're weak and inferior?"

"Hardly." He snorted. "If your stubbornness is any indication, I believe women to be as equally capable and strong as men; perhaps more in some cases." He stepped closer until his jutted chin turned down to face me directly. Sometimes, I hated being short and how my height made everyone look down on me. My insides squirmed to remain firm as he stood so close. And, goodness, what was that divine scent? He had no right to smell that good. That was playing dirty.

His thin lips softened as his glaring brown eyes landed on mine. "I do not work well with women, Ms. Mason," he said, "because I find them distracting."

I struggled to catch my breath. When I found it, it came in a soft gasp. It then quickened as his words sank in.

Distracting? What could I do that was distracting? I was simply trying to work, not flirt or quest for his attention. My stupid, desperate, foolish heart that had never been wanted by anyone romantically was secretly flattered. Stupid, desperate fool. It wasn't personal. I should be irritated that he saw all women the same way.

Mr. Rindlisbacher turned suddenly away. He paced back several feet, closed his eyes, and breathed out, long and deep.

The breaking of the moment and separation screwed my courage into place. I had wilted under his proximity, but now felt the need to defend my gender. I straightened my spine and raised my chin into my business face. My dreams said I was a princess. Even if I wasn't, I deserved respect. "Nobody else in this store seems to have an issue with me, so I think your lack of focus is a personal problem, and not mine. Brian hired me, and I have every intention of working here."

His eyes narrowed. "It's a fine line, Ms. Mason, between bravery and stupidity. Have you gotta dance on it?"

"Fortunately for me, my dancing skills are more than adequate." I smiled, thinking of my dreams of masquerades, where I knew the dances but preferred to watch. "But thank you for your open frankness. I can assure you, I'm only here to work and earn money for college. I hope we can learn to work together with mutual dignity and decency. Good day, Mr. Rindlisbacher."

I gave him a nod, then left without offering him a chance to stop me. I was going to work hard enough to dethrone him as "top sales representative" and leave this store swimming in gold.

Chapter 16

DIA

When I dreamed again of being a princess in another time and place, I wasn't in that grand ballroom with strangers who felt familiar. I also wasn't in that wooden castle that I wanted to call home, or traveling through a deciduous forest.

Instead, I walked through a giant sandcastle. Whoever made the place needed a reward, because it wasn't simply big—it was intricate and sturdy like the Abu Simbel temples of Egypt. Garnet went ahead of us to act as our mediator as Cephas and I were led to the presence chamber. Stepping inside, I smiled at Ame. She stood with her hands resting on her hips, staring at Prince Stanford of Urbanuz. Wait a minute. Did I recognize him from somewhere other than that masquerade?

Ame greeted me with the slightest widening of eyes and mouth. Flicking her eyes to Cephas, she said, "What insanity brings the enemies of—"

"He knows," I said.

"Oh, good." Ame dropped her warrioress stance and ran over to hug me. "Garnet told me everything, but I wasn't sure about your brother. I'm so sorry about your sisters."

I stepped back to offer her a thankful smile. Cephas gaped, then cleared his throat from behind me.

"You were serious? You three are seriously friends?"

"We are," Ame said, linking arms with Garnet and me as she narrowed her eyes on him. "But you're not Dia, so you're still my enemy."

"How about neutral ground?" Garnet offered.

Knowing my brother, I agreed. "If he does anything rude, I'll support your decision to be rude back, but give him at least a chance to become a friend?"

"Neutral ground," Ame mulled over, then stared at my brother with a wolfish grin. "The ground is made for walking. I have permission to walk over him?"

"Hey!" Cephas refuted.

"What confuses me," Ame said, ignoring him to address me, "is that my parents agreed to this arrangement. Garnet of Somnus, I understand, but you two? I had to confess of our friendship to them to let you stay with us, but don't be surprised if they plot to attack you in your sleep. What about your parents? If you snuck away and they discover you're here, they might suspect you were abducted against your will."

I took a deep breath and forced the awkwardness away as I spoke the truth. "My parents expect me to

steal Prince Stanford away from you and take Urbanuz's alliance for Ormio." I decided to both ignore
and address Stanford's gaping by continuing to Ame,
"Which is ridiculous, because you and I know that we
both have no interest in romance, so what's there to
steal?"

"Right," Ame said. Had she hesitated, or were my
nerves messing with my perspective of time? It probably wasn't worth reading into.

"Thus," I said, "I propose we arrange an alliance
here and now. I can draw up the papers in a matter of
minutes. All I need is a scroll and some ink to make it
official. With you, Garnet, and me present, we have
all three Crown Princesses of Rezhina plus the Crown
Prince of Urbanuz. I say we take matters into our own
hands. We need to stop the war between Ormio and
Huiess to finally become a united front against any
and all other threats."

Ame waved her hand to both cut me off and dis-
miss my concerns. "I'm not worried about Tanzi."
Despite Garnet's obvious unease, Ame continued,
"Huiess is stronger than any twelve-year-old, no matter her schemes or influence. Also, this alliance is too
simple. On what grounds will it stand? It won't stop
the hate that's been growing for the past decade between our people. A single piece of paper won't change
that."

Garnet sighed. "Those reasons prohibited us from
drawing up a treaty months ago when we first became

friends, but the situation has changed. We need a united front."

Stanford chose that moment to speak up. "My father, the king, sent me across the mountains for more than an alliance. Sure, two or three kingdoms are better than one, but, according to him, 'nothing solidifies an alliance like a marriage, and Rezhina Valley has a surplus of eligible princesses.'"

He finished his mocked imitation of his dad with a loony expression to turn his serious statement into a joke. Still, I cringed in my dream and mental wakefulness. His words and teasing expressions did more than bring up an awkward topic. They reminded me of how I recognized *Stan*ford in Las Vegas.

"Fine," my dream self said with reluctance. "I'll add our marriage to the agreement."

"*Your* marriage?" Ame frowned. "You don't need Urbanuz's resources like Huiess does."

"Ormio still needs the alliance," I said. "Urbanuz isn't your neighboring kingdom, it's ours. Demographically, it makes the most sense, especially since the only eligible prince in this entire valley is my brother, meaning my only option for a kingly companion is to look outside of Rezhina, to kingdoms like Urbanuz."

Ame followed my gesture back to Cephas. She eyed him up and down before folding her arms and saying, "As if I would take your brother? No thanks."

My brother sputtered with offense, and Garnet raised her hands for a calming motion. I stepped forward to put them outside my peripheral (making them easier to ignore) and lowered my voice for Ame. "Ormio needs this alliance."

"So does Huiess," she said. She stared back with those warrioress eyes, unflinching and unyielding.

"Um," Stanford peeped out, "do I have a say in this?"

I turned to him, half ready to say, "No," but the word stuck in my mouth. Just because I had no choice didn't mean that he didn't.

"Yes," Ame said. "Who would you choose, me or Dia?"

"I think what you mean," I clarified, "is which kingdom does Urbanuz want for a stronger alliance? Ormio or Huiess?"

"Ehh," he slurred and glanced to the sides for an escape, "do I need to decide right now? It's kind of a big choice to make on the spot." His uneasy mouth twitched into a teasing smile. "I mean, there's no need to compete for me."

Ame scoffed with a simple laugh and roll of her eyes.

"A competition," Garnet offered, "might not be a bad idea."

"A sword fight?" Ame grinned. Garnet, Cephas, and I cringed, knowing Ame would beat me with her first lunge.

"Too much blood has already been spilled," Garnet said.

Ame rolled her eyes again. "I can disarm someone without spilling blood."

As could I, but my method was through negotiations. "How about," I said, "we have an open courtship with Prince Muli to help him with his decision?"

Garnet nodded despite her worried frown. "I expect we gave Tanzi the slip for a week or two by coming to Remizio. We have time to begin campaigns for peace, research antidotes for those sleeping, and—" she waved her hand non-consequentially "—woo Prince Muli. May we set a goal for drawing up treaties on the next full moon?"

"I accept," Ame said, instantly warning me. I hadn't expected her to agree so easily since Huiessians never entered fair fights. Did she know something I didn't? "Stanford, what traits do you admire most in a woman?"

"Uh," he stumbled like a deer spotting a hunter. "I like women who are… impressive."

How terribly vague. I panicked, easily imagining Ame showing off her fighting skills. What could I do that was more impressive? Decipher ledgers and an entire city's-worth of budgets? But how could I argue? It was arranged by an objective third party, and the decision ultimately lay with Stanford.

Swallowing hard, I said, "Fair enough. When is the next full moon?" With everything that had happened since Garnet's arrival in Veriae, I had lost track.

194

"Ten days."

Ten days to persuade Prince Stanford that he'd rather align his kingdom with mine, despite whatever impressive acts Ame presented.

I was a lost cause.

My dream shifted to a new scene as I sat on Garnet's guest bed with multiple guards at the door. She sat at a desk, and between us piled the palace's book collection on apothecary drinks, herbs, and medicines. While I enjoyed learning about the various reactions and compounds created by mixing ingredients, my mind was burdened with other thoughts.

"What am I to do, Garnet?" I moaned. "I don't care to win a competition, but I need to."

Garnet shook her head while setting aside a tome that failed to answer her questions. "You should know that I will refuse to take a side between you and Ame. You two are my dearest friends, as dear to me as my own sisters. With my sisters now—" She hiccupped on her words and skipped ahead. "I could not bear to lose either of you, even metaphorically."

I took a deep breath and slowly released it, reorienting my mind to the textbook in my lap about the medicinal uses of moss. She was right. We already had enough going on with our poisoned sisters, and it was selfish of me to ask her to help me over Ame.

"Forget it," I said. "Ame will probably win no matter what I do."

"Now, now," Garnet chided, looking up from her next book to eye me directly. "You cannot give up. While I may not be able to choose sides or assist you personally, perhaps you may ask another."

"Who?" I asked. "Who would help me impress a prince when I'm in enemy territory? I'm supposed to be hiding. I'm already embarrassed enough to ask you for help. Who would help me?"

"While requesting access to the palace library," Garnet said, "I ran into Sapphire. She mentioned that Riddle Maker is in town."

Riddle Maker. The name was more legend than fact, the name of a man so tricky and conniving that no one knew his true identity. Garnet was right. If there was anyone in Huiess who would help an Ormio princess to trick an Urbanuz prince in Huiess, it would be Riddle Maker.

"Where?" I asked. "How do I find him?"

"I believe Sapphire said that he frequented the morning markets under the shade of the cloth section. You may recognize him by the joker card in his feathered hat."

I repeated the details in my mind, memorizing them before jumping from the bed and clasping both of my hands around Garnet's. "Thank you. Thank you!"

"You might want to wait to thank me. You know how Riddle Maker works? You must pass his test of riddles before asking him for a favor. Even still, the favors he grants always come with a catch."

"I don't care. I'll do it. I'll practice solving riddles, outwit Riddle Maker, and he'll help me to win Stanford's heart. For the sake of my kingdom, I'll do it."

"You may need to start right away with that practice. Go on. I can recruit a guard or two to help me study for an antidote to heal our sisters."

"Thank you, Garnet!" I embraced her with a hug, then dashed off to the library to seek the answers to every riddle known.

* * *

I woke with a start, heart beating quickly, sweating, but chilled. Why did my body react to that dream as if it was a nightmare? There hadn't been anything frightening about it—only stressful, as I considered what I'd do to win a competition to impress a prince.

Wake up, Diana. I tapped my face. It was only a dream. Besides, the more I thought about it, the more ridiculous it became. Stan wasn't a prince, he was my co-worker. And I wasn't a princess with the worries of a kingdom. I was a high school graduate working to save money until I could go to my dream school in Stanford.

Stanford. Like Prince Stanford Muli? That wasn't a fun train of thought, especially as it led to my co-worker, Stan. The persistent night dreams were messing with my real dreams.

My first week of work went slowly. Every time I thought I had learned everything, Stan would mention something on the register, or a customer would ask about our inventory, or Mr. Rindlisbacher would frown that I didn't know something about the rules. I finished the binder of instructions and studied through it again, but there were little things that were only gained from experience.

I met my other co-workers. Kevin was an older gentleman with a deep love for space operas and knew the history and quality of their collectibles without needing to look them up. Jay physically resembled a certain young person from that famous pawnshop on TV, but mentally outclassed him. He'd worked at the shop for over ten years but passed on the rumored promotion for assistant management because, "I don't want to deal with the type of customers who want to speak to the manager. I work here because I enjoy it. Being the assistant manager would spoil that." A part of me was jealous of his easy-going attitude.

Mr. Rindlisbacher had taken an interest in the position after working at the shop for only three years, but he had a way with the customers, recognizing repeat customers and their particular circumstances, and keeping his cool, no matter what was thrown at him.

Our boss, Brian, and his family had owned The Golden Pawn for over fifteen years, and he knew our inventory as if he had the whole list of the past ten years in his head.

The minimal turnover rate surprised me. I planned to leave as soon as I had enough saved up for Stanford. California. I was saving up for living in California, not a prince. Annoying dreams.

To my relief, during that first week, my schedule overlapped with Mr. Rindlisbacher's only once more, and he sent me home early again.

I quickly learned that our busiest hours were in the mornings, right after opening and in the evenings right before we closed. Being in a suburb of Vegas, we weren't right next to the strip or Fremont Street to be open late for those who partied like they planned to forget what happened in the morning. Brian didn't want to deal with people who bought wedding bands to hit the next-door chapel or sold their wedding bands to hit the next-door casino.

No, The Golden Pawn was more suburban than that. So suburban, in fact, that Brian invited his employees to his neighborhood park party. Oddly enough, it was Stan who tried convincing me to go.

"They reserved most of the pavilions and baseball diamonds at Arroyo Grande Park. You can bring your bike and try it on the BMX track." He wiggled his eyebrows with a laugh, knowing that my rickety bike belonged on that track as much as I did. Shifting to a more earnest plea, he said, "I haven't been here as long as everyone else, but it'll be like an unofficial work party. Please come. It would mean the world to me."

I pouted my mouth with an exaggerated thought. "Will there be food?"

"Psh, of course. Free burgers and hot dogs. What more could you ask for?"

Now, that was tempting. "Fine, I'll go."

I'd never attempted counting them all, but I was willing to bet there were more baseball diamonds than casinos in Vegas. (I didn't include every gas station or convenience store in the casino count simply because they had the lotto and quarter machines.) Arroyo Grande Park alone had nine diamonds, and the moment the party officially began, Stan texted me to meet him at "the biggest one."

Chaining my bike to a No Parking sign, I huffed over to the shaded stands. That bike would be the death of me, but I could sense my body becoming stronger.

I stood among strangers in the stands, but looking out to the field, I immediately recognized others from The Golden Pawn. Stan saw me and waved, then gestured me over. I met him halfway at the top of the dugout, and he surprised me with a welcoming hug.

"You made it! Come on, you'll be on my team."

He pulled me down to the dugout. I wanted to protest, to say how much I preferred to watch sports—not play them—but Stan *wanted* me on his team. With my figure, no one had ever wanted me on their team unless the game was played at a table. I was last to arrive, but I hadn't been the last pick. I didn't want to let him down.

Following Stan's direction into the dugout, my eyes met Mr. Rindlisbacher's as he stepped out to warm up with a bat. His casual clothes of jeans and a polo showed off his terribly attractive physique. He clenched his jaw at my presence, but said nothing.

To my surprise, some teenage stranger from the dugout called me out.

"Come on, we're playing baseball, not softball."

A tween joined the egging. "I bet she throws like a girl."

Rude. As if that was supposed to be an insult?

"So what if I do?" I called back. "I do a lot of things like a girl that I'm quite proud of."

"Oh yeah? Like what?" the first jerk asked, leaning forward.

With no time to think, my mouth blurted, "Cook."

Stan broke into laughter as Mr. Rindlisbacher's head tilted slightly with surprise, encouraging my next audacious words.

"I also flirt like a girl," I added with a wink at Stan. "You can bet that I'm better at that than anyone else here."

Mr. Rindlisbacher's face turned sunburn red as Stan's laugh burst with joy. "Hah! Somebody get this lady a bat. She's playing."

"But she's—"

"She's got spirit," my co-worker said, "and that's all you need for a good game."

And a good game it was. I ended up watching most of it anyway, but being with the team in the dugout made me feel included. Even if the only people I knew were my co-workers, everyone seemed to know Brian, and Stan made quick friends. He had an easy smile and a friendly attitude. There was something worth admiring about that.

"Hey," a low voice smoldered behind me.

I jumped a whole inch off the bench with a mousy squeak. Goodness gracious, Rindlisbacher caught me staring like a daydreamer at Stan. I turned to glower at him. He smirked and pinched back a teasing laugh.

"Sorry. Didn't mean to scare you. I was just gonna say it's your turn to bat next."

Liar. He was probably testing my security system like a burglar activating a false alarm as a test run. I tightened my glare and turned obediently to grab a bat as Stan hit a homerun.

Chapter 17

DIA

I lay in bed with the sounds of Las Vegas traffic as my lullaby and the glaring blue lights of my alarm clock as my nightlight. 11:46 PM. I'd be late to work if I didn't get to sleep soon. Who was I kidding? I'd force myself to be on time even if I ran on an hour of sleep, but every passing minute was a minute not sleeping, a minute digging into my precious remaining five and a half hours of sleep.

I took a deep breath and counted to eight as I let it out. The problem was, I knew what would happen when I went to sleep. I'd dream of being a princess again. I'd dream of Stan as a prince. Then, I'd wake up unable to dispel the dream until I wrote it down. Next, I'd go to work a little tardy from my morning writing exercise, feeling awkward around Stan and like I somehow didn't belong in this place I've been living in my whole life.

But what else could I do? Stay up all night? That wouldn't make work easier.

When I eventually cleared my head and fell asleep to the hum of cars outside, I dreamed of the sandcastle palace again. I was dressed like a Huiessian with flowing pants of crisscrossing designs and vibrant colors, a top that was more like a bedsheet wrapped around my shoulders and bodice, then tied around my waist to secure it in place. I also wore a silk scarf over my head like a hood. I was a princess in disguise.

Normally, I wouldn't leave the sanctuary of this sandcastle to enemy territory outside, but after three days of studying riddles, filling my head with wit and rhymes, testing my mind with twisting words and symbolism, I felt ready to seek out Riddle Maker.

On my way through the halls, I crossed the path of Sapphire, the middle princess of Huiess. She always had a dreamy look about her, with a little smile that was both sad and secretive. She didn't make eye contact with me, but she squished her eyebrows with concern as she asked, "Dia? Do you remember me?"

"Of course, Sapphire," I said. Did she think I'd forget because we weren't wearing our masquerade masks? "How is Ame?"

"She was alive the last time I saw her."

That was ominous. I sighed, wondering why I hoped to get a straight answer from the odd Huiessian princess.

She turned her eerie smile on me, still without meeting my eyes. "It's good to see you awake. Act natural, and they won't suspect a thing."

"Um, you too," I said. When did she see me sleeping? I was fairly certain that between the two of us, I was the one acting naturally.

She asked, "How are the triplets?"

"Triplets?"

"Your sisters."

I frowned. "You mean the twins? Opal's younger than Dot and Ruby."

"No, I mean Biddy, Dot, and Dorothy." She leaned forward to whisper, "The third one's invisible."

Slanders, she was weird sometimes. I must have misheard her pronunciation of Ruby. "Ruby and Dot are being cared for. We expect to find a cure any day now. Thank you for your concern. Who is Dorothy?"

"Your deaf and invisible sister."

Was this some sick fantasy she made up? Disturbed, but curious, I asked, "Is she a ghost?"

"No, that would be Ruby, the first casualty of this war. Those who do not fall in line are fallen in a line. Why is the line crooked?"

Slanders, her phrases were as confusing as riddles. But maybe that explained it. Maybe she spoke funny because she wanted the world to have more riddles and mystery.

With that in mind, I accepted Sapphire's words as a challenge to test my riddle practices. I squared my shoulders and said, "A line is simply a path between two points. If the line is crooked, it must mean there are multiple points in a crooked path."

Sapphire turned wide eyes on me. For the first time, she seemed to *see* me. Even as our eyes locked, Sapphire's turned watery. "I don't want to be next to fall."

"Who says you will be?"

"The stars. I don't want to die. But Queen Tanzanite needs to unite the valley."

"Queen—Tanzi?" I gaped. Garnet had said Tanzi was behind the poisoning of our sisters. I'd marginally doubted her statement as I questioned Tanzi's motivations. To become Queen? Of the whole valley? Did that mean she would continue until every single one of us was removed? How did Sapphire know?

"Sapphire, did Tanzi tell you this?"

She shook her head. "It's the stars. Are the voices in my head disturbing you?"

"Sapphire," I asked carefully, "what exactly are the voices telling you?"

"We all need to go away. We need to be put to sleep like diseased dogs. That's how Rezhina is united. That's how we have peace."

"What do you mean? What statistics predicted that solution?"

Before she could answer, Sapphire quickly wiped her face clean of any evidence of tears and stared down the corridor.

I stared too. There was no one there. Just as I was about to repeat my question, the door at the end of the corridor opened.

Sapphire whispered, "Act natural, and they won't suspect a thing."

The repetition of her phrase sent chills up my arms. It didn't feel like a repeat of her earlier phrase. It felt like the earlier phrase was a repeat of this moment. How was that possible? Could Sapphire somehow divine the future? Even if she could, I didn't believe the stars decided our fates. People created their own fates. That was the only way for me to save my kingdom.

The servants down the corridor passed without issue. Sapphire bid me a good day with, "Don't forget me." I pulled my headscarf over my nose to cover my whole face except my eyes, then slipped out of the sandcastle.

Outside, the sun glared down from the harsh angle of morning. It knew I didn't belong in these open streets of sand and rocks. I wished to hide behind the leaves of a green forest. The few trees in this desert land were tall and naked until they branched at the very top like a witch's bad hair day.

Checking the map drawn on my hand, I wove between the streets to the market, bustling with people, singeing my nasal hairs with spices, dizzying my eyes with vibrant fabric colors. The kaleidoscope of colors, throngs of people, and music playing in the distance reminded me of the midnight masquerades.

Today, my mask was simply a headscarf, but it was enough. As much as I wanted to find a wall to lean

back and observe the social interactions, I pushed forward, checking every stand and alley for the fabrics
section. When I found it, I scoffed for trying too hard.
There was no way I could have missed the giant rugs
rolled and stacked high against the wall, the light silks
that draped between them, or the great overhangs that
offered me sweet, sweet shade.

I walked up and down the alley twice, checking
every man (and every woman just to make sure) for a
joker card in their headwear.

Again, as soon as I spotted him, I scoffed at myself
for working too hard. He walked in with a sea captain's hat folded into a triangle and displaying a
peacock's worth of feathers. Tucked like a babe in its
featherbed was the joker card. I approached him from
behind, hoping that the surprise attack would keep
him from running away for any reason.

"I seek Riddle Maker," I said.

He kept his back to me and continued to sort
through the rugs against the wall.

"What is your business with him?"

"I need a favor."

"Everyone needs favors. What is yours?"

"I need to impress a prince."

He spun around with incredible grace and control,
his eyebrow high with assumptions.

That was when it clicked, and I gasped.

Why hadn't I recognized him before? His fluid
movements, his allusiveness, his shorter height, strong

208

build, black hair, and light brown eyes. This was the mystery man from the masquerades. Somewhere in the back of my Nevada mind, I groaned with extra recognition.

He bent low into a courtly bow. "Consider the maker of riddles at your service."

I gaped. "You're Riddle Maker?"

He straightened and gave me a teasing smirk. "Were you expecting someone else?"

"No, just—" I stumbled on my words and re-sorted my thoughts. "I need your help. Prince Muli of Urbanuz is visiting—"

"I know."

"—and there's a competition to marry the one who best impresses him. I need to win."

His eyebrows shot up. "This is the first I've heard of a competition for the prince. The participants must be highly limited, which makes you—" He stepped to my side and eyed me up and down. "—someone who took a great risk to meet me in Remizio. My, you've got to be desperate."

I gulped. He recognized me as the Crown Princess of Ormio. What would he do with such knowledge?

For the moment, he beckoned me to a secluded corner in the alley, then stepped behind a curtain to a small storage room, lit by a single oil lamp, crowded with dusty rugs, and barely enough room for five people standing.

He lit two more candles with the lamp to lighten the clouded room. "Welcome to my office."

"Your office?"

"It's temporary." He smiled, falsely sweet. "But private. You were correct to assume that I have the know-how to impress royalty. I've helped lonely souls to woo their true loves of any status."

I cleared my throat, knowing all too well of his tactics and practices of wooing during the masquerades. "Prince Stanford is not my true love."

His eyebrows somehow went higher. "No?"

"No." I was half tempted to confess my attractions to another man—to him. But the image of Opal lying too still in that bed, of the possible future, of my people starving on the streets (and my Las Vegas connections to the man before me) directed my tongue. "Prince Stanford is a necessity."

Riddle Maker eyed me carefully. "Without love on either side, that makes this a little harder."

"But you can help me?"

He looked sideways at me and folded his arms again. "I suppose. For a price."

I slipped open the knot around my purse. "Name it."

"Oh," he chided, "I do not exchange with money, Princess. My needs are far more complicated than gold and silver."

I gulped, my mind betraying myself to the worst possible implications.

"I require knowledge," he said. I immediately relaxed. Knowledge was something I had more than most. He continued, "Answer three of my riddles, and you've got my services for free. Fail to give the correct answer, and we'll talk…business."

I squared my shoulders. I'd practiced for this. I would solve his riddles and earn his help to save my kingdom. My people depended on it. "I'm ready."

Riddle Maker tilted his head and spoke slowly, studying me as I studied his words.

"Roses are pink, but I make them red.
Two petals part, and rub in my blood.
Roses are red, and I am encased.
May two bloody petals always be chaste.
What am I?"

He finished with raised eyebrows, anticipating my answer. I held up my index finger for him to wait. Riddles were all about metaphor. I needed to pick apart the details, ignoring most of the nouns and focusing on the adjectives.

Something was pink, but became red. It had two moving parts that became colored by the insides of the mystery item. The mystery item was "encased." That seemed like an interesting word, but maybe it was used simply because it rhymed with "chaste." That was also an interesting word choice. What could be chaste?

People? Relationships? Were the two petals two people? How were they pink?

I felt the Mystery Man's eyes on me. He'd never stared at me so intently during the many masquerades. I dared a glance at him, at his cunning smile that thought he beat me, at his lips as soft as… rose petals.

"You are lip paint," I declared.

Instead of frowning at being beaten, his smile grew with pride.

"Good job. Now, for riddle two:

> "Though my body is like a bird's,
> I never fly.
> Though I speak unlimited words,
> I have no mouth.
> My blood can be worth more than gold,
> But people spill it freely.
> I'm gripped, clenched, or stroked in their hold,
> But I have no arms to hold back.
> What am I?"

I grumbled. He had switched tactics. This type of riddle required a focus on the nouns, considering puns or twists of phrases to determine their deeper meanings.

I went line by line through the riddle again. Its body was like a bird, but it didn't fly. That eliminated my options to flightless birds, something shaped like a bird, or simply similar to a bird in some way. It spoke
212

without a mouth, meaning it probably wasn't a living animal.

"Again with the blood," I muttered. "Are all of your riddles this gory?"

He chuckled, and I nearly lost my focus within the sound. "Do you give up?"

"Never," I muttered.

What was worth more than gold yet spilled freely? Though it was probably the most revealing clue, the trivia led me to dead ends. Considering the last clue, the item seemed to be some sort of tool. What tool resembled a bird and created words?

Words!

"A quill," I said.

"Good, now—"

"I have a riddle for you too," I said, unable to constrain myself.

> "I dress up as one does to the masquerades on
> Noz Isle. What is my code name?"

"That's not a riddle. That's a personal question."

"A riddle is defined as a question or statement that requires creative thinking to answer, usually as a game. Thus, I ask again; what am I?"

He stared at me again with that tilted head, as if he wasn't sure whether to take me seriously. Seeming to make a decision, he walked around me, studying me.

Coming full circle, he folded his arms. "It's a trick question. You don't go to the masquerades."

"Yes, I do."

"We're talking about the midnight masquerades on Noz Isle? I'm there every week and I've never seen you."

Gut me, why don't you? He'd never noticed me? "I know you're there every week, because so am I. You wear a jester's mask with diamonds of gold and black on your cheeks."

Riddle Maker twitched. Still annoyed that he'd never noticed me, I grinned at making him uneasy. I would win this battle.

"Fine. I have one more riddle for you. It was originally easier than my first two, but your challenge has persuaded me to give you my hardest one yet. You don't need to answer right away, but whoever answers the others' riddle first is the winner."

The next masquerade wasn't for another six days. Six days would be plenty of time for me to find the answer to his riddle. "Fair enough. Give me your last riddle."

"You know me as the Riddle Maker.
I mold words like dough by a baker.
You answered two and played my game,
But here's the last; what's my real name?"

What was his name? I frowned. "That's not a riddle."

"By your definition of the term, yes, it is."

I gulped, as if I could swallow back my words. Did anyone know Riddle Maker's real name? After calling him Mystery Man for so many months, I had felt accomplished enough to learn his second identity as Riddle Maker. Now, I had six days to learn his true identity despite his mere existence being a legend. Meanwhile, he'd be seeking the answer about my identity and codename from the masquerade. Six days suddenly felt too fast. I had to find his name before then.

"What are the consequences?" I asked. "If I don't solve your riddle, you won't help me win Prince Stanford's contest?"

"No, no. I'll help you with that, anyway. A chance to dupe royalty is hard to pass. No, if I solve your riddle before you can solve mine, then you must employ me as the court jester to live in the castle for as long as you reign."

I swallowed. All he asked for was employment and comfortable living conditions. He couldn't know that he also asked to live in my future home with me, to torture my heart with his handsomeness while I served as wife to another man. He couldn't know that his mere presence in the castle would test my loyalty and constantly remind me that he was the only reason I won the prince.

Catching a glint in his eye, maybe he did know that last part. He would hold this moment as blackmail over my head.

I couldn't let him win.

"If that's your condition," I said, "then if I solve your riddle first, my condition is that you leave Rezhina, never to set foot in this valley again."

He narrowed his conniving eyes and pursed his lips. "A high price for a game of guessing names."

"This is the price for failing a kingdom. Factually, I have the feeling that if I fail to win Prince Stanford's competition, you may wish to flee this valley, anyway."

His eyebrows twitched with interest. "Is that so? In that case, we have an accord. We shall woo this prince of yours. Tell me, what are the exact parameters of this competition? Are there any loopholes?"

"Too many," I mumbled, then explained the agreement.

Riddle Maker hummed and tapped his chin. "What is your most impressive talent?"

I huffed. "None of my talents are 'impressive,' especially compared to Ame's combat skills. Hence my coming to you."

He raised an eyebrow. "And what do you expect me to do for you?"

"Whatever it takes. I care little what it is as long as I win the stupid little contest." My people needed my victory.

"And what happens when you marry the prince and he discovers that you used questionable methods to win?"

I gave a half shrug. "I think he's concerned less about how we win and more about being entertained. I plan to tell him everything after my victory."

Riddle Maker smirked. "You expect him to understand or fall instantly in love with you simply by revealing the truth?"

I clenched my teeth to bite back the blood rushing to my cheeks. "I don't expect it to be simple, but like you, I have a way with words. I believe he will understand the reasoning for my deception, as it is the only option to save my kingdom."

Chapter 18

EMER

The morning after waking Opal, Emer woke up shivering. But for the first time since seeing the mære, her nightmare wasn't the only reason for her shivering. She sat up on her bench and peeked through the window. The white fog greeted her, as usual, but the scene before her was extra white.

"Pearl!" Emer shook her sister's shoulder. "Pearl, wake up! It snowed!"

Her sister woke with a gasp, shaking and blinking away her sleep before climbing up to peer through the window with Emer. She gasped again, this time with delight.

"Have you ever seen anything more beautiful?"

"Snow in Somnus," Emer said, remembering Somnus trees that kept their dark greenery all year long to become blanketed by white. In Ormio, these trees and abandoned buildings had abandoned their leaves, creating a dead scene beneath the white dusting of frozen mist. Still, the silence and softness of their powdered surroundings inspired awe.

Pearl scrambled for shoes and a cloak to wrap around her shoulders before opening the door. A burst of winter air flooded their coach.

Pearl apologized before stepping out. "I hope the others slept well."

With ten people in their company, they had utilized Opal's magic to command rocks to build huts out of abandoned rooms of the Veriae homes for shelter against the cold weather, but Emer worried if they had enough blankets to stay warm. Sleeping in the state coach with Pearl had given Emer a cushioned bed and a small space to lock in their body heat. She shivered as she stepped into the cold.

Marin and Ranae were already up, huddled together at the flickering fire pit. Emer followed Pearl to the large, white-dusted men's hut. Pearl stopped at the entrance, bent over, and called, "Good morning!" to those inside.

Bent over and unsuspecting, Emer couldn't resist the temptation. She squished the fine layer of snow into a little ball and tossed it at her sister's backside. Pearl squealed and stared at Emer. Emer bit back her laugh and pointed at their older sister. "It was Marin."

"A likely story!" Pearl laughed, crouching to make her own snowball. Emer laughed and ran for cover behind the coach. Marin didn't take kindly to the false blame and joined Pearl's team to ambush Emer. The sisters laughed as they tossed wet snowballs and tackled one another into the frosted grass.

Their attention became diverted as the Braeder brothers emerged from the men's hut with flexing stretches. Next door, a small pack of wolves exited the Ormio sisters' hut with Dot and Opal.

Emer stared with wide eyes at the tame beasts. "You invited a den?"

Dot stroked the back of the largest wolf and explained, "They cuddled with us to keep us warm."

Chase elbowed his brother with a teasing grin. "Looks like we've got competition."

Leo cleared his throat and pointedly ignored his brother, though his reddening neck said otherwise. "We should pack and start moving to stay warm. We can have breakfast on the way to Huiess. Caden!" His shout back into their hut was answered with a froggy grumble. Emer pinched back her smile, expecting he'd stayed up late to record their adventures. The last of the sleeping men exited their shelter and made quick work to pack their horses.

"Is it time to go?" Mica asked, ready to mount his horse with Pearl. "Are we actually going to the golden city of Remizio?"

"Golden?" Ranae asked, helping Marin to situate herself on Tucker with a blanket wrapped around her. "Is that a reference to its beaches?"

"No, it's literal," Mica said.

Caden paused before climbing onto the state coach behind Emer to rummage through one of his packs of scrolls. "Don't get too excited. Every legend says the gold is cursed."

"What gold?" Marin asked. "What legends and what curse?"

Unrolling his map of Rezhina Valley, he pointed to a small peninsula on the south side of Lake Imazhin. "According to Opal, this is where Crown Princesses Diamond and Garnet were headed, correct?"

Emer nodded. "Yes, that is the location of Remizio. Why?"

"Because that's the reported location of the cursed city of gold."

Mica picked up the explanation. "They say the entire city is made of gold. Every building, every street, every brick—"

"Every tree, piece of food, and *person*," Caden finished with a warning look, rolling up his scroll and replacing it in his bag. "The city's cursed. Touch the gold, and you join it."

Leo grunted from Dot's wild horse and started their procession southward. "I bet they add that as a way to keep people from flocking to the city for fortunes. I'll believe it when I see it."

"It's true," Chase said quietly from another one of Dot's horses. When every eye turned on him, he shrugged. "Queen Tanzanite instructed me to visit the outskirts of the city soon after she took me in. The entire city is a cautionary tale of what happens to greedy people."

Renae frowned. "I understand that Veriae was destroyed by mære as a way for Tanzi to prove her power and cause fear of her demons, but why would she essentially destroy the port city with gold?"

"I think," Caden called from the top of the coach, "it's the poisoned curse. Every princess has been surrounded by a curse-like protective barrier. Emer's briars, Marin's whirlpool, Pearl's midnight forest, the animals around Ruby and Dot, then the hazardous rocks around Opal. These curses protected the princesses while they slept for the last century. So, gold seems like a strange curse, but maybe you can all help me piece the legends together."

He and Mica shared parts of a story about two witches contesting to win a princes' heart, leading one greedy witch to seek help from an outsider. The legends broke into different directions about her reasoning for turning the city into gold, but either way, the results were the same as Remizio's golden curse.

Dot folded her arms with a frown. "Is the 'greedy witch' supposed to be Ame or Dia? My sister's ambitious, not greedy. She's one of the most selfless people I know. I looked forward to her becoming queen, knowing how she always put the needs of the kingdom before her own."

Marin tapped her finger to her chin. "The same could be said of Ame."

"Regardless," Emer said, "the legends twist our friends into villains. If history is written by the victors, then that means Tanzi endorsed those legends."

Chase wiggled uncomfortably from his horse. "It's easier to keep citizens away from a cursed golden city by describing it as a prison for greedy people."

Caden frowned thoughtfully. "The tales are more legends than history, but if the people accept it as truth without knowing the true history, then history is doomed to repeat itself."

Chase turned in his saddle to eye each person carefully. "I've been meaning to ask; what are your plans? I understand you mean to wake every sleeping princess, but rumors from the west claim you're starting a revolution to overthrow Queen Tanzanite."

"So," Caden said, rubbing the back of his neck, "the original plan was to recruit an army to help us fight the ogres up north. After waking Emer and causing the death of Ogress Charlotte, we understood that Queen Tanzanite would side with the ogres because of her treaty, so recruiting soldiers meant recruiting people despite her ruling."

Chase narrowed his eyes at the Uldran Prince. "But she's helping to fight the ogres now."

"Why?" Leo grumbled. "No one joins a war without something to gain from victory."

"Also," Marin said, "Tanzi must stand trial for her crimes. She orchestrated the downfall of every royal in all three kingdoms in order to take the throne."

"She betrayed us," Emer said. Her voice grumbled and her face grew hot. "Everything wrong with this valley—our cursed poisonings, the nightmarish mære, the persecution against the merpeople, even the sleepy mists that forced people away from the lake—every-thing happened because of her."

Chase's tight eyes and mouth landed on Emer and her sisters. "In a fair trial, what would be her punish-ment?"

"I say," Marin spoke, "that she deserves the same punishment she bestowed upon us. Justice would place her in captivity for a hundred harvests."

Pearl whimpered lightly. "What if she says sorry?"

"What?" Emer's face became incredulous. "Pearl, she tried to kill you three times!"

Her younger sister tucked down her chin. "She never went through with it."

"Just because we saved you does not excuse her at-tempts."

"Emer," Marin said, mimicking Chase's narrow expression. "What would *you* call justice?"

Emer did her best to swallow her emotions, but found them steaming up her throat. Tanzi had been so young and unassuming. If she'd wanted to make a change in the world, she could have simply asked Gar-net. Garnet would have listened and considered every possibility and outcome.

Emer wished she could do the same as her older sister looked to her for an answer. She wasn't the only
224

one. With every eye on her, Emer had a shocking realization. Everyone wanted to know her opinion because they valued it. Her opinion was worth something to her friends and family.

While this thought flattered her, it also terrified her. What if her words came out wrong and offended someone? What if her opinion was too contrary to everyone else's? What if her decision was the wrong choice? Would they disregard her? Would she lose her influence and become discredited in a time she could truly help?

She had tutored herself to be an aide to Garnet, to be an advisor to a great leader, not to *be* the great leader.

She tasted a sample of the anxiety that had burdened Garnet on a regular basis as she considered her solution to Tanzi, wondering if death was too simple for her traitorous sister.

With another heavy swallow, she managed to squeak out, "I cannot say." She coughed and started again. "Perhaps we will test her heart to determine an appropriate consequence."

Chase didn't seem satisfied with her vague answer, but Opal nodded and rested a hand on his. "There needs to be consequences for our actions. Even a queen must be held accountable."

They continued their travels as they slipped into more amiable conversations and the snow thinned into patches on plants. The trees grew farther and farther apart. Going directly south, they veered away from the lake and Noz Isle, enjoying wider views as the mist cleared. When they stopped to eat, Emer persuaded the plants to bear fruit and Dot asked the animals if there were any in pain so Leo could end their suffering. She and Marin still refused to eat the meat, though she didn't scowl at the others while they dined on a deer that had broken its spine from a recent fall.

On their third day of traveling, Opal checked the mountains between a break in the trees. "The Western Canyon is almost due west. We should be close to Ruvuz Gaudez."

"Ooh," Pearl said. "Never have I seen the red cliffs of Ormio."

Dot smiled. "They're a lot like the red plateaus of Utah and Arizona but in a straighter line."

Pearl squished her eyebrows in confusion. "What are the plateaus of You-tah and Air-zona like?"

Leo laughed. "Dot, I think we're the only two who understand that reference."

Dot scoffed and gestured with a quick sign that made Leo laugh.

Emer shuffled out Caden's map and rolled it open. She didn't mind when he leaned closer to analyze the map over her shoulder. Didn't mind at all. In fact, she was a little sad when he turned away to keep from shouting in her ear. "Do you think we'll meet any

Urbanuz people? I've heard they have advanced technology. Maybe they can help us improve our phones and cameras."

"Oh!" Emer reached over the carriage to grab one end of her vine phone. "I had an idea to try propagating my vine. It may be possible for the sibling vines to connect without roots. I hoped to make a new basket pot before we left the woods entirely."

They paused to rest the horses and discuss their route while Emer worked. After instructing the fern leaves to weave into a large basket, she cultivated a tree branch into a sturdy cane for Caden.

Marin shook her head. "If we are almost to the canyon, then we are too far west. We should turn eastward to reach Remizio on a more direct route."

"Marin's right," Dot said. "The Ruvuz Gaudez are impassable on the western side. Toto said that only their assassins were brave and trained enough to dare climb the western cliffs."

"Toto," Caden echoed. "As in Princess Topaz from Huiess? Why were Huiessian assassins training in Ormio? I thought your kingdoms were at war."

"The cliffs were part of the war," Ranae explained. "Huiessians believed the border between the kingdoms began at the cliffs, but Ormio claimed the border at the more southern divide at the Remizio River."

"Either way," Leo said, "turning east means turning toward the lake." Addressing his brother for confirmation, he asked, "The farther away from the lake we are, the less influence the mære and mists have, right?"

Chase nodded. "Yes, but Dot's right. The cliffs are impassable to horses—not to mention a state coach—even a kilometer west from the lake's edge."

"Hold on," Opal said. "The cliffs are rocks. Rocks obey my words."

Chase's eyes brightened with realization until he laughed and smashed a quick kiss to Opal's forehead. "You're right! Who cares about some rocks in the way? We'll make our own path!"

Marin gaped. "You will deface the iconic Ruvuz Gaudez for our personal convenience?"

Opal rolled her eyes. "I'll put them back exactly as they were before as soon as we reach the bottom."

Emer's environmentally minded sister huffed.

Within the next half hour of travel, they reached the southern point of Ormio where Western Canyon was due west and they stood at the top of a dangerously steep plateau of red.

"How incredible!" Pearl said.

Emer agreed. It was like standing at the edge of the world with a winter forest behind them and a rocky desert ahead. They could see for miles as the mountains slowly curved from their right until they became merely bumps on the southern horizon. Lake Imazhin continued to shape their eastern horizon, but Emer couldn't even pick out its beaches behind its curtain of mist.

"So, Opal," Caden called, "how do you plan to make our path downward?"

"I may need your help instructing the rocks again," she said, glancing at her sisters and friends. Emer and the other princesses guided her with specific words to create a long ramp for the horses and carriage. Observing the new and gradual slope downward, Chase leaned over Opal's shoulder to whisper, "It's almost like a slide."

A devious light settled into Opal's expression as she took command of the rocks to create a second—steeper and smoother—ramp.

"Oh, shrews," Marin swore.

Holding hands and laughing like children, Opal and Chase jumped off the cliff and slid hundreds of meters to the bottom within seconds.

Emer's eyes glinted as she smirked at Caden. "Remember when you said that you would follow me off the edge of the world?"

"I definitely don't remember saying that."

"You were sleep talking. Mica can verify."

He glared at Mica then cringed. "Are you going to make me regret my words?"

"Jump on three."

"That phrase is supposed to be hypothetical," he said, his voice nearing panic.

"Are you going to jump with me or not?"

"I suppose," he said regretfully, "but I want the record to show that I thought this was a bad idea."

"What record? Your history accounts? You can only record this misadventure if we survive it, and if you plan to write this all down for history, the least we can do is make it entertaining."

Caden grinned back. "You'll be the death of me, you know that?"

"One…"

Chapter 19

DIA

I did my best to forget my dreams every day after waking up and heading to work. Stan wasn't a prince. Mr. Rindlisbacher wasn't a court jester. I wasn't a princess secretly attracted to my co-worker while attempting to woo another co-worker.

It helped when the men in my dreams acted differently than their real counterparts did. Stan was less awkward than Prince Stanford, and Rindlisbacher was more grumpy than Riddle Maker. At least toward me.

I blushed to imagine Rindlisbacher acting like Riddle Maker. Goodness gracious, I'd be the one struggling to focus on work if that were the case. The thoughts helped my afternoon bus ride slip by, so I entertained them a bit longer than I probably should have, especially since Rindlisbacher was the one to greet me at the back door when I arrived at the shop. Maybe I shouldn't have been surprised. I was supposed to learn how to close the store that night.

He stood with his arms folded and pointedly not looking at me. "You didn't get my text?"

"What text?" I asked, heading for the office to clock in. I paused to pull my phone from my bag and read the notification from an unknown number. "We're slow. You can come in later." It was sent twenty minutes ago. "Sorry," I said. "I was already on the bus and hadn't noticed."

He worked his jaw, tapping his finger against his muscled arm. "If you have errands to run in the area—"

"I need the hours," I said.

He dared to glance at me, then looked back to the storage room. "Fine. You can check the dates on the loan items for anything that's expired."

In other words, "get out of my sight." At least I'd be paid for it.

He left me alone to clock in, then I slipped into the storage room where we kept the items purchased by a loan to customers who basically used us like an expensive three-month storage unit. I spent the next hour going over every piece on the rusted shelves that were built more for strength than display, rotating older items to the front to call the customers for a two week's notice before we'd move their items to the store for purchase. Eyeing a particularly chunky golden necklace, I wondered about its purity. But that would mean going up to the front of the store and "playing" with acid around Rindlisbacher.

With a relenting little sigh, I intentionally mis-quoted, "Everything that glitters is gold," and set the necklace down. After an hour, I had everything organized, categorized, and customers notified. Half of me wanted to linger in the storage room to avoid my co-worker, but I couldn't let him catch me doing nothing back there.

Thankfully, customers kept us both relatively busy and separated until Jay arrived for the closing shift. Seeing his release, Rindlisbacher excused himself and went to the office to complete manager-ly things for Brian. Whatever those were.

One of our regulars came in, asking to buy back a necklace he'd put on loan a month ago. Jay went back to retrieve it, leaving me to chat idly with the customer while we waited. Jay returned with empty hands and a confused expression. He held up a finger and explained, "Hold on. I need to check something." He grabbed the set of nitric acid and retreated back to the storage room. I attempted to keep the customer occupied with chit-chat for ten-ish minutes until Jay exited the storage room again, this time with a golden necklace in hand. Instead of coming up front, he held up his finger to have us hold longer as he went into the office.

The customer and I shared confused looks.

Curious and hoping to learn something, I joined Jay and Rindlisbacher in the office. Though we weren't supposed to leave customers unattended, Jay gestured for me to close the door behind me.

"I don't understand it," he said. "We purchased a twelve karat gold necklace from him last month, and it looked exactly like this one. This has the same tag and everything, but feel it! I even tested it with the acid—see?" He showed off the rubbing stone to Rindlisbacher. Speaking through clenched teeth like a ventriloquist, he hissed, "It's twenty-four karat gold! We have no record of a golden necklace with this purity level."

Rindlisbacher frowned and studied the necklace. "You think someone switched out the fake with a real one? Why? Like it's a reverse robbery?"

"I don't have the foggiest clue. What do we do with it? Do we sell it back to him based on its original price? Or put it on our shelves like it's a new item? I say we sell that piece as fast as a shotgun wedding."

Rindlisbacher chuckled. "Tempting."

"Are we supposed to report it to the police? What if a thief is trying to use us like a fence?"

"Then they're doing it wrong." He grunted. "But that brings up a good point. I don't want to be caught with jewelry like that with no records. I'll tell Brian, and he can write up a report."

"Okay. Then, here." Jay handed over the necklace like it was a grenade. "If we're giving it to the cops, I don't want my fingerprints all over it. What do we tell the customer?"

Rindlisbacher smirked and grabbed a tissue from a Kleenex box to wrap around the necklace. "Tell him we're sorry, but we're unable to return his item for undisclosed reasons. Say we'll get it back to him as soon as possible at the original price. Supposing this is the original item. If he needs something today, let him buy another piece with a special full-refund option."

"Cool. Thanks, Mr. R." Jay nodded and returned to the front.

I lingered. "How will you return it to him if the cops take it?"

Rindlisbacher grunted. "We'll buy him a new one if we've got to. It might put us in the hole if the police don't reward us for that piece, but it's not his fault if things got switched around."

I tilted my head as if to see my co-worker from a new angle. He wasn't like my expectations of Riddle Maker in my dreams. He didn't lie in wait to trick or ensnare anyone with riddles. He was fair.

"If you're a diamond," I asked, "why do you act like coal around me?"

The man blinked at me, though his expression opened a little more.

When he said nothing, I explained with a shy shrug, "Your integrity says a lot about your character. You're a good man, Mr. Rindlisbacher."

He continued to stare at me until the edge of his lip lifted with a hint of a grimace. "No, I'm not." He punched the buttons to unlock the office safe.

I folded my arms and leaned against the wall of the small office. "Do I make you uncomfortable?"

A faint growl rumbled in his throat. I could practically hear his jaw hardening as he placed the necklace inside the safe and hissed something unintelligible.

"Sorry—"

"Yes." He slammed the safe door closed as his passionate eyes met mine. I gasped and drew back.

"Why?" I whispered.

He jerked away to jab his name and password into the computer to clock out for the day. No, I wasn't going to let him run away from my questions that easily.

"Why?" I demanded. "Why do you hate me?"

With a heavy calming breath, he turned on me as if I'd issued a challenge and he was gearing up to fight till the death. He stepped toward me with slow and calculated steps. I backed up until I bumped into the wall. The door was partially open and within arm's reach. I could easily slip out and run to the public space of the shop, but I needed to know Rindlisbacher's mind.

"I don't hate you," he said, continuing to measure his footsteps with slow deliberation toward me. "That's the problem."

His palms slammed against the wall on either side of me, locking me in with one swift motion. Though he was far from touching me, I pressed my spine into the wall.

236

He whispered with hunched shoulders, "It would be hard enough if you were only beautiful and intelligent."

If I thought he couldn't surprise me any more than he already had, I was wrong. First, the honesty with Jay and the customer. Then this confession of attraction? I didn't know what to think or feel. As my heart beat wildly, I wasn't sure if it was with flattery from his attraction, excitement from the sudden adrenaline rush, or fear of what he might do.

The bell jingled from the front to announce a new customer. Rindlisbacher didn't even glance away. I wondered if I should slip past him. Did I want to escape? I was equally intrigued and nervous for his next move. We both stood with bated breath as he quivered with restraint.

The bell jingled again. My stomach and heart rose as I braved to meet the passionate eyes before me. Another jingle. Jay was probably overwhelmed with customers. We remained, each trapped in our own prisons. How long would this last? It already felt like an eternity had passed.

Just as Jay called his greetings, Rindlisbacher yanked himself away to dash through the half-closed office door. I remained standing against the wall, gasping for air. How long had I been holding my breath?

Jay thanked someone for coming in, and I found my legs to step out of the office. I half expected to find Rindlisbacher waiting just outside. He was nowhere in sight, having either hidden behind a storage shelf or bolted for the back door. I dashed from the little room of extreme emotions, nearly running into a customer who stood at the corner. He wore a hoodie and headphones, singing to the collection of vinyls.

For the rest of my shift, I failed to comprehend Jay's instructions about closing the store. I couldn't stop reliving the moment from the office. Every time I closed my eyes, I saw the passionate face of my co-worker: his wild brown eyes that weaved between desire, restriction, and pain. His heavy breathing lips, open with want, and quivering with indecision. I rubbed my arms from chills and thought of his sleeves pulled tight against his muscles. I shivered and remembered how he shook with hunger and restraint. He was both feral and leashed. The look in his eyes thrilled me with both fear and excitement. He had basically called me more than beautiful and more than intelligent, to the point that it drove him crazy.

Conclusion: he was right. Mr. Rindlisbacher was a dangerous man. All sources of wisdom screamed to avoid him at all costs. All sources from my stupid heart yearned for another encounter.

I mentally slapped myself. Fool of a woman! I shouldn't be attracted to such a monster! I should call Brian and ask him to separate our schedules! I should call the authorities and tell them… what? That he cornered me in the office? But I'd chosen to stay and confront him. And he hadn't even touched me. No harm, no foul.

Thoughts of accusing him of harassment left me with a guilty after-taste. I wasn't entirely innocent either. I had provoked him by demanding answers. Also, could I honestly say his attention was unwanted? As much as he unnerved me, part of me enjoyed his attention. His brown eyes were like a milky chocolate truffle sprinkled with edible gold leafing and set on fire. His trembling mouth and honey-lemon breath begged to be touched by—

Stop! I forcibly banished such thoughts. My emotions were untrustworthy. I considered cold hard logic to focus.

Fact: Mr. Rindlisbacher was dangerous.

Fact: Mr. Rindlisbacher was my co-worker.

Fact: Mr. Rindlisbacher was practically a stranger.

Fact: Mr. Rindlisbacher—

I paused as a new realization hit me.

Fact: I didn't even know Mr. Rindlisbacher's first name.

Chapter 20

DIA

I knew my dreams after the incident in the office would be unbearable. Between the risky consequences of sleep deprivation and the risk of dreaming about my co-workers, I chose sleep deprivation. With Cherie and Steve gone for a biking trip in the canyons (crazy people), I stayed awake by blasting energizing music through my bedroom. I turned it down with each angry knock from our shared neighbor's wall until the fourth knock convinced me to turn it off. I drank coffee and researched the chemical compounds between various golden alloys until even the traffic settled to a quiet hum. Then, I played tug-o-war between "I'm so tired, I should sleep" and "No, I have to stay awake, I can't sleep" until…

I was back in the life-size sandcastle, staring out the window of my bedroom. Movement caught my eye as a young man leaned against a window in a lower turret. Prince Stanford. Was he alone? Maybe this was my chance to talk with him. Every other time

240

I'd seen him, Ame had been present, and I had to wonder if she was somehow influencing him against me. Not that I'd hold it against her. It was politics, after all.

I didn't have plans to meet up with Riddle Maker until later that evening (unsurprisingly, the man was a night owl), leaving my afternoon open and available. I stepped to my door to leave and considered what I'd say to Stanford. In all of my studies of solving riddles, maybe I should have studied the art of persuasion. Idiot. That was obviously what I should have done. If I could persuade Stanford to forget the competition, then I wouldn't need to worry about impressing him, or working with Riddle Maker, or guessing Riddle Maker's name.

Yes, that was a good idea.

With a plan in mind, I marched out of my room and circumnavigated the castle to find the prince. After hitting a couple of dead ends and turning around three times, I found him walking toward the gardens.

With his back to me, I called, "Prince Stanford?"

He turned, surprised. "Yes? Princess Fashio, was it?"

My cheeks flushed with heat. I'd jumped to his first name, forgetting formalities until he used my last name. This was why I preferred to converse with books and food more than people. Social expectations were such a bother. As if I could keep them straight among my own people, throw in international customs, and I was as lost as a fish in the sky.

"Yes, please forgive me, Prince Muli," I said with a little curtsy. "I mirrored my familiarity with Ame—or Princess Zhenero—onto you." Wait a minute, could I use that? "See, I feel like we are already friends. Forgive me if this was a misconception."

As expected, his jaw bounced with uncertainty. Denying my friendship now would seem insulting. Yes, I was socially inept, but that didn't make me clueless. My mom and dad had taught me how to fool a room of nobles into believing me capable of being their queen someday.

Prince Muli bowed. "No, the fault is mine. You can call me Stanford if you wish."

I accepted with another little dip, waiting for him to ask for my name in return. He didn't. Maybe I wasn't the only one who was socially inept.

Clearing my throat, I offered, "Only if you return me the favor with Diamond."

He frowned. "You want me to pay you with a diamond for using my first name?"

A laugh escaped me before I could stop it. With one released, I let them all go until I was holding my stomach and fanning my face. "Oh, what logic would make sense of that? No, my given name is Diamond. I'd like you to use my first name if I use yours."

"Oh." His shoulders and smile relaxed. He had a sort of boyish and naïve smile that I would call more adorable than handsome, but not unattractive. "I recall Ame referring to you with a similar name."

Ame. Not Amethyst or Princess Zhenero. Slanders, she had beaten me to the punch for using first names—nicknames at that. How was I supposed to convince him to choose me when she had a head start?

Speaking of the slanderer, she poked her head around the garden door. I knew the Huiessians well enough to know that they never accidentally entered a room or conversation. How long had she been standing there, waiting, listening?

"Stanford?" she called. "Oh, Dia, how about you join us? We were going to stalk around the hunting grounds."

I replied with a tense smile. I didn't "stalk." I didn't know anyone in Ormio who did. But I couldn't let Ame have more time alone with him. Cringing behind my smile, I said, "Sure."

Thankfully, my dream skipped over the next couple of hours of humiliation as Ame stalked like a lioness while I reportedly "stomped like a toddler." At least Ame and Stanford had some laughs over my embarrassment. Unfortunately, my dream didn't skip every miserable part. I ended up at my next moment of humiliation as I snuck out of the castle after dinner to meet with Riddle Maker.

He asked to meet me at the temple, which was already playing dirty. If he knew I was an Ormio princess, he would know that stepping between those giant pillars of sandstone was blasphemy against the Words. Our temples were inscribed with words of inspiration and aspiring qualities. The temple of Remizio was carved with stars and constellations. What was so inspiring about them?

Feeling like an infidel, I found the closest priest or priestess. It was hard to tell with their shaved heads.

"I'm supposed to meet someone here." I estimated Riddle Maker's height with my hand, saying, "He's a shorter man with black hair and light brown eyes. Almost dismissible without his wicked smile."

She raised her shaved brows. Oops, maybe I shouldn't have described someone as "wicked" in the temple. But it was the most accurate word choice for the way his mouth quirked and his eyes smoldered like he knew exactly what stupid affect it had on people. At least I hadn't called him "devilishly handsome."

She gestured with her hands like she was pushing air upward, down a side hall. My Las Vegas mind laughed a little at the single pump to "raise the roof."

Confused, I asked, "I'm sorry, I don't understand."

The ridges above her eyes squished together. She grabbed my hand, making me involuntarily flinch. Our holy people never touched others. But this was Huiess, where their holy people were apparently as silent and rough as the surrounding stones. She pulled me down a long corridor and up a set of stairs. Ah, maybe her earlier gesture meant "he's upstairs."

Indeed, he was. Riddle Maker wore a creamy and flowing shirt, sleeves rolled up to his elbows, and hung loosely around his neck enough to reveal curling chest hair. He leaned against a window overlooking the front entrance, picking at his nails. He must have seen me enter, yet waited there for me like he didn't have a care in the world. His attitude made me both angry and jealous. I stood a few paces away, waiting for him to acknowledge me as the priestess left us alone.

In greeting, he said, "You've got a lot of work ahead if you want to win your competition."

"What do you mean?" I asked. "Are you surprised? What other reason would I hire you than to lessen my work?"

He didn't even grace me with the courtesy of looking up from his nails as I approached. He simply leaned back more casually. "Hiring a second servant to care for an entire castle doesn't mean there's less work to be done."

I folded my arms and asked, "Then why do you want to help me? You say that you do this out of the gleefulness of your wicked little heart, but your doubt and aloofness make me question your end goal. Why do you test my resolve? Do you have a reason that I shouldn't marry the prince?"

He couldn't possibly have feelings for me and be jealous of my desires to marry someone else, right? Even if he was, that wouldn't save my kingdom.

He mimicked my stance by folding his arms and staring back. He dared to add a little smirk. "I told you. I get a kick out of tricking royalty. I'm getting a two-for-one with this trick. You and the prince."

I challenged him with my eyebrow. "You plan to trick me?"

"Please," he scoffed. "As if you didn't know my reputation or what you were getting into by 'hiring' me? Also, based on your own riddle to me, I've got an inkling that you plan to trick me in return, so it's all mutual."

A small part of me panicked. Like Ame, he was two steps ahead of me. "You have a victorious spirit. Did you also discover my codename from the masquerade?"

He straightened and pouted. "Not yet. I'm still convinced that it's a trick question. I would have known if the heir of Ormio frequented the island. I know that the crown princesses Garnet and Amethyst attended regularly."

"It's no trick question," I said. "I know you danced the night away with various women until settling on one to pull away from the party. Then you would return at the end of the masquerade and move on."

He raised his eyebrows. "You are an observant one, aren't you," he stated. "You recognized my meetings with my informants?"

Informants? Not lovers then.

I contained my stupid heart's measure of relief at that mystery solved. "Maybe you're not as sneaky and clever as you think."

"Then what about you? Are you as clever as you think? Have you learned my name—this most simple piece of my identity?"

I scoffed. "Information is rarely simple, especially when it's guarded by secrets and lies. Speaking of which," I said, "I want to know why you chose this place to meet. If you know who I am, then you should know that this place offends the Words."

He smirked, and I almost wished the priestess was still around so I could point and demonstrate, "See? Wicked smile."

"Because," he said, "I like heights, and this temple has one of the best views—other than your guest chambers, of course."

I stepped back. "When were you in my chambers? How do you know where I'm staying?"

His smirk glinted. "Wouldn't you like to know?"

I squirmed before remembering his mention of informants. I should have known this would happen. I should have listened to the warnings to stay away from Riddle Maker and listened to the stories that said how he swindled people.

Thankfully, the logical part of my brain hadn't completely shut off. It analyzed his tactics and found a pattern.

He knew I was a Princess of Ormio, but he chose to meet in a Huiessian temple. He liked heights, though heights made many people uncomfortable. He claimed to know where I slept and to know what the view was like from the inside. Everything he did was to make me uncomfortable, throw me off balance, and control our situation.

I refused to be controlled.

Marching right up to him gave me the pleasure of faltering his smirk. I hissed, "Even without your mask, you're a fool. If there's no other reason for meeting here, I will take my leave and take my chances with the competition."

He reared back a little, evidently surprised. Then he barked a joyful laugh. I narrowed my eyes and spun on my heel.

"No, no, don't go," he said, still laughing. "This is the best place in Remizio for a secret conversation, because the only people who might be listening have taken oaths of silence."

"The priests and priestesses?" I asked, sparing a half turn. That explained the priestess's actions. I put my back to the wall opposite of the windows to keep both Riddle Maker and the exit in my sights. The temptation to leave rose as his smirk returned.

"At least this is the best *public* place for a secret conversation. There are plenty of private and more intimate places—"

"This is fine," I said, annoyed at the heat in my cheeks and wandering thoughts. "With all of your research on me and my chambers, did you find anything useful about the prince?"

He chuckled and settled into the window corner again. "About that, I got it on good authority that you, Princess Amethyst, and Prince Stanford went on a nice little walk through the gardens today."

"You spied on me?"

"Correction, I got others to spy on the prince for me. I have people in place gathering information, even as we speak. About your possible Noz Isle codename and anything on the Urbanuz Prince. To impress a man, you must first know what impresses him. You know what I learned?"

"Tell me," I said, expecting nothing new while making a mental checklist of ways to hide my Noz Isle identity.

His smirk disappeared into a serious stare. "You're doomed."

Chapter 21

DIA

I was doomed? Lifting my chin, I told Riddle Maker, "I refuse to give up."

He sighed dramatically, as if to say, "Don't say I never warned you." Out loud, he explained, "This prince you're so determined to win is a mere boy. He doesn't care about love at all. He doesn't even care for an impressive woman. He might be daft, but even he knows he can't love a woman solely based on her talents. All he wants is to please King Daddy like a good little boy. So, how do you get a woman good enough to please Daddy without emotionally getting a wife? You choose a wife who's 'impressive,' someone so distracted by her arts and hobbies that he'll never see her."

"You dare to slander his good name?"

"You think what you will, but that boy isn't interested in a wife. He wants a bond to satisfy the king so that he can return to playing mindless games."

I mentally shrugged. I wasn't interested in being a wife either and made no attempt at fooling myself into

250

thinking I would find love in Stanford. Oddly, our disinterest in romance might have made us a better pair. Maybe I could tell him that.

Riddle Maker frowned at me. "You have no idea how much harder that makes this."

"In what way?"

"My original plan had a plan B, that even if your talent was subpar, he'd choose you anyway because you make him fall in love with you."

"Factually," I said, "that's the main idea of the competition, but to do so in a week is one hundred percent improbable."

His frown deepened. "It wasn't a bad idea until I found out the prince was a dolt. You're not unattractive, but quite memorable."

I scoffed. "Liar. If I'm 'quite memorable,' why don't you remember seeing me at the masquerades?"

He opened his mouth, only to close it again.

Despite the sting of his words, I grinned. "Look, I stumped Riddle Maker."

"That!" he said, pointing. "That's memorable. Your words. You're a true Princess of Ormio who has studied Words with reverence and devotion. Use these next few days to talk with Prince Stanford, and even a dolt like him will see there's more to you than what's on the surface."

I raised a challenging brow. "Are you saying that what's on the surface isn't enough?"

He rolled his eyes and chuckled. "Stars, you've got to be as bad as I am with turning a phrase? But that's plan B. For plan A, we've got to amaze him. So, what are your talents?"

I listed my skills in arithmetic, event planning, budgeting, organizing, finding patterns, and critiquing food.

He shook his head, a little incredulous. "While commendable, none of those will work. We need something creative, artsy, a real crowd pleaser. What are your hobbies? What do you do for fun?"

I paused to think of my daily activities and the little things I did between duties. "Reading, solving puzzles, conversing with my sisters and friends, critiquing food, and watching people."

Riddle Maker blinked. "There's got to be more than that, right?"

I shrugged. "I'm a princess of Ormio. I have little time for anything else."

"That's depressing," he muttered. I didn't know whether to agree or take offense. "Fine. How's your acting?"

"Amateur at best," I said. "Why do you ask?"

"Because our next best option is to *pretend* you're good at something."

Confused, I said, "Please explain."

"I've got many skills," he said, "talents, hobbies, and natural presentation techniques to impress people.

But, most of all, I've got the skill of a conman. I'll provide the crowd pleaser. All you've got to do is act like you're the one doing it."

At that, I took offense. "You want me to lie? To con the prince into choosing me?"

"Think of it as a magic trick. All you need to do is impress him, right? He never said anything about continuing your performance after you're stuck together. And put that anger away. If you didn't doubt your abilities in the first place, you wouldn't have hired me. Did you want my help or not?"

Clenching my teeth, I muttered, "Fine. We will take the night and morning to consider which 'trick' to present, but no more of this slanderous talk in a temple, even if it's to the wrong gods. Next time, I choose the location."

I woke up in Nevada and immediately began my new ritual to write down the dream. These dreams had come maybe once or twice a week at the start, but lately they came almost nightly. While it bothered me to imagine such vivid and insane realities with my co-workers, I also anticipated the next part of the story.

The next few nights explored the next two "dream days" as I shadowed Stanford every morning and afternoon, asking him questions about his interests and favorite hobbies. The best way to impress someone was to perform on the master level something that they enjoyed spectating or practiced on the amateur level. For instance, I was highly impressed by Ame's fighting skills because I knew a lot about it without being able to do any of it myself. I was also highly impressed by my twin sisters' musical talents because I knew the basics of trumpet and flute, but hadn't ever practiced enough to become as skilled as they were.

Unfortunately, Stanford enjoyed watching dueling tournaments and had always wished to practice more winery crafting. Any fighting displays I'd attempt would be dwarfed by Ame's, and even if a wine-tasting session could be impressive, one week's worth of effort wasn't enough time to take credit from a winery.

Still, I hoped that I was improving slightly on Plan B to woo the prince as my personal questions inspired enthusiastic conversations. The prince acknowledged my entrance and presence with smiles, and we talked easily. I thought it was going rather well until I met with Riddle Maker that evening in the palace's library of ledgers. With rare visitors, only one entrance and exit, and many large shelves to hide behind, it made a decent place to meet an indecent person.

He was already inside by the time I arrived, disguised as a palace servant. He greeted me with a frown and folded arms.

"What?" I asked.

"Are you even trying to woo him?"

"Of course I am! Every moment I'm not with you, I'm with him. Why—have you been spying on us again?"

254

"My informants say you talk, that you are 'perfectly polite.' Princess, if you want to win his heart, you've got to flirt a little."

I cringed, and his shoulder sank with dismay.

"What's that face for? Are you serious—even the thought of flirting disgusts you?"

"Not disgust," I murmured, "just unease."

With an exaggerated sigh, he beckoned me. "Have I got to do everything around here? Here, I'll show you how it's done."

I started to approach, then backed off when I realized what he meant. "This is ridiculous. I don't need you to teach me how to flirt."

"All my informants say otherwise. Besides, you've got to practice acting so that he'll believe it's you performing your impressive feat."

"Exactly what will I be pretending to do?"

"I've got to figure that out still. I'm working on it. You, meanwhile, need to work on your courting techniques. Show me what you've got. Pretend I'm Prince Stanford. We're walking through the rock gardens, alone. What do you do?"

I folded my arms and stared him down. "I asked him earlier about his interests, hoping for inspiration for my performance."

"Alright, first of all, this has got to go." He took my elbows and pulled them outward to unlatch my folded arms. "You've got to appear open, comfortable, and genuinely interested. Try this; we're walking side by side, right? Slip your hand around the inside of my elbow. It's no more than a non-verbal request for an escort while you walk, but the key is you've made physical contact. Come on, give it a go. We're walking side by side…"

I blushed furiously with the thought of forcing physical contact with a man—not to mention the Mystery Man I'd once longed for. Yet he stood beside me with his hands in his pockets as Stanford often did, waiting for my boldness.

Feeling like a rodent stealing cheese, I tucked my chin down with nerves and slipped my hand around the nook of his elbow.

Slanders, his arm was solid with muscle. Maybe I shouldn't have been surprised, knowing how often the man danced for recreation. Whereas I had the body type of someone who sat, ate, and watched everyone else dancing.

"There," Riddle Maker said softly. "Was that so hard?"

I slipped my hand away and refused to look in his direction.

"Let's try another scenario," he said. "The prince typically sits between you and Princess Amethyst at dinner, right?"

"Right," I said, still staring at the wall, away from Riddle Maker.

"In that case…" He tugged on my elbow again to stand side by side against the wall, forcing my sights
256

back to him to watch where he directed me. "Imagine we're eating dinner. I say something foolish because I'm Prince Stanford—"

"You slander him—"

"—And I quote, 'Sometimes, I swear, gullible really is written on the ceiling!' Then you laugh like I'm terribly funny."

I bit the insides of my lips to hold back my laugh. His imitation of Stanford's relaxed body language and Urbanuz accent had been spot on.

"No," he said with a point, "don't hold it back. Laugh like you agree."

I released my laugh, though it felt less like an agreement than a mockery. All the same, Riddle Maker's smile spread with success. He stared at my mouth as if analyzing my laugh. Was I too high pitched? Too fast? Too loud? I turned away and stifled myself.

He rotated to face me and leaned his shoulder against the wall. "And when you've got him alone somewhere, get in close, like this." He slid closer and tenderly touched my chin to direct my face toward his. "Speak low and quiet, like you're sharing a secret meant only for him and to encourage him closer. Make sure he gets a good look into your beautiful golden eyes."

I inhaled his scent of sandy palm trees and forgot to exhale at his proximity and compliment.

"Then," he whispered, "when his lips part like yours have, you let your eyes wander to them and let yourself imagine what they might feel like against your own."

Oh, I was imagining, but not with Stanford. Riddle Maker's eyes focused on my mouth as he started to close in. My eyelids fluttered between acceptance and light-headed panic. As much as I wanted it, I couldn't let him kiss me. I was a princess, heir to Ormio, and he was… a stranger?

"Then you pull away," he said, pushing himself back and severing my hypnosis. "You've got to leave Prince Stanford wanting."

Right, Prince Stanford. He was the one who would help me save my kingdom. Riddle Maker was no more than a means to an end.

I shook my thoughts back into order and huffed. "That's the backup plan. When establishing the competition, he stated that he likes 'impressive' women. Have you had any thoughts about my performance?"

"I've got a few, but the challenge will be teaching you to pull them off. Magicians work with three main techniques: skill, misdirection, and showmanship. Male magicians often use female assistants to help misdirect and distract the audience, but if you're the one who's supposed to be fooling the prince without months of practice, you've got to rely on showmanship."

I tilted my head. "If you failed to notice me all these years at the Noz Isle masquerades, what makes you think I can keep his attention or put on a show?"

He rolled his eyes. "It's precisely because you claim to have attended the masquerades all these years that I know you can do this. As I said, you're memorable. You must have had quite the costume to hide, disguise, or distract from your words, royal posturing, and even your hair."

"My hair is nothing special. I don't have curls like Opal or red highlights like Ruby. It's yellow and straight, like straw."

For some reason, Riddle Maker didn't seem to like that. He stepped close and reached up. Before I realized what he was doing, he slipped his fingers through my hair. I froze. Only men of my family had ever touched my hair with fatherly pats or brotherly teasing.

"It's not straw," he said. "It's gold. Like your eyes. Like you."

My breath caught. My masquerade codename was Gold. Did he know that? I was no closer to discovering his name.

Even as we stood there, his face grew with a mischievous smile. "I know how to impress the prince."

"Oh?"

He started to laugh. "It's got to be the best magic trick ever, one worth writing home to the king, one so incredible that the king will insist Stanford chooses you." He laughed harder. "We're going to win, Princess!"

His laughter was contagious and hopeful, though a worry warned my gut. "How? How will we win?"

Gleeful, he whispered, "We're going to turn straw into gold."

Chapter 22

DIA

It seemed odd that no one knew Mr. Rindlisbacher's first name.

"I bet it's something embarrassing," Kevin figured.

"He probably lost his first name with his sense of humor," Stan guessed.

"Don't you know? His first name is Mister," Jay joked. "He was a businessman from the womb, and his parents named him appropriately. That's my story, and I'm sticking to it."

As much as I wanted to speculate, I preferred to occupy my thoughts with other subjects like the history of our items. I learned fun facts about our inventory to add interest to customers, how to kindly deny unsellable pieces, and how to estimate values for sellable pieces. I worked hard to prove my worth as the newest, youngest, and only female employee.

After four weeks of working at The Golden Pawn, I joined everyone in the storage room before opening for our monthly report. Five of us squished around a cheap foldable table that was made extra crowded with breakfast muffins, doughnuts, bagels with cream cheeses, and jugs of juices. Rindlisbacher was notably the only one absent. Once everyone had served themselves and was quietly stuffing their faces, Brian stood for everyone's attention. "Alright, you all did a great job this last month, some more than others—or you all did well, but you know what time it is."

My co-workers half-heartedly cheered.

I questionably "wahoo"ed with the others and leaned over to Stan beside me. "What's going on?"

"Employee of the month," he explained. "Brian rewards last month's top sales rep with a free meal from a restaurant of their choice. And I mean *any* restaurant. It would be more exciting if any of us stood a chance against Rindlisbacher."

Brian gave a knowing look to Stan. "You know, the reason he works so hard is because he has a wager—or bet with me. If anyone outsells him, he'll personally provide the lunch and an additional prize. Jay's won before. What did he give you, again?"

Jay grinned. "We went for lunch at The Wicked Spoon to discuss my prize. Then he gave me VIP tickets to Amazing Comic Con."

That was generous. With more than a few Michelin Star restaurants uptown, the free lunch could be quite the expense. Then he gave a high-priced reward on top of that? Why? To challenge his co-workers (possibly future underlings) to try beating him in sales?
262

Admittedly, knowing about the possible prize did bolster my desire to do better.

"Cool, right?" Brian said. "Any of you can compete with him, and this last month's top sales proves it's possible, because Rindle's going to take care of—or pay up! We'll have to see if she can keep it going."

She? That narrowed down the options fast. All eyes turned on me as Stan leaned over in preemptive excitement.

"Everyone," Brian announced, "give it up for Dia!"

The cheers continued as my co-workers stood in my honor. Stan nudged me with that playful grin of his while I remained stunned in my chair. The honor swelled my heart with pride and joy, but the thought of sitting down for a meal with Rindlisbacher tightened my heart with worry. The contradicting emotions left me motionless until Stan stepped around to lift me by my shoulders. He hugged me and whispered in my ear, "You deserve it."

Brian moved on to other matters, explaining what to expect with the upcoming fall season and heading into the winter holidays.

"Also," he added, "there's been some discrepancies—or mix-ups with our jewelry inventory. When a customer brings in a piece, be sure to test its purity. We've had more than a few pieces that were cheapened—or low-balled—and we've needed to adjust. It hurts us and the customers when their pieces are under appraised of their true value."

I frowned. Was that the explanation for that twenty-four karat necklace? A necklace with that level of purity was improbable and illogical, so maybe the employee assumed it was a lower quality from the beginning? But he said there were a few. What other pieces had been undervalued? How many?

We finished eating and chatting until it came time to open the store. Stan was scheduled for that morning, leaving the clean-up of the food, tables, and chairs to the rest of us.

Business quickly returned to usual for everyone except me. My thoughts were consumed by my upcoming meal with my co-worker. It didn't help when Brian said, "Rindle had a meeting—or appointment this morning, but he should be by in an hour so you can talk to him about your lunch date."

Date? Panic mode: on.

"Or lunch," Brian flustered to fix his wording as if he saw the rising heart-rate on my watch. "Just lunch. It's the same offer he gives to anyone who beats him. Anyway, I know you bike here, so it's not a lot of time to go home and back."

Sure, but that gave me an hour to over think the whole situation. With little else to do, I spent the time scrolling through restaurants and menus, loitering in the front, and distracting Stan. As much as I wanted to visit a Chef Joël Robuchon restaurant, I really didn't want the Michelin Star experience tainted by Rindlisbacher's presence. Also, those required reservations, and I figured the sooner it was over, the better.

I picked The Pepper Club for its proximity, take-out option, and its prices well beyond my budget. Even the sides were double dollar signs. But, gracious, it all looked beautifully prepared and appetizing. It was the kind of food I hoped to study and make someday.

Looking through the menus and gallery of photos helped ease my nerves, but ten minutes before the hour, I reached for Stan with trembling hands.

"I can't do it, Stan. Will you go for me?"

He scoffed. "I wish! I don't say no to free food, but Dia, you know I can't. He's expecting you, and the whole luncheon conversation is supposed to be about how he can reward you based on your wants. What would I say? Buy you a box of chocolates?"

I laughed, but it came out shaken. "I wouldn't want chocolates from that man." Goodness gracious, what kind of rumors would that start?

"Can you imagine his face if I showed up instead and asked for girly stuff?" Stan laughed. I, however, suddenly found it difficult to imagine anything except Rindlisbacher's handsome face.

"Here." Stan took my elbow. "I'll walk you to the office to get your things."

The thought of the office and that memory against the wall ambushed me.

I grabbed Stan's hand before he reached for the door handle.

"Stan, wait. What if..." I lowered my voice. "What if he tries to take advantage of me?"

Stan blinked. "Rindlisbacher? Why would he—"

"I never told anyone because he didn't touch me, but—"

"Hold on, you're serious?" Stan grabbed my arm and jerked me toward him. "Did he hurt you? Dia, why—why didn't you say something?"

Stan hurt me more with his yanking than Rindlisbacher had when caging me even as Stan demanded information of the possible harassment. The irony shocked me.

"Ow," I said with a glance at Stan's hand on my arm. He released me like a hot iron, only to reach gently for my hands. I swallowed and tried to shrug like it was no big deal. "I didn't say anything because nothing factually happened that would be taken seriously. It was just words as he said what he thought of me."

Stan squeezed my hands, his worried expression taking me very seriously. "Words can lead to actions. No one has rejected employee of the month lunches, but I'm sure we could find a way around it if you think he'll do something."

The front door opened with a happy chime, calling for Stan to return to the front. Considering Rindlisbacher's restraint in the private office versus what could happen in a public restaurant, I mustered my courage and shook my head. "No, I don't think he'll go that far."

"Well," Stan said, his thumb stroking mine, "if he starts making unwanted moves toward you, tell him you have a jealous boyfriend. You can claim me if he asks for a name."

My mouth dropped to gape and reply, but the customer up front called for assistance. I had to choose. Enjoy a luxurious and free meal or bike home to make my fanciest of ramen recipes and rant it out with Cherie. Shove my value in the man's face or deny the honor and rewards of employee of the month. Meet with Rindlisbacher, or excuse myself with Stan.

As much as Rindlisbacher's face haunted me, it also taunted me. I had every day opportunities to eat ramen, but only this moment to prove my worth to Rindlisbacher.

Last second, I slipped from Stan's grasp and into the office. "Thanks, Stan," I said. "I'll be back soon."

The door closed behind me, and I steadied my breathing. I would say hi, accept congratulations, request a visa gift card, then excuse myself to take my meal To Go.

Gathering my possessions and willpower, I went out to meet with Rindlisbacher. I passed Brian in the storage as he scratched his head over a ledger.

I stepped outside to find the aspiring assistant manager locking his Ford Mustang. That car and his prizes validated the rumors that he came from old money.

"Rindlisbacher," I announced with a high chin, "the number one sales rep is here."

"'Kay. Brian warned me I'd be paying up. Give me a minute, then send him out."

I raised an eyebrow. "Him?" My thoughts of quiet dismissals were wedged aside by my pride. I stood my ground with my hands on my hips. "I'm not your secretary. You didn't think a woman could be the number one sales representative?"

"Dia?" His jaw slackened. "It wasn't personal. I just assumed it would be a man since ninety percent of the employees are male." He looked back at his car and muttered, "That changes things. Did you choose a restaurant?"

"The Pepper Club." I considered explaining my reasoning but paused as he strode past me to the back door and called into the storage.

"Brian, will you join us for lunch? Dia chose The Pepper Club, and I think they do take-out. We can pick up the order and eat here."

Our boss looked up, though he only seemed half surprised. A joyous grin spread across his face as he wrote down our orders. With a call ahead, our boss went to pick up the food, leaving Rindlisbacher and me exactly in the scenario we'd both hoped to avoid: alone.

268

Hating the awkward silence, I said, "Too bad they put the tables and chairs away from this morning's meeting."

"I'm taking counseling."

If the man's random proclamation had surprised me, his posturing doubled it. He stood with hunched shoulders, staring at the corner between the wall and floor. I likewise kept my eyes averted as I pulled out three chairs. "That's not something to be ashamed of. Is that why you missed the meeting?"

"Yes. But I am ashamed," he said, grabbing the table and setting it up. "Mostly, I'm ashamed of the way I acted toward you. I just wanted you to know that… I'm working on it."

I couldn't confess how his actions had factually affected me, especially as his humility was one more way he took me off guard. I wasn't ready to accept his apology yet, but I could encourage him to keep trying.

"What's more impressive?" I asked. "A man who's a gentleman because he's never been tempted to be otherwise, or a man who's a gentleman despite his temptations?"

He didn't answer, and I forced myself to face him. He finished setting up the table and stood tall, blinking at my feet. His eyes rose to mine for the briefest second before I looked away like he'd caught me staring.

"Thank you for lunch, but a reward isn't necessary. I was just doing my job."

He returned to staring at my shuffling feet. "You did your job better than everyone else, despite being the newest and youngest employee. You even beat me. You deserve to be rewarded for your hard work."

"I've heard about your prize rewards," I said, forcibly stilling my shuffles. "A Visa gift card would be just fine for me."

He pretended to busy himself by shifting loan items on the storage shelf. "That's all? What would you get with your gift card?"

"I don't know." I shrugged. "Food?"

That caught his attention as he raised an eyebrow at me. "You'd get a thousand dollars worth of food? Are you that strapped for cash, or is there a Michelin restaurant downtown you want to visit? You're too young for alcohol, so it's not like you'd spend it all on a bottle of wine."

Goodness gracious, a thousand dollars? My eyes widened as I considered what foods I'd buy with that kind of spending money. Caviar? Wagyu beef? Truffles?

"Mostly," I said, "an unspecified gift card would help me save money for housing at Stanford."

However the generous man planned to respond, he was cut off as Brian entered through the back door, holding two bags of take-out from The Pepper Club. The aroma was heavenly.

"Ah," our boss said. "You set up the table and chairs again. Excellent."

"Thanks for making the trip," Rindlisbacher said with a wave. "What did you order for yourself?"

Brian smirked. "Atlantic Salmon."

I was pretty sure that was the most expensive item on the brunch menu. Rindlisbacher gave our boss the stink-eye, but didn't dispute.

Brian set out the meals on the card table, handing a poke bowl to Rindlisbacher and a box of stuffed French toast to me. Glorious scents of cooked salmon, sugary bread, and Asian spices overwhelmed the storage's usual smells of oiled tools, dusty electronics, and metallic jewelry. I took a picture of the thick bread with its decorations of cream and fruit.

Rindlisbacher raised his eyebrow again. "You post your food on social media?"

I couldn't stop my tease from rising to the surface. "Right, because the best way to display this incredible food is in to-go boxes on a card table in a warehouse. No, I take pictures to try to replicate the dishes at home."

He tilted his head with curiosity. "You mentioned going to Stanford. Do you know your major?"

"Food Science," I said. "Stanford is among the top universities for it. I have a half-scholarship when I start in the fall, but the student housing makes me strapped for cash."

"I gotta wonder," he said with a hinted smile, "with food science, do you enjoy cooking or just playing with your food?"

Despite my uneasiness in his presence, I had the delectable meal, Brian's company, and the topic of food to relax me. I rattled off my favorite chefs and styles, only half surprised when Rindlisbacher said he was familiar with them. They were the best, after all. I went on about facts I'd learned from baking shows, like the various effects butter could have in pastries depending on its temperature, how yeast created chemical reactions with water, and the components of gluten.

I savored every bite of food as Brian snarfed down his salmon. Our portions were small, though the flavors and textures justified their price. Despite our warehouse surroundings, I couldn't remember the last time I'd enjoyed such an exquisite meal. Unless I counted those in my dreams as a princess served by castle chefs. Even if they were dreams, I sat with a straighter back and covered my mouth before speaking.

Seeing Brian's empty plate, I laughed. "You're done already? Ah, now I'll feel bad for eating in front of you."

He shrugged. "Don't. I'll let it settle as I chaperone—or crash your party."

Chaperone? I cleared my throat as if to clear my mind of any romantic inclinations and murmured, "I'd feel better if you were distracted."

Rindlisbacher muttered back, "You're plenty distracting."

That wasn't the response I'd expected. I turned away to hide my heated cheeks. Wanted: new topic.

My turn from the table put my gaze toward the office. A curiosity came to mind. "Whose puzzles are those in the office?"

"Mine," my co-worker said. "I find it helpful to occupy my hands while considering how to answer difficult emails from angry, frustrated, or desperate customers."

"You answer the emails?" I asked, landing my question on my boss for his explanation.

Brian shrugged sheepishly. "He's better at wording things so customers complain less—or are more satisfied."

I couldn't say that surprised me. Back to Rindlisbacher, I asked, "Can you solve all of your puzzles?"

He raised an eyebrow. "Is that a challenge?"

Would I regret asking? I couldn't see how, so I chirped, "Sure."

Without another word, he stood and retrieved several small silver puzzles from the office. I ate and watched him separate strange shapes, remove rings from chained cuffs, and slide open hidden compartments from boxes. Brian tried a few, but usually ended up shaking them like a rattle before giving up. The first few, Rindlisbacher did with ease, and he always returned his silver puzzles to their original positions.

"Can you do them all that easily?" I asked.

He grunted and began another.

"I hope not," I added. "I thought puzzles were meant to work your mind and challenge you. What's the point of a puzzle if you don't need to work at it?"

"The point," Brian said to the side, "is to show off."

"They help me consider things with new perspectives—again, helping me to answer difficult emails." Rindlisbacher continued to solve puzzle after puzzle. Some required multiple steps. One in particular kept his hands in motion for several minutes as he pulled a silver wire back and forth through golden rings.

Even with his mind occupied, he managed to carry a smooth conversation as he asked me more about my life goals.

"You still haven't told me what you'd like as your reward. You said you want food, but I gotta wonder if there's a certain spice or restaurant worth your interest."

I pondered on that. "As much as I love the smell, appearance, and history of wagyu beef or truffles, I don't think I could ever buy them just to try them. They're more expensive than I'm usually willing to spend on a single meal, and I would only have one. One beautiful meal between a slew of peanut-butter sandwiches would spoil my palette."

A thought crossed my mind, and I wondered if I dared to voice it. "Maybe you can reward me with the answer to a riddle."

He raised an eyebrow. "You're correct to assume that I'm just as capable of solving word puzzles as these little gadgets."

I leaned forward. "Oh, it shouldn't be a hard riddle—not for you, at least. As far as I know, you're the only person who knows the answer."

Rindlisbacher's eyebrow went higher. "Alright. Shoot."

I squinted, feeling bold and nervous to tread on personal ground. "What is your first name?"

Brian stopped chewing. Our boss failed to keep an uninterested face as his eyes glanced sideways. Of course, he probably knew. It must have been on Rindlisbacher's résumé when he applied. The man himself met my gaze like a challenger: confident, measuring, and with a slow growing sly smile.

He leaned back in his chair and rolled his shoulders. "Guess."

I huffed. I preferred researchable questions over guessing games. Annoyed, I said, "Half of us are convinced your first name is Mister."

Rindlisbacher laughed. It started as a single bark, then multiplied as true humor lit his smile. I found myself tittering as well.

"Now really, I want to hear your guess."

"I don't know. You look like a Leonard, but you act like a Damian."

He laughed again. Even Brian coughed to hide his chuckle.

"Why those names?"

"I'd rather not say," I said, while thinking how Leonard sounded intellectual, mature, and formal, whereas Damian sounded intriguing, strong, and devious.

"Hey, Brian!" Stan's voice shouted back to us, saving me from any explanations. Brian dropped his failed little puzzle to dash over to the curtain door.

"You need something?"

"Yeah," Stan said, still audible from our table. "Freddy's here to re-purchase his grandpa's pocket watch."

"I'll grab it." Brian went to the storage shelf to search for the watch on loan, then muttered a curse. "Not again. Rindle?"

My co-worker set down his puzzle (solved, of course) and stood to join the boss, eyeing the watch. "What is it?" Curious, I stood to join them.

"Freddy's pocket watch," Brian muttered. "He brings this thing in almost every month."

"Like clockwork," Rindlisbacher said, like quoting an inside joke.

"Right. We've tested it more times than needed—I know it was only ten karats. But feel it—or test it."

Rindlisbacher took the golden watch in his hands, scratched at the metal, then muttered his own curse. "How does this happen?"

"Beats me," Brian said. "It's like something out of a book—or fantasy. But even if the sorcerer's stone was

276

real, why would someone be playing with it in our pawnshop, turning things that are already gold into more—or purer gold?"

Rindlisbacher's face frowned with disbelieving skepticism at Brian, but flashed toward me with a hint of doubt. "Like something from a fantasy, huh?"

"But it's Freddy's pocket watch, for sure," Brian said. "Do we sell it back to him at our initial estimated price?"

"You're the boss—"

Rindlisbacher's watch beeped at the hour, and he blinked in surprise. "It's been an hour already?" He returned to his business posture and held out his hand for me to shake. We shared a firm pump of the arms, but didn't release. "Well, congratulations again, Dia, on earning the top sales rep for the month. You deserve it."

"Thank you. I feel like we talked so much about me and my likes that all I learned about you in return is that you can solve all of your little silver puzzles."

"They're steel—"

"I'd better get back to Stan," Brian said.

"Right. Thanks for joining us, Brian," my co-worker said. He still held my hand in a motionless handshake. As Brian disappeared behind the curtain to the shop, a small step brought Rindlisbacher closer and my eyes up to his. I could see the battle within him. It wasn't a full-out war between desire and restraint as it had been in the office, but a battle nonetheless. His subdued passion encouraged my attraction more than my fear of the man. My growing attraction, however, scared me just as much.

I forced myself to step back and give another solid pump of a handshake.

"Thanks for the lunch, Rindlisbacher."

He blinked, then released me with a curt nod. I was halfway to the store curtain when — "Dia."

I turned around. Rindlisbacher remained where I'd left him, with his hands in his pockets. "You asked for my first name. I'd rather that you called me Rindle."

The corners of my lips lifted as a small reflection of the jumping rocks in my stomach. "Have a nice day, Rindle."

I went up front to say bye to Stan, and he straightened with attention. Brian was busy with Freddy and his pocket watch, allowing Stan to rush to me as soon as the curtain closed behind me.

"Are you okay?" he whispered, clasping my arm. "How was it?"

"It was fine," I said. "He was a complete gentleman and asked Brian to join us."

"He didn't touch you, leer at you, or say anything demeaning?"

"He—" I cut off as I remembered our lingering handshake. "I'm fine, Stan, but thanks for your concern."

He let out a heavy breath. "Good. I'd hate it if he mistreated you. I hate the idea that he already did something to shake you. I mean, he could be a great assistant manager one day, and I'd hate for either of you to quit working here because of something like that. Most of all, I'd hate it if something happened to you, Dia."

He reached for my hand again to give me a squeeze. I smiled back, grateful for his unique kindness and friendship.

Chapter 23

DIA

I dreaded going to sleep that night, knowing I'd dream of my co-workers again. Fortunately, when my dreams came, they weren't the first people I saw.

I wandered through the sand-palace halls, giving myself another tour of the place while looking for the perfect spot to perform Riddle Maker's trick.

Amethyst appeared from the end of the corridor, walking with her own air of searching. Spotting me, she asked, "Dia? Have you seen Sapphire?"

As if I knew my own whereabouts in this giant sandcastle? Even after a week of hiding away in Remizio, I only knew the direct routes to the dining hall and the bedchambers. "No. Why?"

"No one has seen her since she took off after breakfast. She said she had a meeting, but there was nothing scheduled for today."

Considering Sapphire's typical behaviors, my initial instinct was to shrug and assume she was off doing who knew what for any reason a fourteen-year-old could concoct. Except recent revelations questioned her words. Were they somehow a foretelling of the future? She had a meeting that no one else knew about? With whom? About what?

Unable to share a properly coherent response, I simply said, "Odd. If I see her, I'll tell her to report to you."

"Thanks," Ame said, her smile friendly. "And if you're looking for Stanford, he said he'll be resting until dinner. Apparently, our morning ride along the lakeshore exhausted him."

I didn't bother restraining my scowl. "Clever. You wore him out, so now he has no time for me?"

Ame's smile turned patronizing. "Dia, you know I love you, right? But you must know how this will end. Why bother trying?"

I tilted my chin up at her. "You should know by now how competitive I can be, especially when my kingdom is at stake. By the way, I have a performance planned that will shock off Prince Stanford's boots and stockings."

Ame laughed with sarcastic surprise and eagerness. "I can't wait to see it. But honestly, why? Stanford is far from your only option. Your brother, Cephas, might be the only son of a king in the valley, but you have plenty of sons of nobles to choose from your own kingdom or even Somnus. I have…" her voice drifted, "limited options. I must marry someone outside of

Huiess to strengthen our kingdom, but foreign men…
well, apparently I intimidate them."

While I'd never seen Ame look so vulnerable and
shy, her last statement made me bark with a laugh. "I
wonder why. You're only the best swordswoman in
the valley. Add your throne, and it's a guaranteed death
sentence if they displease you."

"Stanford doesn't seem intimidated."

A thoughtful downward turn of her eyes and suppressed smile was the closest I'd ever seen Ame blush.
When considering Stanford?

I mentally guffawed. "Probably because he's too
naïve to know better."

"Maybe," she said with a little shrug. "But I've
already reached out to every eligible noble I'm not
warring against. Even the reclusive Lord of Noz Isle."

I raised a dubious eyebrow. "The one with the
name that no one can pronounce? Whom nobody has
seen for over a decade? I figured he was dead since we
go to Noz Isle every week and never hear of him."

"If I counted the harvests correctly, he's a bit older
than we are. I've heard no news of his death or marriage, and that must make him eligible, right?"

"I've heard no news of him at all. When that happens for a decade, that usually means they're dead."

While my dream-mind pondered a backup plan to
reach out to the nobles on Noz Isle (maybe they could
help in this internal war against Tanzi?), my Las Vegas
mind connected dots and plots.

"Either way," I said. "I am committed to winning Prince Stanford's contest, so be prepared."

Ame raised a smirk and threw back, "Prepare yourself. I'm performing my piece tomorrow."

"Tomorrow?" Slanders, I wasn't ready. Considering performances I'd attended, there were reasons for simpler entertainment performing before the main event. The first pieces were always impressive. I needed to amaze Prince Stanford and upstage Ame before she had a chance.

"Golden," I said. "Then I shall perform my feat tonight. I shall require a spinning wheel, bale of straw, and a moment with my… assistant."

Ame gave me a confused smile. "A spinning wheel and straw? What absurdly cunning scheme have you planned?"

I answered her with a secretive and teasing smile. "You shall see in the morning."

Except now I was in a bigger hurry than ever. I still needed to find the perfect room for turning straw into gold. I also needed to send a note to Riddle Maker to expedite our plans.

Continuing my search through the sandcastle, I eventually wound my way down and through the corridors to the ground level. I needed a room that was close to the outside where Riddle Maker could sneak in to do his "magic." Spotting a young servant boy, I called him over.

Hoping to gain his confidence, I asked for his name and interests. Derrick happened to enjoy many games and sports, including night-time possum hunting.

"That sounds fascinating," I lied. Alright, I was mildly interested, but not to the degree that I played. Like a proper and pleasant dignitary, I said, "I would love to try that, but—oh! They have a curfew after sundown. I would never be allowed to leave the castle after dark."

Derrick pondered with his fist to his chin. "Hmm. I always leave before sundown, but one of my friends might know how to sneak out of the castle after dark."

"Who?" I asked.

The young boy referred me to a youthful guard, stationed near the kitchens. With Derrick's introduction of night-time possum hunting, the guard whispered of a loose sand stone in the wine cellar that—if pushed out—created a hole large enough for a person to crawl through.

I thanked the boys with a vow of secrecy but immediately went to the documents room to pen a letter to Riddle Maker. I explained the situation to move up the performance and the setting in the cellar with the loose stone. The sun slipped its face behind the mountains just as I sent the letter with a bird. Then I headed toward the cellar to scout the place.

Passing Crown Princess Garnet's room, I poked my head in to say hello when a cry of alarm broke. It wasn't a cry of intrusion or warning. It was a cry of terrible deeds already done.

Garnet stood from her desk and stared with an ashen face.

She trembled and cried, "No, no, no!"

"What is it?" I asked. "What happened?"

"I-I cannot say, but those cries sound all too familiar. Someone else was poisoned. Tanzi found us."

"Impossible," I said. "Let me go find Ame. I'll be back with the truth."

"Let me go with you. I need to put them to sleep. Whoever it is. I cannot save them now from the poisoning, but maybe, one day…"

Ame rounded the corner. I'd never seen the Huiess princess look scared, but at that moment, she was terrified.

"Thank the stars," she said, running to Garnet and me. "You're safe. But not for long. Tanzi's here. She…" Her bottom lip trembled and the warrior princess sobbed.

"Good heavens," Garnet whispered. "Who was it? Who did she poison this time?"

"Not poison," Ame sobbed. "She's dead. Your crazy little sister killed my crazy little sister."

While talking about Tanzi, Ame's words had spat venom, but when referring to her own "crazy" sister, her voice turned painfully tender.

"Words," I swore. "Sapphire?"

Ame choked on her words, but managed to speak. "They found her at the graveyard an hour ago. Dead."

Garnet's eyes widened with panic. "An hour ago? I need to give her a sleeping potion immediately! Then we will need to flee. There is always a curse that surrounds the sleeping victim. It comes fast, without warning—"

"She's not poisoned or sleeping," Ame cried. "She's dead. She's cold. She was stabbed in the heart!"

Garnet and I shared horrified looks. Garnet had described her sisters as only sleeping, and Opal hadn't turned cold. She had been poisoned and put to sleep. We would wake her and the others as soon as we found an antidote, but a piercing to the heart… My mind refused to even imagine.

Garnet's lip trembled as she reached for Ame. They fell into one another's arms. Unsure what to do, I stepped in to hug them from the outside.

"Ame, dear Ame," Garnet murmured. "Forgive me for not finding a solution sooner. I fear that I still have no answers other than to run and hope that answers will come with time."

Ame raised her tear-blotched face. If that wasn't unusual enough for the Huiess Princess, she was also doubtful. "Running is the coward's answer."

"We run only until we have sufficient strength to fight back," Garnet urged. "All of us. The three of us can still fight back with the strength of our kingdoms once they understand the threat upon us. We shall

286

take Toto and Cephas too, perhaps to Levamen. Tanzi would never dare to follow us into the Sesso Desert."

For good reason. Thoughts of fleeing into that wasteland gripped my heart with fear. For some reason, Ame responded with a determined look. "If you plan to travel through the Sesso Desert, you'll need my help."

No, I had already set plans in motion. "Not yet," I said. "Ame and I have our competition for Prince Stanford. With Urbanuz, we can defeat this. It's only one more day. I have arranged to complete my performance tonight, and then Ame can perform tomorrow. Stanford will choose, and—"

"Do you even hear yourself, Dia?" Ame guffawed, tears streaming down her cheeks. "You of all people want to continue with this charade of romancing Stanford? My sister's dead. I can't perform tomorrow."

Swallowing my sorrows, I forced myself to remain strong. "Then we give up creating an alliance with Urbanuz? If we all run now, what will Stanford do? He's not likely to flee with us to that forsaken land. He would return home with wild stories about our crumbling kingdoms. I refuse to give up one day before making an alliance with all of our kingdoms in your capital city. Will you?"

Ame hardened as I successfully bolstered a smidgen of her determination. "A Huiessian Princess never gives up."

"Golden," I said, smiling despite my growing headache from restraining my tears. "We'll complete our contest as planned, then we'll escape."

Chapter 24

DIA

Waking up in Las Vegas, I sat up and replayed the scenes from my dreams. I pulled out my half-filled dream journal, wrote down everything I remembered, then went over the details of the previous nights and dreams. Ame's sister had died? But hadn't she been the future-teller? How could anyone kill someone who knew the future?

Then there was a separate part of my dream that made more sense. If my guess was correct, I knew Riddle Maker's name. I wouldn't lose my bet against him! I wouldn't be forced to hire him as a jester with him constantly reminding me of my secret attraction or of his part in winning Prince Stanford's contest. I would banish him from Rezhina Valley and banish him forever from my thoughts.

I smacked my forehead. It was only a dream. There was no bet in real life. I wasn't a princess, and Rindlisbacher wasn't a jester. Only a pawnshop co-worker with an unknown name.

Still, I couldn't help but connect the dots. Riddle Maker was always at the Noz Isle masquerades, and nobody knew his real name or where he came from. But having an outside perspective, I had figured it out. He was the "reclusive" noble of Noz Isle, always hiding behind fake names and masks while putting on dinner parties (gifting lunches and rewards?) with his family's fortune (from his "old money?"). I wrote down my guess of Riddle Maker's name with its pneumonic pronunciation. Was it even a real name? Maybe my lucid and sleep-deprived brain was making things up. Considering the rest of my dream journal, I wouldn't be surprised.

I shook my head. It was all made up. It was all a dream. It couldn't be real.

Despite it being my day off, my dream angled my thoughts toward work and those I worked with. Turning straw into gold was different from transforming one gold alloy into another, so what were the possibilities of it happening naturally? What science could explain the changing metals?

Pulling up the internet on my phone, I typed in a vague search about metal transmutation. I received equally vague answers about alchemy, nuclear reactions, and supernovas. All three were highly unlikely in a pawnshop, but I read a page about the history of transmutations and the search for the philosopher's stone, which could turn any base metal into gold through purification. That was all before the world understood the periodic table with set protons and neutrons. Radioactive decay could change an element, and apparently, in 1980, the Lawrence Berkley National Laboratory managed to produce a small amount of gold from bismuth and a ton of energy. They proved it possible, but not worth the cost. Still, they estimated the possibility of using iron, which was a closer element to gold. Some white-gold jewelry alloys were mixed with platinum, which was next to gold on the periodic table. Would that make it easier to transmute?

I rubbed my temples with frustrating thoughts. Even if it was "easier" to transmute platinum than bismuth into gold, that wouldn't happen naturally in our pawnshop storage room. Still, with no other explanation, I printed off the webpages and articles and filed them into a folder. Maybe I could share them with my co-workers for more ideas.

Cursing the work schedule and my lack of patience, I rode my bike through the streets. I was going to work on my day off. I could wait until my work schedule lined up with Brian or Rindlisbacher's again, but that wouldn't be for another week. At least the heat was slowly cooling for the oncoming fall months.

I rubbed my eyes, hoping that the agitation would help me wake up. Similar to every night this last week, I hadn't fallen asleep until past midnight. Parking my bike in its usual spot, I carried my morning research folder as I walked into the storage room. I rubbed my eyes again as the door closed behind me, removing the natural sunlight. The dream of Ame's distress hadn't helped my sleep, and now the scene before me looked like a dream.

They had replaced the sturdy shelving of industrial metal with gold. Every bar and wire shined with the purest yellow. The effect was absolutely stunning, but ridiculous. Why? Pure gold wasn't meant to be worn— let alone support storage.

Kevin entered from the front room, and surprise lit his face. "Dia? Are you scheduled today? I thought it was—"

"I had something to drop off," I said, thinking, Really? I was the most surprising thing in this room? "When did they change out the shelving for gold?"

"They changed the shelving?" Kevin asked, looking around as if he couldn't see the gold.

Was it just me then? Was I going crazy or seeing things because of my eschewed sleeping schedule?

Kevin's head tilted curiously. "Are you alright? Did you forget today's your day off?"

"No," I said, subtly answering both questions. I needed to return home and take a nap. "But I had something I wanted to discuss with the manager."

"Is it that urgent? Brian's not here, but Mr. R might be able to help."

"Um…" I fidgeted. "Yeah, he was there when we discussed it the other day, and I wanted to share some research. Sorry, I don't mean to distract you guys from work. I guess I'll…"

Without a real plan of what to do, I considered leaving my file on the office desk, then leaving, feeling an utter fool.

"Dia?"

I pivoted. Rindlisbacher stood at the office door. He seemed just as surprised to see me as I was to see him. Again, me, not the golden shelves.

In my mental embarrassment and affirmation that I was seeing things, he spoke first. "Isn't it your day off?"

Mustering a smidgen of confidence again, I met him halfway to present the file. "I hope it wasn't out of line. I did some research for transforming metals."

My insides squirmed while waiting for his response. He thumbed through the pages, skimming the proof of my sleep deprivation. After a few painful seconds, he said, "You didn't have to do this."

"I know, Rindlisbacher," I said, praying he didn't already have a file of his own with more complete information. "I wanted to do it." It was something to keep me awake instead of dreaming of him and Stan.

"Thank you," he said, a genuine smile teasing his lips. "I didn't tell you to do this, but I did say you could call me Rindle."

My cheeks heated. "Sorry… Rindle."

"That's better," he said as his tease of a smile widened. My blush deepened. His smile was a beautiful thing. As much as I wanted to stare at it all day, he was on the clock. I stepped back to leave, when he asked,

"Do you have a moment? You can review my notes, and maybe we'll find a solution together."

That had been my purpose in coming. I passed Kevin while following Rindle to the office. He wiggled his eyebrows suggestively, and I rolled my eyes back.

Rindle led me to the office but left the door open. That put us out of sight, but within Kevin's hearing. Rindle sat at the office computer with its captain's chair.

"How are you?" he asked.

"Golden."

His lips twitched with some secret joke, and he murmured, "Yes, you are."

I snapped toward him. "What was that?"

Suddenly terrified, he raised his hands in surrender. "Nothing. At least, nothing meant in offense."

I frowned. It had seemed more like a tease than a compliment. As if he knew that Gold was my Noz Isle nickname. That secretive smile spoke of a victory, as if he'd discovered my masquerade codename before I'd discovered his name. As if he knew he'd win the bargain.

Stop, that was impossible. They were just dreams, and the bargain was only in my dream. He was simply complimenting me—flirtatiously, I might add.

Still, a part of me worried about Princess Diamond of Ormio. I'd figured out Riddle Maker's name, but did my dream-self know?

I sat on the opposite end of the desk in a fold-out chair and watched as Rindle thumbed through my file to separate it into the different piles.

"Looks like we have some redundancies in processes of purifying gold and the experiment by the Berkley lab. Last night, I did some investigating into reasons someone might target our shop for their experiments, but a new development might put a wrench on that theory." He picked up one of his puzzle boxes. "This was wooden yesterday. Now, it's silver with over ninety-percent purity."

He turned the box in his hands, sliding parts to solve the puzzle. "Why on earth would someone replace every one of my little dollar-store puzzles with silver versions? Silver has a similar softness as gold and makes for poor construction for daily objects. These are meant to be handled, twisted, and maneuvered."

I picked up one of his puzzles to evaluate. "First gold, now silver too?"

"And not just metals. That box was a mixture of woods before. That's why I've been back here researching instead of helping Kevin up front."

I reached over to one of the piles of papers. "Are these the articles you found? Can I look through them?"

"Go for it." He waved nonchalantly to give me access.

I skimmed through the pages as Rindle typed away at the office computer to categorize my notes. After a few minutes, he said, "Now, that's something. Look at this." He turned his monitor toward me, but even leaning forward wasn't enough to clearly read the fine print beneath the article on biological transmutations. I pulled my chair next to his at the desk. Rindle might have shuffled in his seat, but my attention was focused on the screen.

The article explained the physics-breaking transmutations of mitochondria and the chemical reactions through simply breathing in oxygen and expelling carbon dioxide.

"Our bodies naturally transmute with a minimal amount of energy. That's incredible!"

"Notice," he said, "how it mentions people living in desert habitats are known for transmuting potassium into calcium as a cooling mechanism. Maybe there's something in this hot summer air that's affecting us or the metals."

"It sounds far-fetched, but the more I research, the more it seems possible."

I turned to him and suddenly became aware of his proximity. The light in his eyes shifted into something warmer.

"Thank you," he said. "I think we're… on the right path."

"Yeah," I said. Was he talking about the project or… another path we could be on together? I wasn't sure where either path led, but my stupid heart beat with anticipation for the journey.

"I," he whispered, like speaking a secret thought, "honestly forgot that you were a woman for a minute there."

And the journey fizzled. I gave him a downward stare.

He flustered. "I'm sorry, that came out wrong. I meant it as a compliment."

"You'll have to do better than that to compliment a woman."

He paused. "You'll let me try again?"

"If you think you can do better, sure. Compliment my feminine and scholarly work." I grinned like a goof, and his eyes drew down to my smile. Why was he glancing at my lips?

"You, um, are an amazing woman."

Oh. Hold on, that wasn't my intent when fishing for a compliment. All I'd wanted was some validation for my research. I wanted him to compliment my work, not me.

With a low voice, he confessed, "I'd like to share lunch with you again. Outside of work. Without Brian."

Goodness gracious, what was he saying? Did he just ask me on a date? Of all the words to say, those were the most terrible. Either they were a lie that played with sensitive feelings, or worse, they were a truth that made me feel those sensitive feelings. He really was a wicked man.

But he was a respectful, wicked man. Despite his quivering hands and deep breathing, he waited patiently and didn't move.

How could hearts pound so fast while sitting so still?

"Please," he whispered, "say something."

"What?"

"Anything."

My brain was too muddled by his closeness to come up with anything, so I said, "I believe I just said, 'what?'"

His smile broke free, and his tension loosened. Slightly. "I feel… a little transmuted when I'm with you."

"Are your counseling sessions going well, then? You need to learn to not be a sucker for a pretty face." How I managed to tease him at a time like that was beyond me.

His brown eyes widened incrementally before squinting with a smirk. "I'll pass that on to Brian when you ask for a raise."

His hand slowly inched toward mine, and my mind panicked. Hold on—did I want this? How could I want this—I didn't even know his first name!

"Is it Roald?"

He froze and stared at me like I'd said the most extreme profanity.

"How did you find out?"

Wait, my dream was *right*? Logic failed me as I attempted to justify and explain the premonition of my dreams. It could still be a wild coincidence. Of the millions of possible names, he just happened to have the same name as the Noz Isle noble that I suspected was Riddle Maker. Well, not the exact same name. Attempting an old Norse accent, starting with a breathy rolled R, I asked, "Hróðvaldr?"

He jerked away and stood with a step back like I'd turned into a snake. "Where did you hear that pronunciation? Who told you?"

A dream. How could I have known? I wasn't sure whether to be more astonished by my prophetic dream or by his intense reaction.

"Which is it?" I asked, standing to meet his level. "Roald or Hróðvaldr?"

"Roald, but everyone else says it like 'rolled.' It's Roo-ald. How do you know it—especially that *other* version? You couldn't have read it anywhere—nobody pronounces it right from reading. Who *told* you?"

One massive step and he towered over me again, but the passion in his eyes wasn't the tethered yearning from seconds ago. It wasn't even the barely leashed desire from the wall incident. This was furious confusion at the end of a burning rope.

His expression twinged with discomfort. "Not even I'd heard that version until the dreams."

I stumbled and stared, too terrified to take my eyes off of him. "Dreams?"

He glared at me, hiding pain. With a low grumble, he muttered, "Why won't you get out of my head? You're not a princess."

Wait, how —

"How do you know about Hróðvaldr?" he growled low with his shapely lips and quick-sand eyes. Like a whisper to himself, he added, "Will Gold banish me?"

Gold. Not the material, but the person. How did Rindle know my Noz Isle codename and about my bargain to banish him? Did Riddle Maker know my codename then? Did that mean Rindle had the dreams too? Did Rindle know I also had the dreams?

Before I could gather my breath to ask my dozens of questions, footsteps announced someone approaching, and Rindle flinched away from me like I'd burned him. Kevin stepped around the open door. "Mr. R? It happened again."

As soon as I was free, I scrambled away and ran until I was through the doorway.

Somewhere behind me, I thought I heard Rindle swear. "Sorry. I need a minute."

Only a minute? The whole day wouldn't be long enough to let me regain composure.

I ran from the office and that building of memories. My heart beat too fast for walking. I ran through the storage room and out the back door, jerking my bike from its lock and speeding home. Cherie asked where I'd been, but I ignored her to hide inside my bedroom until my breathing slowed.

My dream had been correct about his name. And
Rindle had dreamed of a bargain of banishment between Hróðvaldr and Gold. We couldn't have the
same dreams, could we? It was impossible… but so
was a wooden box turning into silver. Was this real
life?

Chapter 25

EMER

Despite finding a worn path midway between the Urbanuz Mountains and Lake Imazhin, Emer and her friends traveled slowly through the southern part of Ormio. The path led them through several villages and small towns, where they received a variety of welcomes. Most townspeople hid away at their approach, then refused to open their doors. Some citizens gave in to Leo's demands for sanctuary, but many remained in fear regardless of the princesses' attempts to cheer them.

They did manage to make progress in one small village where a homestead offered bread to them. They had a young boy who walked with a stick, blinded from a mære scratching his eyes.

"How horrible!" Pearl sympathized as Dot stood and departed toward the forest. Emer swallowed back her emotions, realizing the reminders of Ruby. At least she had Opal, who followed her older sister.

The blind child named Demetrius spoke with an uplifted smile despite his blindness and natural downcast eyes. He shared a story from his day of braving the lake to fish at the docks. By the time he had everyone laughing, Dot and Opal returned. A small coyote trotted between them.

All attention jerked toward the oddly tame animal, and the parents asked, "You have a trained coyote?"

"Not exactly," Dot said. "She volunteered from her pack to come be with your boy. She will be his seeing-eye-dog."

Before the parents could manage to work their dropped jaws, Demetrius jumped up with excitement. "You're giving me a pet coyote? Where is she? Can I pet her? Does she have a name, or can I name her?"

Dot grinned and instructed the canine to go to Demetrius and obey his commands as if they came from her. The coyote ran to the young boy and nuzzled against his leg. He laughed and rubbed his hands all over her coat.

"I've never petted a live coyote before. She's so warm! I bet you're beautiful. What big ears you have!"

The father finally found his voice again, asking, "Please explain this gift. You are giving us a coyote?"

Dot shrugged, half in shyness, half in a lost memory. "My sister was blind. She had a dog that helped her with directions and to run for aid when she could not. I—" she paused to shuffle bashfully "—have a way with animals, so I called for a volunteer to join your

303

family as such an aide. This coyote answered my call. She will serve your boy well."

Opal took her sister's hand with reassurance. "I saw Ruby's pet too. One of the best-behaved dogs I'd ever seen."

The mother blinked wide eyes between the dog licking her son's laughing face, her son, and Dot. Tears moistened her eyes before she sniffed them away. She bowed to Dot. "Thank you, Your Highness. We will treasure your gift and care for her as she cares for my son. Thank you."

They left the homestead with a sweet parting to continue their journey southward. Unfortunately, the next afternoon, they left an oasis town with heavy feet and hearts, and had little hope when the population density grew around the once-great city of Remizio. Crossing a wide bridge with nervous lookouts for mære, they met Ormio's definition of Huiess and a woman blocking their way with several armored guards.

She looked Huiessian by descent with overall tones of dark brown save for the highlighted hairs that framed her face like a halo. She wore pants as they did a hundred harvests ago, but instead of flowing loosely around the ankles like disguised skirts, hers were cropped and tied tightly just below her knees. Instead of the traditional Huiessian top that draped with a simple tie at the waist, this woman's top was likewise cropped and secured at her waist, revealing her toned stomach and pierced belly button.

Marin gasped at the immodesty while Caden narrowed his eyes. Before Emer could be jealous, he said, "If my research is correct, we are in the presence of nobility."

Of course, Emer scolded herself. He hadn't been admiring her physique, he'd been analyzing her likeness and apparel to recognize her status.

Leaning over his shoulder, Emer whispered, "We should probably dismount to look less threatening."

Caden nodded, but grimaced the moment he put his injured foot on the carriage ladder.

"Men," he said to the other princes, then he grunted with a gesture of his head that somehow translated as "off your horses, you dolts." While the riders dismounted, Caden stayed and explained, "If you'll pardon my manners, I'm suffering from an injury that makes dismounting and walking difficult."

The woman acknowledged his excuse with a twitch of her eyebrow, then turned toward Chase as he stepped forward and bowed low on one knee. "Chieftess Olga of the Remizio Tribe, heiress of the Lady Remizio named by Queen Tanzanite. We are glad to meet you and seek safe passage through your lands."

"Rise, huntsman," she said in a strong voice. "Have you come to draft us for the war again?"

"Draft?" Ranae asked from atop the carriage. "Which war?"

"Against the ogres in the north," Olga explained. "Queen Tanzanite is drafting all able bodies to help the northern kingdoms with their plight against the ogres."

Emer shared a look with Caden. As much as it relieved Emer that Caden's people were receiving help, she worried about Tanzi's goals. He likewise frowned in thought without an answer.

Emer hoped to discuss it further, but the chieftess lifted her chin to speak first. "Who are your companions, huntsman?"

"Ah-uhh," Chase stumbled.

Pearl mouthed up to Emer, "Do we pretend to be someone else?"

Emer answered with a subtle shrug. She still stumbled over the puzzle of Tanzi's motivations. Only after her shrug did she recognize Pearl's request for guidance. And Emer had let her down without direction.

Before Emer could reprimand herself or compose a proper response, Pearl stepped forward to bow as Chase had before the chieftess. "Chieftess of Remizio, I am Mearl from the distant land of Warcastle. We are acquaintances of Queen Tanzanite, and are well met."

"Warcastle?" Chieftess Olga asked. "I've never heard of it."

"It's distant," Mica said, jumping in with an emphasized London accent. "Actually, very distant, but
306

near my own homeland. Honorable Mica at your service. Please, forgive our sudden and frazzled appearance, as we've traveled far."

The chieftess raised her chin again, though the smile on her face accepted the apology. When she lowered her gaze again, it landed on Caden. "And the injured coachman?"

He cleared his throat, then leaned forward to bow from his seat. "Honorable Caden from London. High Chieftess, if I may introduce my darling, er—"

"Amber Princeton from Tintagel," Emer said with a similar bow. Caden mouthed her a, "thank you," and she winked back. He'd forgotten her doppelgänger's name, thinking of her only as Emer.

Marin squirmed in the back, hissing to her husband, "I do not remember my dream name, and you were a frog."

Thankfully, the chieftess seemed satisfied and stepped aside to let them walk beside her and her guards. Emer smiled, relieved and remembering how Ame, Sapphire, and Toto never turned their backs on anyone. Some traditions never died.

"Come, Honorables," she said, gesturing toward the city outskirts. "We have lodging and dining available in the city."

Except she didn't lead them to the left, toward the lakeshore and location of Remizio. She led them directly straight and southward to continue on the well-worn path. Pointing at the dirt path, Chieftess Olga said, "We tend not to cross the north side of this road toward the lake. I advise you to do the same."

Emer whispered to Caden, "Is it because of the mære appearances near the lake?"

"Maybe," he said. "Or it could be Princess Diamond's curse. We may need your powers for a scouting mission again to see what surrounds her."

Emer nodded, hoping to be useful.

Without hearing Emer and Caden's whispers, Marin asked, "How do you survive out here without the lake's resources? With its distance away from Noz Isle, the mist is much clearer here, yet you still avoid it? Is it because of the mære?"

The chieftess twitched at Marin's mention of the monsters, but explained, "We have a channel that brings the water to us, but the road serves as a safety boundary to guard citizens away from Old Remizio. The temptation's too great."

"Temptation?" Pearl asked. "Then is the city truly golden?"

Mica grinned. "Will we actually get to see the golden city of legends?"

"Only fools go any closer," the chieftess said. "Since you truly act like foreigners, let me tell you a tale. When each citizen in Remizio comes of age, their guardians take them to see Old Remizio. I was once like you, imagining a great city with streets and houses made of gold. Except it isn't only the city." A haunted look widened her eyes and snarled her lip. "To become a woman, my papa and the chief took me up to the city. Not too close to tempt me to join it, but close enough to see the lost ones."

"Join it?" Emer asked while Caden echoed, "The lost ones?"

"The citizens of old Remizio," she scoffed. "See, once upon a time, Remizio was a normal port city. Busy, but normal. Then, a prince from a faraway land came looking for a wife."

"Yes," Caden said, "I've heard the legends and informed my friends about the curse."

Chieftess Olga nodded, grateful. "Then you know how a witch turned straw into gold and made a fool of the prince. He didn't really want to marry the old hag, so he threw her in the dungeon anyway, with a demand to turn all the straw in the land into gold to make him rich. In her vengeance, the witch cast a final spell on the land, to turn more than just the straw into gold, but anything and anyone who touches it."

"Any... one?" Pearl whimpered as Dot signed curt gestures to Leo. He signed back with motions that even Emer recognized as calming.

"That's right," Olga continued. "When my papa took me to the golden city, I saw the streets and houses made of gold alright. But what I can never forget is the expressions of the golden statues. They're all dead, every one of them turned to gold as soon as they touched the smallest piece of the cursed metal."

"You can't even touch it?" Mica asked.

The chieftess shook her head. "The witch cursed this kingdom with a fortune that we can never use. You can't eat gold. Gold can't teach us trades. Gold can't make a bed. It can't even be used for comfortable clothes. Rumor says that the witch still sleeps in the castle, spreading her useless gold to make sure that anyone as greedy as that prince will be cursed the same way."

"Brilliant," Caden said with sarcasm, writing furiously to capture every word.

Emer was tempted to nudge him as a reminder to be more considerate, but a nudge would smear his writing and only sour his attitude.

Dot frowned deeply at the chieftess and signed furiously at Leo. He responded with more calming gestures and sympathetic expressions. Chase eyed their signing, and Opal asked, "Can you tell what they're saying?"

"Parts," he said.

Unfortunately, he left everyone hanging until they reached their own community residence that was built from large bricks of mud and decorated with colorful tile mosaics. They were welcomed into a central courtyard with a small fountain and archways to individual bedrooms.

After the departure of the chieftess, Dot hissed, "That was my sister she slandered! She is no witch! She is the heir of Ormio, the most clever and passive person I know!"

Chase grimaced. "I agree with what I recognized from Leo's signs. We don't know if the witch refers to your older sister. Regardless, it doesn't matter what kind of person she was, the curses each of you created around yourselves made you look like terrifying witches."

Caden grunted. "Rumors will say what they want about people, but I'm more interested in these rumors about Queen Tanzanite drafting an army to help us fight the ogres. I cannot trust this sudden interest in aiding us. What does she hope to gain from it?"

Mica shrugged. "Maybe she heard of our plight and finally decided to help."

"Five years after the first attacks?" Leo growled. "Why help now?"

"She had a treaty with the ogres, right?" Emer asked. "Charlotte, the ogress said that she did."

"This is true," Chase said. "We left them alone as long as they remained outside of Rezhina Valley. The mære and I were given charge to slaughter any ogre that entered the valley. It was my honor and privilege to serve that charge."

Leo shook his head. "You wanted to kill ogres, but that was the coward's way. You let them roam freely through our lands while you sat and waited for them to wander your way."

"Perhaps," Emer said, purposefully interrupting Chase's retort, "Tanzi withheld her aid, but then the ogres sent a battalion through Somnus. Maybe she saw that as a breach on their treaty."

Marin shook her head. "It cannot be that simple."

"Maybe it is," Caden said. "On the surface, Queen Tanzanite sees herself as a savior. She united the three kingdoms of Rezhina. She kept peace in the land for an entire century. She even took in Chase—a would-be slave or victim to the ogres like Shinópu."

Chase nodded slowly. "She often told me of the sacrifices she made for the sake of her kingdom."

"Sacrifices?" Opal cried. "I was one of those sacrifices! She was one of my best friends! I trusted her!"

"Underneath," Dot said through gritted teeth, "she betrayed us all to get what she wanted. She's a devious usurper. I agree with Marin. Something more is going on than a broken treaty."

Chapter 26

EMER

Emer and her friends spent their first day in New Remizio exploring the city, resting from their travels, and planning their search for Dia. Emer attempted to dive through her plants' roots again, but the desert was too sparse and the golden city was too solid. Pearl asked Lucy to search from the sky, but all the little ball of light conveyed was "Gold," and "Palace in center." Dot's birds gained the most information as they flew over the city and back. However, Dot cringed to send the flock into the golden city as fewer returned each time.

"They become tired," she explained. "They search the palace through its open doors and windows, but if they land or even brush their wings against anything, they turn to gold."

Marin cried in dismay and joined Dot's insistence to use another option to find and reach Dia.

On their second day, Chieftess Olga invited them all over for breakfast, offering delicacies from her city.

Compliments and gratitude echoed around the table, though Pearl refrained from partaking from any of the gifted food. Emer struggled to eat the fruits and vegetables—knowing of their rarity in the desert, while Marin and Dot likewise abstained from the meat. The chieftess seemed to take no offense as she ate plenty and chatted amiably, asking about their homelands and travels.

"Honorable Caden," Chieftess Olga said, standing and beckoning him. "I had a question for you about your research. Would you mind joining me in my study to consider some of my own notes?"

Caden set down his drink and shuffled with his new cane to stand. "Sure. Give me a moment. This leg…"

Emer tried and failed not to worry as he followed the chieftess out of the dining hall. She trusted Caden, but she didn't trust Olga. Something in her smile reminded Emer of Tanzi.

She stalked them around the corners until they disappeared into a room behind guards. Emer clenched her teeth, undeterred. Dashing outside to the carriage, she grabbed the vine phone and found a secluded corner in the stables.

"Burrow beneath the ground," she told one end. "Wiggle and stretch like a root, going south-west until you come underneath a dwelling, then sprout upward until your tips reach the clear air."

She encouraged its path and growth, all the while worrying about Olga and Caden's private discussion.

Finally, voices echoed back to her through her end of the phone. She listened with bated breath as she recognized Olga's voice.

"—queen's draft for soldiers to fight in the northern kingdoms. I did some research. It seems that the heir and Prince of Uldra has been seen traveling through Rezhina with several companions, including the former princes of Braeder and Zubra. If my research is correct," she said, a softer imitation of Caden's words, "I am in the presence of royalty, Prince Caden Seaver of Uldra?"

Caden cleared his throat before replying, "Your research is correct. Forgive me and my companions for our deception. We weren't sure of your alignment with Queen Tanzanite at the time and thought it best to disguise ourselves."

Olga laughed warmly, a sound that Emer found a little too friendly. "You mean you didn't want to proclaim to a stranger with noble standing that you're traitors to the crown? Raising monarchs from the past is a sure-fire way to start a revolution. I'm impressed."

"Chieftess—"

"I know your true name and title, Caden. You have every right to call me Olga."

"Olga, about our alliances—"

"Say it again," she whispered. Regardless of her pounding heartbeat, Emer had no problems hearing with her speaker pressed firmly against her ear.

"Say wha—beshrews!" His curse came with a clatter of something wooden and a few small objects hitting the ground. "Chieftess, forgive me if I gave any inclination of my interest, but I'm already, and *firmly*, attached."

A small foot tapped the floor with anxiety. "You'll reject me then? What of the other princes?"

"Er," Caden slurred. "I believe they're also all attached."

"To your companions? The fallen princesses?"

"It seems so. If there was nothing else, the chieftess would like to discuss…" Emer strained to decipher the following sounds of Caden's muttered apologies, quick and lopsided steps, and a little moan from Olga. Emer continued listening, hoping for clues about what had happened, but the room was mostly silent. Feet shuffled, wood scraped against the floor with adjustments, and someone sighed heavily. The chieftess muttered, "Not even the cripple. No use wasting my time with the others, then."

Emer sorted through what she'd heard, replaying the scene in her head with various scenarios. Inclinations of interest… attachments to the princesses… Emer's face flushed as she considered the probability of Olga attempting to ensnare Caden romantically, but her heart soared with his refusal and loyalty.

She nearly tossed her vine phone to run to Caden—probably halfway back to the others by this point—

and kiss him with her appreciation, except a word from the chieftess caught her attention.

"Your Majesty."

"Chieftess," a new voice said with a slight warping of a glass barrier. Emer gripped her phone tightly. Was that Tanzi? She sounded older, like their mother, but harder. "Did you win over the northern princes?"

"I'm afraid the witches have poisoned their minds."

Her younger sister hissed. "Then onto the alternative. Kill them all."

"Yes, Your Majesty."

Emer almost dropped her vine phone in shock. Olga had direct contact with Tanzi? Did she have her own phone? More importantly, Emer needed to warn her sisters and friends. Clenching her vine phone, she spoke new commands to split into a new vocal phone and burrow through the ground toward the dining hall.

The chieftess's voice echoed again through the phone as she called for her guards. "Captain Stone. I have orders for you and your team concerning the guests in the dining hall. They are traitors to Queen Tanzanite. Kill them."

As soon as the voices of her sisters and friends returned through her speaker, Emer shouted, "To arms! The chieftess sent her guards to kill you!"

"Emer?" Pearl asked as stone chairs scooted against the tile floor. "Where are you?"

"Meet me in the stables! Run!"

Emer didn't wait for her sisters to respond. She commanded the vine phone to retreat to the stables as she hurried to saddle the horses. There wouldn't be time to hitch the carriage. Saddling the horses was tricky enough as they fed on her anxiety.

"Come now, Tucker," Emer murmured to Caden's horse. "Caden will need your speed to compensate for his injured leg. Unless you would rather that he take another horse?"

Tucker snorted and stilled enough for Emer to saddle him. Just in time. She had Tucker and two other horses saddled with the vine phone as Marin, Pearl, Dot, and Opal dashed around the corner. Shouts followed them as Mica came into view, carrying Caden over his shoulders. Emer's breath of relief was stuttered with a laugh at the sight of Caden dual wielding his sword and cane behind Mica's back.

"Are the horses ready?" Mica asked.

"Only three," Emer said.

Dot moaned. "Bareback riding isn't preferred, but we have no time. Your warning came just in time for us to prepare ourselves before the Huiessian guards attacked. Leo, Chase, and Ranae are holding them off."

"We must be prepared to flee," Marin said, "as soon as they join us."

Opal frowned, dismayed. "What about Dia?"

"What if," Emer said, an insane idea forming, "we flee to the old city? The people refuse to go near it."

Marin huffed. "For good reason, by the sounds of it. The city turns them into gold!"

Ranae, Leo, and Chase came running around the corner with their weapons drawn.

"Hurry!" Ranae shouted, and there was no time to discuss more.

Mica hefted Caden over Tucker. With his arms and good leg, Caden situated himself before pulling Emer up to join him. She gave him a quick kiss on the cheek. "Thank you for being who you are."

The others were ready to ride before he could question her. Pearl, Marin, Mica, and Ranae took the other two saddled horses while Chase, Dot, Opal, and Leo hopped on bareback. They galloped out of the stables as Olga's guards charged inside. A bell rang from somewhere overhead, announcing their escape to every warrior in the city.

"Toward the city," Emer called to her friends. As the last word escaped her, a worry took its place inside. She'd acted as a leader again. What if escaping to the city was the wrong call? What would they do once they reached it? What would they do if they didn't reach it?

They galloped through the sandstone streets with calls of alarm chasing them. Arrows zipped overhead. They made some quick turns when seeing the road blocked ahead with soldiers. "This way!" Chase called, urging his horse to the front. Emer cringed, hoping he led them correctly with his knowledge of the city and not to a trap set by Tanzi.

Relief and fear settled in her heart as they reached the main roadway between the new and old cities. Running through the open left them vulnerable to attacks.

"Shield us!" Marin shouted, calling for a wall of ice to rise behind them, blocking the path and view of their attackers.

"Brilliant!" Caden grinned. He allowed Tucker to slow to a canter as they crossed beyond the edge of the abandoned buildings.

Emer joined his smile, though her worries remained. "How are we supposed to enter the city of gold? We cannot swing on a vine to the golden center, and Pearl's light would do nothing to change our circumstances. Only Dot's birds were capable of entering the city."

Caden nodded and shouted over to Dot and Chase, "Can the birds carry us over the gold and into the city?"

Dot balked. "Birds can only fly because of their light weight and aerodynamic bodies. Even horses shouldn't carry more than twenty percent of their own weight. It would take an entire flock of eagles to lift a single person."

Before more could be said, all horses skidded to a stop. One block ahead, the sun-bleached sand and stones of the old Huiessian city shone with bright yellow metal.

"The golden city," Mica breathed, tapping his horse to go closer.

"Don't touch it," Dot said. "My birds have confirmed the rumors about it being cursed."

Opal frowned. "Then how can we reach Dia? And are we safe from Olga's guards?"

To answer her second question, an arrow stabbed the ground at the edge of their group. Emer followed its angle of trajectory to find two archers standing on rooftops several blocks behind.

"Take that as a 'No,'" she said, urging Tucker toward the gold. The horse stepped to the side, unwilling to go forward. Caden convinced his horse to hide behind a crumbled house wall as Leo and Chase released their own arrows at the archers. An agonizing cry reported their aim.

"You were supposed to aim at the one on the left," Leo said, smacking his younger brother's shoulder.

"I did aim at the one on the left."

"*Our* left—"

"Men!" Ranae scolded. "Incoming from the west!"

More arrows launched toward them from an outcropping cliff.

"Shield us!" Opal shouted, and a wall of stone rose three meters into the air beside them.

Mica moaned, "What can we do? They'll box us in at this rate."

Emer studied the new wall. "Can we use that to enter the city? What if we built a bridge of stone over the gold?"

Opal shuffled nervously. "I can try."

"Do it, Opal," Chase said eagerly. "I know you can."

Swelling with his encouragement, she commanded the stones again. Starting from the outside edge of the gold, the rocks arched over with a pathway.

Caden frowned at the slow progress of the narrow bridge. "I doubt that will hold all of us and our horses."

A glance was enough to confirm the thin bridge. Another glance at each of her friends and sisters provided an idea. "Caden, I know how much you want to be at the forefront of history in the making, but you need to stay here with your injuries."

"But—"

"No buts." She slid off the back of Tucker and waved for Opal and Dot to join her. "I have an idea to find your sister. Dot, can you send some birds to scout one more time for us? Opal can create our walking path and a landing place for them. Pearl, can you blind the archers or create an area of darkness like you did in the Midnight Forest?"

"Oh!" Pearl said, happy to be of help. "I suppose I can."

"What of me?" Marin asked.

"Protect the men with your ice shields. I assume Leo and Chase will continue to attack with their long-distance bows. Caden, Mica, and Ranae can be ready if any come within short-range. All in favor?"

To Emer's surprise, no one argued, but immediately began their new duties. Caden, still atop Tucker, smiled and beckoned her.

"I hate this plan, but I can't disagree with it. You're brilliant, you know that?"

"Am I?" she asked, doubting. "I expected others to pitch in with ideas."

Caden chuckled. "I thought I was supposed to be the questioning one. Don't you see? They trust you. Trust yourself."

"I shall try. Thank you." She wanted to climb up to him and share one more kiss before parting, but there wasn't time. Instead, she blew him a kiss and tried to convince herself that she'd have another chance, that this wasn't goodbye, and she would see him again soon. Grabbing one end of the vine phone, she bid farewell with, "Keep in contact, and stay safe."

Opal's wall cracked as some weapon speared it from the other side. She couldn't reinforce it as she continued commanding the bridge into the golden city. Emer snatched the two Ormio sisters by their arms.

"Time to go!"

Chapter 27

DIA

I kept to my usual work schedule that thankfully kept me away from Rindle. In the rare moments when we worked as a replacement for the other, I managed to leave a few minutes early or he arrived late. We still caught each other in passing at times; in the parking lot as he locked his fancy mustang, in the storage room as I discussed new changes with Jay, in the office as I clocked out. Thankfully, in that last instance, he waited until I was done before he entered. In every encounter, Rindle became awkwardly nervous, like he half expected me to shout his real name for no reason at all.

On my next day off, I decided to do a different kind of research. If gold transmutation was possible by accident, there had to be some records of it. Considering my dreams and their similarities to the Rumpelstiltskin tales, I expanded my research into fairytales. They were part of history, and they had to be inspired by some facts, right?

I read over every version of the tale I could find, discovering the tale was factually named after The Miller's Daughter. Also, the mystery man's name changed between four different versions of The Brothers Grimm, naming him Trit-a-Trot, Tom Tit Tot, Terrytop, or Whuppity Stoorie. I laughed a little at that last one. The closest to the English Rumpelstiltskin was a version from France which named him Ricdin-Ricdon.

Considering another historical tale, I expanded my research into the tragedy of King Midas. The Greek legend seemed to fit The Golden Pawn's situation better. I was halfway through the Wikipedia page when someone knocked on the front door.

I frowned, instantly suspicious. Cherie and Steve weren't home to expect visitors, and nobody came to visit me at home. Were my guardians expecting a package?

Checking the peephole, I spied a delivery man in gold clothing with a large golden package at his feet. Did he have the wrong address? I hadn't ordered anything. Especially with a box of that size.

I opened the door. "Hello?"

"Diana Mason?" The middle-aged delivery man read my name off of a gold page.

"I'm Dia," I said.

"This is for you. I'll need you to sign for it."

I scribbled a messy signature and attempted to lift the box. Nope. The delivery man left, shaking out his arms from the release of the heavy box.

Dragging the package over the threshold into the townhouse, I tore off the shiny tape and opened the box. Inside was a collection of fifty small jars, labeled with whole spices. I couldn't believe my eyes at first. There was also a mortar and pestle set for grinding and an extra set of empty jars with resealable lids. Lifting the cinnamon jar, I pulled the lever-lid to reveal five sticks and the sweetest aroma. It smelled like the holidays, as memories of pumpkin pies and homemade cider drinks filled my mind. I closed it reluctantly, then my eyes bulged with disbelief at the jar of saffron. Those little flower stigmas could be worth more than gold! Examining the rest of the collection, I noticed a small yellow note on the side of the box.

"Sorry it's late," the note read. "Congratulations to my favorite Employee of the Month. Stan said you'd mentioned this spice brand as the best. Also, please be patient with me as I work to become a better man."

Tears welled in my eyes. I choked on a sob as gratitude and appreciation filled my heart. He could have given me a Visa gift card like I'd asked, or a gift card and reservation to a fancy Michelin restaurant. Instead, he'd given me something to experiment and learn from, to turn my daily meals into next-level experiences for months to come.

The saffron jar probably cost Rindle more than what he spent on the average employee of the month, and he bought me the entire spice collection. I thought back on our luncheon and mostly remembered his puzzle-solving and the beginning of the transmutation theories. But Rindle had remembered my love for cooking and my hopeless desire to study food science. And Stan had remembered a single conversation when I'd mentioned the best spices and storage supplies.

I couldn't stop the next sob of sweet joy. Hugging the jar of vanilla beans to my chest, I released my ugly cries, suddenly grateful that my guardians weren't home. No one interrupted my moment of utter happiness. As soon as I regained my breath and controlled my tears, I wiped my make-up clean, then called The Golden Pawn.

Brian answered with his usual greeting.

"Brian?" I asked, my voice scratchy from crying. "Who's working today?"

"It's me and Rindle right now. Stan's coming in an hour for the closing shift."

Perfect. I warned him I'd be stopping by, then hung up. I didn't want to wait. Bursting with emotion, I hopped onto my bike and set my jar of vanilla beans into my front basket. The warm air helped to dry my tears as I pedaled like I was late to work.

Arriving at The Golden Pawn, I stepped into the back storage room, then stopped. The entire warehouse was gold. From the shelving to the walls, the

327

power tools, and signed posters—everything was gold. I called out to Brian, but no one answered. I went to the office to search for Brian or Rindle but found it empty. They were probably up front with a customer then.

Remaining in the office, I blinked again at my surroundings. The computer and desk were also gold. Praying it still worked, I pressed on the monitor's power button. It hummed awake, though the screen remained golden. A light shined behind it, but I could barely make out the login screen behind the golden shine. I leaned back, confused, but what could I do about it? Even if I called maintenance, what would they do? Sell the computer for a melt-down price and buy a new one?

I called out for Brian and Rindle again. With no answer, I wondered if I should call tech support about the golden computer. I picked up the work phone, relieved when it still beeped with function. Before I could search for the IT number, Rindle popped his head around the doorway, surprised and confused to find me.

"Dia?" Rindle asked. "Isn't it your day off?"

As if my presence was the only matter of confusion, and all was well in the office of El Dorado.

"What's wrong?" he asked. Did he not see the gold around him? Did that mean these golden visions were false? Was I hallucinating?

He approached me, concerned, but stopped a few feet away. I didn't stop. I'd come to thank him for the gift, but now I craved support and the touch of reality. Holding the vanilla with one hand, I threw my arms around him. I curled my face under his and wept. Eventually, his hands came up to rest on my shoulders.

"Thank you," I whispered. For the tender hug or the spices? I clarified, "For the spices. They're the best gift anyone has ever given me."

He exhaled near my ear and relaxed into the embrace. "You're welcome. You're worth it."

"I don't know about that," I said, shifting away. "I think I'm going crazy."

"What do you mean?"

"Why is everything gold?"

"Gold?" He frowned.

I gestured to the computer and desk only to find that everything—from the shipping boxes to the coffee maker—was now golden. I didn't know whether to step away and spread myself for balance or hold tighter to Rindle for support.

"Everything," I whispered. "Everything is gold! What's happening?"

"What are you—" Rindle looked around his fancy golden office. His eyes widened with fear as he pointed at his golden puzzles. "I swear those were silver just a moment ago."

"Only the puzzles?" I groaned to myself. "*Every-thing* is gold! The carpet, the walls, even the coffee! Why am I the only one who sees it?"

Why couldn't I see colors beyond the metallic yellow? Was it everywhere or just the warehouse and office?

Rindle's face opened with terror at the walls as I ran out to the shopping area to check. Sure enough, the warehouse and computers hadn't been the only "upgraded" sections. Every display case and crack in the flooring was golden. Was it all in my head, or had everything been replaced with gold? No, I'd only been off for one day. The gold couldn't have possibly taken over every single product to buy—from the stereos to the guitars.

I almost didn't notice Brian at the register. I yelped when I did. He was a solid gold statue.

Chapter 28

EMER

Emer, Dot, and Opal ran through the crumbled city of Old Remizio as Pearl commanded the light to fade to shadow. The scene behind them darkened as twilight, then to midnight with a full moon, then no moon.

Dot laughed nervously. "Last time this happened to me, I was running with Garnet and Ruby through the Somnus Forest."

Emer joined in her humor. "I was running away from ogres."

Opal whimpered. "In that case, I hope this is the only time I experience this."

"Sorry," Pearl's voice echoed from Emer's side of the vine phone. "I can stop if—"

"No," multiple voices said. Caden added, "They'll have a devil of a time finding us in this."

Leo said, "It feels cowardly to hide."

"A hunter knows when he has become the prey," Chase said. "Survival instincts are never cowardly."

"Stay safe, Chase," Opal said in return. "Our stone bridge needs support from below, but I think the gold will only transform the moving rocks."

"You think?" Emer asked, voice wavering with worry more than fatigue from their run. They slowed to a stop as they reached the base of Opal's bridge, at the edge of Pearl's darkness and the golden city. Without the shadows to obscure her surroundings, Emer saw with horror every building, plant… and person frozen in gold. Hundreds of human statues stood at the edge with gaping eyes and mouths of terror. Their styles of clothing ranged from ragged to royal throughout the last century. The people rimmed the city as the gold had slowly spread itself with each victim over the past hundred harvests.

Opal cleared her throat. "Stone bridge, please don't let us fall off."

With that, a thin railing curled over the edges of the narrow bridge even as it continued to stretch deeper into the city. Caden had been right about the structure of the bridge. It wouldn't have supported their horses or every person, as it was barely wide enough to let two people walk side-by-side. Afraid of falling off, the princesses walked in single-file with Opal leading and Emer in the rear, dragging the phone vine along.

"Dot," Opal asked, "which way is the castle? I've never visited Remizio."

"Neither have I since the war started before I was old enough to join excursions." She turned toward the sky, then pointed north-east. "See that flock of black birds circling overhead? They're directly over the castle."

Opal nodded and instructed her bridge to expand in that direction.

"Thanks," Emer said. "Have the birds found Dia's location in the castle yet?"

"Not yet," Dot said. "They started on the top floors and have been slowly exploring downward."

They walked carefully along their stone bridge, occasionally glancing back at the massive shadow where they'd left their friends.

"Are you staying safe?" Emer asked through the vine.

Caden whispered back, "Yes, but we're trying to stay quiet in case Olga's soldiers are listening for us."

Dot peered over the railing to gasp at a litter of kittens in an alley. They stood frozen in gold. Dot's leaning crumbled some stones beneath her feet. Emer grabbed for her as she stumbled back. The stones fell from the bridge and broke against the gold streets below, instantly transforming.

Twisting Emer's phrase, Dot panted, "I hope *we* stay safe. Opal, can you build this bridge any faster?"

Her younger sister turned back with frustrated and worried eyes as she continued to mutter instructions to the rocks.

Emer gripped Dot's shoulder. "Her magic is still new to her. Thank you, Opal. Your efforts are wondrous."

Opal smiled thinly with the little boost of confidence, and their pace quickened through the golden city. Their bridge curved through the streets, taking the most direct path to the castle. Song birds frequently landed on the bridge railings, resting from their search for Dia. They were only one bend away from the castle when Dot exclaimed, "They found her! She's in a cellar on the west side."

Opal nodded and began constructing their bridge accordingly. Dot praised her birds with compliments and promises of treats. Emer dared to hope for an easy rescue until they reached the outer wall of the cellar. Pointing at a hole in the golden wall, Emer asked, "Is that the only entrance?" They would need to crawl to fit.

Dot bit her lip. "Um, yes. How are we supposed to reach her without touching the gold?"

Opal mimicked her sister's worried expression. "Maybe I could line the opening with stone?"

Emer shook her head. "That would make the hole significantly smaller."

"Lucky for you, I'm small," Opal said.

Emer folded her arms. "But if you accidentally touch the gold, then Dot and I are trapped here. We need you in order to leave the city if Dia's curse remains."

Opal, again, mimicked Emer's posture. "We didn't come all this way to turn back. My magic works on rocks, right? Isn't gold another form of rocks?"

Emer grimaced, unsure of the technical answer. It wouldn't hurt to try. "Can you control the gold?"

"Um," Opal shuffled. "Gold stones surrounding the hole in this wall, can you make the hole larger?"

Nothing happened. Emer huffed. "It seems that gold is too much of a mineral. How do we go through?"

"Try lining it with dirt," Dot suggested.

Opal swallowed and began to instruct her rocks. They crumbled to small stones, pebbles, then fine dirt and reached down from their bridge to the hole in the wall. As soon as its bottom touched the gold, all moving pieces transformed.

"Create a frame," Emer instructed, "then connect it to the edges of the hole by filling in the gaps."

Opal nodded and changed her wording to build a small square that would fit within the opening. She stabilized it with supports below as it tunneled through the hole in the wall. Emer crouched to check that the tunnel reached the other side without turning to gold but cringed at the results.

"Opal, only you will fit through that."

"I know," she said. "I'm just the right size."

Dot blinked at her younger sister, then pulled her into a hug. "Though I'm happy that you've grown more daring from your dreams, be careful. I cannot lose you too."

The youngest Ormio princess gulped and nodded, then crouched down to her belly to slide down the bridge to the hole. "Careful," Dot urged. "Better safe than sorry. Take it slowly."

"I know," Opal said through gritted teeth. Emer and Dot crouched to watch her progress into the dirt tunnel.

"What do you see?" Emer asked. "Is Dia inside?"

"I see, um, wow, a lot of gold yarn. Mounds and mounds of gold yarn." She crept farther, her head disappearing from view as the tunnel swallowed her. "The room isn't large, but it's pretty full with yarn, spiraled like giant hay bales and draping down the walls. Hold on, I think I see—it's Dia!"

"Dia!" Dot shouted.

"She's… There's someone with her, but I don't recognize him. I don't know if I can reach them. Maybe I can try something."

"Be careful, Opal," Dot warned.

"I'm just…maybe if I—Words," she cursed. Dot's face slipped into a reprimand for her language, but Emer's blanched. Her worst fears were confirmed as Opal began screaming.

"Dia! Wake up, Dia! It's turning me into gold!"

Chapter 29

DIA

"Brian!"

The store boss didn't respond. He remained frozen at the register, forever holding his finger against the touch screen.

Rindle joined me in the hallway. "Whoa! Brian?"

I turned on him. "You see him? Is he golden to your vision too?"

"Yes," Rindle said. "And the office is too. Either your sickness in seeing gold is spreading to me, or the walls and coffee listened to your words to transmute as you said it. What happened to Brian?"

"I don't know. This is the first time it's taken something alive. Do you see the rest of this room as gold?"

Rindle shook his head. "Everything's normal except Brian. And the entire office. What do you mean 'this is the first time?' Do you know what's happening? Is he still alive? Can we save him?"

"I don't know!" I shouted. "This is supposed to be impossible. Things don't just transform into gold! I'm no King Midas. Even if I was The Miller's Daughter, she wasn't the one to spin the straw into gold. It was Tom-Tit-Tot who factually performed the magic." I couldn't help the subconscious glance at Rindle, the man who played Riddle Maker or the figurative Rumpelstiltskin in my dreams. He was the one to "transform" the straw into gold, even if it was by trickery.

He caught the look and underlying accusation. "What?"

"It's you. It has to be you! You're the one doing this!"

"What?" he shouted and backed away. "I have no idea what you're talking about. You were the one saying you've seen this before."

"I thought I was just going crazy—too stressed, not enough sleep, working too hard. But you were the one who suggested we turn straw into gold—"

"What?"

"—These stupid dreams are driving me crazy. I couldn't turn anything to gold before, so why would I now? I need to stop these dreams. Everything and everyone in this building is turning into gold."

"Dia!"

Who was that? The voice called to me like a distant memory.

"Wake up, Dia!"

I knew that voice. How? From a dream?

"It's turning me into gold!"

338

"Dia! Please, can you hear us, Dia?"

Another familiar voice, female, similar to the first. Similar to my own. My family?

Sisters! My sisters! And friends! From my dreams? Goodness gracious, I really was going crazy.

Rindle waved his hand in front of my face. "Dia? Are you okay?"

I moaned and grabbed my head. "And now I'm hearing voices. But I think they want to help."

"Please, wake up, Dia, and stop this curse!"

A third voice. One of my friends? Where were they? Why were they telling me to wake up? I was awake. My fast-beating heart was proof of that.

"This isn't working," one sister cried. I recognized that voice if only from a dream. My sister, Dot! Garnet had said she'd been poisoned, but she sounded fine—asking me to wake.

"How do we wake her?"

"I don't know. How did you wake up?" a younger sister asked. Opal? My heart plummeted with relief and sadness from hearing her. Did that mean she was awake too? Except hers was the voice that cried about turning into gold.

My friend huffed, *"I woke up as I nearly died in my dream."*

That didn't sound like a good idea. I paced back and forth, struggling for a solution and coming up empty.

"How did you wake up?" Dot asked.

"I discovered my rock magic to fight my shadow monster hallucinations, then, um, Chase kissed me." None of that made sense. Magic? Shadow monsters? Maybe I could relate to the hallucinations, but who was Chase? Shouldn't I know my sister's boyfriends? How had I missed my youngest sister's first kiss?

"I guess that's right. Caden kissed me right as I was dying in my dream."

"I woke with a kiss from Leo. But if all it takes is a kiss, then why didn't Ruby wake when she kissed Leo before I did?"

"I kissed multiple people," Opal's crying voice confessed. *"That's why I was so ashamed to tell you about my dream. It was only when Chase kissed me that I woke."* Wait—she kissed multiple people? Apparently, we had a lot of catching up to do. *"Oh Dia, please wake up! The gold is almost to my heart!"*

"Then only true love's kiss breaks the spell?"

"Dia! Have you dreamt of your true love? Is Stanford with you?"

"Yes, find Stanford! We heard of your attempt to win his affections. Did you end up falling in love with him?"

"Dia?" Rindle asked. "You spaced out on me again. Care to clue me in?"

"I—" I stuttered. "They're telling me to find Stan." I wasn't sure whether to squirm or blush as I added, "They think I should kiss him."

Rindle snorted. "How's that supposed to help any of this?"

"I don't know, but he should be arriving soon for his shift." I nearly grabbed Rindle by the hand to pull him to the storage room, but hesitated. "Just in case one of us is the cause of this, we probably shouldn't touch."

"Um, kay?"

"King Midas. If we touch, one of us might turn into gold. I vote not me."

He smirked. "Then that would make you the cause, wouldn't it?"

"Whatever, there isn't time to debate." Even if I was somehow the cause, I didn't know how I did it or how to make it stop. I wanted to make it stop. I wished to the heavens to make it stop as Dot and my friend screamed Opal's name. Opal. My youngest sister. Even if she was only a dream or hallucination, I didn't want to lose her.

Rindle thought it wise to temporarily close the store, locking the front door and turning off the neon OPEN sign. Meanwhile, I studied Brian, his patterned clothing, and terrified expression. Like Opal's transmutation, it hadn't been instant. He'd felt and anticipated the transformation as it spread through him.

With Rindle close behind, I ran to the storage room. The curtain had changed to golden drapery. Rindle paused at the open door to the office.

"What the? What's with the computer? And the shelving in here. Who makes golden shelves?"

"You see them? Good. I really hope Stan isn't late because he turned into gold."

"Why? Does he know what's going on?"

"Doubtful," I muttered.

Speaking of the devil, the back door of the storage room opened. Stan appeared around the frame and stared wide-eyed at the golden walls and products. The longer he stared, the more his mouth dropped.

"Stan," I called, and his eyes snapped to mine.

"Dia?" He ran to meet me halfway through the room, grabbed my arms, and pulled me into a hug. That debunked my King Midas worries.

"What's going on? What are you doing here? I thought it was your day off. Why and how is everything turning to gold? It's spreading like some mad scientist unleashed the sorcerer's stone on us!" Philosopher's stone, but now wasn't the time to nitpick words.

I pulled away to look him squarely in the eyes. "Then you don't know what's going on? The voices in my head say that you can help us solve this."

"What?" Stan blinked and screwed his expression into confusion.

"These voices in your head," Rindle said, "why are you the only one who can hear them? I think that indicates you to be the mad scientist."

"I am not!" I automatically defended, then reconsidered. "But it might be my fault. Apparently, true love's kiss can cure this curse. My sisters say—"

"Dia…"

I followed Rindle's concerned voice to his attention on his feet. They were transforming to gold.

"I can't feel my toes," he panicked. "You're seriously turning me into gold? You did this to Brian?"

The pain in his eyes broke my heart.

"No—no! I can't be the cause of this! I don't know what I'm doing! I don't know how to stop it! Wait—Stan! I just need to kiss him like he's my true love or something, and it'll fix everything, right?"

Rindle grimaced. Was his discomfort from the growth of gold up his ankles, or from the mention of Stan as my true love?

My eyes met Stan's.

He blinked his surprised eyes. Yeah, I doubted he'd woken up that morning expecting this to be his work day. *Welcome! Everything is turning gold! Now, kiss your co-worker to save the store and everyone inside!*

"True love?" Stan asked. "I mean, I care about you, Dia. A lot. I've even had these dreams lately…"

He drifted like he didn't want to explain, but I needed to know.

"Stan? What dreams?"

He shrugged. "They're just crazy dreams, right? You wanted to turn straw into gold like you were some fairytale—"

"Princess?" Rindle finished.

I bit my lip, unsure whether to be terrified or relieved that I wasn't the only crazy one. "Prince

Stanford?" I directed at Stan, and he flinched like I'd insulted him. To Rindle, I asked, "Riddle Maker?"

Rindle's face drained of color even as the gold reached up his feet. He swore. "That's how you learned my name? How you knew that weird pronunciation?"

Stan frowned at Rindle. "I don't remember seeing you in the dreams."

Rindle's painful grimace twisted with a smirk. "That's because I didn't want you to see me."

"Dia, quick! Opal's bridge is collapsing! If we fall, the gold will transform us!"

"Alright, guys," I said. "Now that we're all on the same page, you might recognize the voices in my head as the other princesses. My sisters, Opal and Dot. You might have known them as Lucky and Feathers from the Noz Isle masquerades. I think they're joined by my friend, Emer, from Somnus. Flora?"

Rindle scoffed. "I knew you were Gold, but my dream self refused to—gagh!" He cried in agony as the gold grew over his knees.

Stan cringed with sympathy. "I don't know if we're true love, but I'm willing to give it a shot."

I stepped up to Stan. Was that it? One kiss to stop this madness? One kiss to save my forgotten sisters? One kiss to save Rindle and Brian? Stan took my hands in his and nervously bit the inside of his cheek.

"You've been the best of friends to me," I said. "And you're a good man."

Rindle groaned with pain. "Kiss him fast or don't kiss at all. Heaven knows I'll be miserable, anyway."

"Rindle?"

"Don't look so surprised, Dia," he muttered. "I never tried to hide my feelings from you."

"Rin—"

"Dia!"

"Dia?" Stan piped in. "I never wanted to rush a relationship, but if you say a kiss will stop it, we should probably…"

"Gagh!" Rindle cried. His legs were entirely gold.

I turned back to Stan, my heart screaming in my chest.

He squeezed my hands. "It's your choice, Dia."

He really was a good man.

Tears streamed down my cheeks as I threw my arms around the man I loved and pressed my lips to his.

After a second to recover from his shock, Rindle kissed me back.

I became lost in the sensation of his arms around me and his lips against mine. I had forgotten the sensation of touching reality. My mind had pulled in memories to fill in my gaps of dreaming. For the first time in so long, I felt real. I felt awake. I felt alive. Kissing Rindle overwhelmed my senses. Everything about him was real—from the softness of his facial hair to the scent of dryer sheets on his collar. He was passionate, like I expected, but also unpredictable as he kissed me hard, then soft, excited, then relieved.

The world shifted around me, but I didn't pull away until I heard the voices from my dreams calling.

"Opal! Dia! Are you alright?"

I opened my eyes to find myself and Rindle lying on a pile of yellow yarn in a stone room that was crowded with giant balls of more yellow yarn. Two women in fine clothes that had seen too many days in the woods and deserts crawled from a hole in the stone wall. They embraced a younger woman who stood at the entrance, gold melting away from her feet. They were all women from my dreams. No, not dreams. Memories.

"Oh!" Opal—my youngest sister!—accepted the embrace, but searched for me across the room. "She's awake! What happened?"

"The castle is no longer golden," my friend said, awed and excited, like a castle turning from gold to stone was equally as impressive as turning stone to gold. "I shall check outside and call for the others."

"It's real," a voice whispered beside me. Rindle lay on his back, staring at every single stone and trail of yarn. My two memories collided, throwing me back like whiplash. Something similar must have happened to Rindle as he moaned and palmed his forehead. I bit my lip and reached for Rindle's hand.

"Welcome home."

"Home? Weird. Oh." Rindle grimaced and cursed. "Looks like I'll never get to be assistant manager, and I'm going to miss that car. Dia, did we have to wake up?"

I ducked my head and bit harder on my lip. "I'm sorry. You lost everything."

His eyes lit with a tease as his lips lifted in a flirtatious grin. "Did I?"

He pulled me in for another kiss. I kissed him back with relief. He traded a life of comfort and luxury for a relationship with me. I would make sure he never regretted it.

Chapter 30

DIA

Dia sat at the spinning wheel bench and rubbed her temples as her two worlds collided. Opal and Dot had embraced her with tears until they were joined by Emer, Marin, and Pearl. They were accompanied by Marin's husband and four other men.

A man who introduced himself as Prince Caden Seaver of Uldra explained, "Our time is short as we have a few hundred people outside who have a lot of the same questions that you probably have."

Dia shook her head. "I can't believe you're all here. Factually, I can't believe *I'm* here. Las Vegas felt so real. And you say that a hundred harvests have passed? And that little pipsqueak Tanzi is queen over the whole valley?"

Marin sat next to her and took her hand. "I know. It is a lot to take in. What do you remember of the days before you were put to sleep?"

Dia cringed. "I was an idiot. Desperation makes fools of us all. After Opal was lost, I ran to Remizio with Garnet and Cephas, hoping to build a treaty. As heir of Ormio, my parents demanded that I marry and strengthen the kingdom. You remember how I was back then? The last thing on my mind was romance. But Somnus had fallen, my sisters were in comas, and Prince Stanford was pitching offers. I was desperate to win his alliance. Especially when Sapphire was—" A thought struck her. "Sapphire! Could she be under the same spell?"

Opal perked up. "You know where Sapphire is?"

"She's here, in Remizio. She's—" Dia's heart sank as she remembered the Huiess princess's condition. "They buried her."

Opal gasped as everyone else was stunned to silence.

"Could she…" Emer began, but seemed unable to finish.

"We have to try," Opal said. "It wouldn't be the same without her. Besides, she might know more about the other Huiess princesses."

Dia shook her head. "Unlikely. She was killed the day before I was put to sleep. Garnet made plans to escape to Levamen with my brother and the other Huiess princesses, but we stayed one more night to complete our competition and settle on a united treaty. I also wanted to win my bet with Riddle Maker." She stole a small smile at the quiet man in the shadows. She earned several odd looks from that, but Dia wasn't sure if the looks were from her uncharacteristically romantic smile, or the fact that anyone could smile fondly at

Riddle Maker. They had no idea what kind of man he was, but that wasn't their fault. Lord Hróðvaldr was difficult to understand and let very few enter his confidence. Dia blushed to think that she earned that honor, though her blush enhanced the incredulous looks in her direction.

"So," Prince Caden said, "the Crown Princesses Garnet and Amethyst went to Levamen? Is that where we're headed?" He looked at Emer and his fellow princes. Dia had mentally repeated their names as they'd been introduced to help her remember. She never wanted to forget anything or anyone again.

Opal folded her arms. "I'm not leaving Remizio until we find Sapphire first. She might be sleeping like the rest of us were."

"Great," Hróðvaldr chuckled darkly from the shadows. "I always wanted an excuse to grave rob."

Dia pinched back her laugh as those close enough to hear answered him with a sour look.

Caden—not close enough to hear—shrugged. "Each of you were preserved from Princess Garnet's sleeping spell. So, all we'll need to do to confirm is… open her casket."

Marin shuddered. "I may stand in the back for that."

"Perhaps she was preserved in a glass coffin as I was," Pearl said, then leaned down to peer through the wall hole. "The people are gathering. With our personal experiences of waking up to this new Rezhina, we should be the first people to explain their situation."
350

"Agreed," Caden said. "It also won't hurt to gain their loyalty before Chieftess Olga and Queen Tanzanite call us traitors."

They began to filter out of the cellar, but Dia remained seated on her wooden bench with Marin beside her and Hróðvaldr in the shadows. The princesses sat in silence for a moment, Marin rubbing Dia's back with soft and encouraging strokes.

A grunted cough startled them in Hróðvaldr's direction. "Aren't you leaving?" he asked Marin.

"Excuse me?" Marin asked, her eyebrows high.

"I thought it was obvious that Dia and I've got a lot to discuss."

Dia's cheeks burned pink, and Marin's eyebrows arched higher. She looked to Dia for confirmation. Still burning with uncharacteristic shyness, Dia answered with a nervous little nod.

"Huh," Marin guffawed, but stood to leave. Her baffled expression remained as she left to join the others.

Alone with Hróðvaldr, Dia asked, "Why do you hate your name?"

He gave a half shrug. "Nobody can say it right, especially my Rezhina version. It's easier to go by aliases. They let me be whoever I want."

Dia nodded sadly. "I can understand the limitations that come with titles. What name would you like me to use for you?"

"You?" He flashed her with crazy eyes. "Hot Sauce Rapscallion Casanova."

She fingered her chin, pretending to take him seriously. "No, that's far too many syllables. How would I shorten it when I'm angry with you? Hotty? Maybe if it's spelled as H-A-U-G-H-T-Y that could be appropriate for you."

He chuckled. "Most people here know me as Riddle Maker, but I liked it when you called me Rindle."

"In that case, Rindle, will you sit with me?"

Like a stealthy cat, Rindle glided from the shadows to sit beside Dia. Before he even settled onto the bench, Dia grabbed his vest lapels and latched her mouth over his.

"Dia!" Rindle laughed. "I said that we've got a lot to discuss."

"It can wait," she said, roaming her hands around his neck and down his back.

"Will you hear my elevator pitch?" he asked between kisses. "I love you, and I can't believe you chose me."

"Of course," she said against his cheek.

"I even chickened out from our bargain. I learned your masquerade name after meeting in the temple, but you'd already captured my interest. Having a front-row seat to your marriage with Stanford would have made me miserable. I couldn't let myself win, so I hoped you'd never guess my name and that we'd end with a draw."

352

"That's exactly why I gambled on your banishment. I was in love with you even then. I didn't understand it, but I knew that I could never see you again if I was to remain loyal to Prince Stanford."

"Oh, Dia," he whispered into her neck. "We were such fools."

She tittered, stroking her fingers through his hair. "Apparently, it took some Las Vegas perspectives for us to see each other straight."

As if to prove her correct, Rindle raised himself to meet her gaze straight on, then lowered again to catch her with breathtaking kisses.

He set her heart on fire. No man ever made her feel so alive—so needy.

A yelp at the cellar doorway distracted their attention. Dia caught the departing colors of a turquoise dress and sounds of scampering footsteps.

Dia sighed to slow down her quick breathing. "Slander it all. Welcome back to royalty life, where my love life is everybody's business and scrutinized with mannerisms."

"Ugh." Rindle collapsed to become a dead weight on her shoulders. "The many reasons I lived under my alias…"

"Rindle." Dia laughed, bouncing him lightly.

He shifted his arms to hug her like a favorite pillow. "I've waited too long for this moment to let go of you now."

"I know the feeling," she said, pressing a kiss to his temple. "I daydreamed of your passion when we were dreaming. Now, we're awake and it's better than I imagined." She held onto Rindle and the mere sensation of his affections. She chose Rindle and had no regrets. "Just five more minutes," she whispered, "but then I will need to stand. This bench is really uncomfortable."

Rindle chuckled in her ear and held her tighter. "Five more minutes."

Eight minutes later, Marin returned with her husband in tow at the cellar's doorway, finding them still on the uncomfortable bench. While Marin's expression could rival a storm, Ranae gave them a thumbs up.

"Ranae!" Marin backhanded his arm. "We are not encouraging this!"

"We are not encouraging love?" her husband asked, confused.

"Not without restraint!"

"Marin," Dia snapped. "I kissed him first. And just because Rindle's not a dispassionate bore like the rest of you doesn't mean that he's a wild hog."

Rindle bent close to loudly whisper, "I could be a wild hog if you wanted."

Dia bit her lips inward to keep from laughing, though her heated cheeks said enough about her humor.

Marin gasped and fumed. "Ranae, please remove Riddle Maker. I do not care where. Just try to talk some sense into him somewhere else. Such language is not appropriate in front of royalty above his station."

Dia scowled, tempted to reveal Lord Hróðvaldr's true station despite his wishes.

"Sure," Admiral Ranae said. Stepping over to Rindle, he spoke quietly, "You can talk that way all you want around other scoundrels like a navy admiral." He added a wink, then said loudly, "Come on. Shall we grab a drink? I want to hear all about your dream."

Rindle rolled his eyes but followed him out with a secretive smile at Dia. As soon as they stepped away, Dia glared at Marin. "You're not my mother."

"No. Surely your mother would be even more appalled. Did you forget that you are Ormio's heir? Your younger sisters look up to you! Your people should look up to you!"

"They're no longer my people," Dia said. "I don't know what happened in your dreams, but I did forget those exact things. I became a working-class American, and I thrived. I was a commoner who proved my worth with my own intellect. I had a GPA and SAT score to earn a scholarship to—oh, you don't know what I'm saying. My point is, I chose my path, and I chose Rindle."

"Maybe in your dream, though now that you have returned—"

"No," Dia cut off Marin's words. "I love Rindle. I never wanted a powdered gentleman who put me on a pedestal. Rindle doesn't treat me like I'm fragile. He challenges me. He makes me proud of who I am—even when I'm not a princess—and makes me want to improve as he works to improve."

Marin stared back, confused. "Wha-what about your people?"

Dia shook her head. "Ormio hasn't existed for a hundred years. The people I wanted to serve—the young boys in the army, the little girls with their donation baskets—they're long gone. I don't know the people who live there now. I can't be a queen to strangers."

Marin's confused expression didn't leave. "Forgive me. I do not understand."

Dia sighed. "I don't expect you to."

Marin winced from the unintentional jab. "Would your response be the same if my words came from Ame or Garnet?"

Dia frowned, taking her own turn to be confused.

"I know you were closer to Ame, and you always listened to my older sister."

Dia shook her head. "No, they wouldn't change my mind, either."

Marin sighed. "Then no one would. I suppose your heart is settled. Shall we join the others? We have a sudden humanitarian effort to aid everyone else who woke up with you."

Dia followed Marin up the stairs, around corridors that were exactly as she remembered them, and to the great hall. They stepped through and shattered Dia's expectations.

While the sand palace was exactly as she remembered it, its largest banquet hall was stuffed with several hundred people sitting at stone tables on stone chairs. A dozen lights lit the room from above like the buildings in Las Vegas. A large pig roasted over a long fire trench, and vines blooming with fruit and leafy greens streamed down like table runners.

Dia gawked. "I don't remember those being here before I fell asleep."

"The people?" Marin asked. "Most of them are residents from Remizio when your curse took over. The others were trapped by the curse of gold over the years."

"Okay, now I have more questions," Dia said, "because I was initially talking about the lights and—are those plants moving?"

Caden, ever recording notes, chuckled from a wooden desk and stool that continued to grow leaves. "That's because they weren't here until ten minutes ago. Every princess gained a power in their dreams. Princess Pearl created the lights, your youngest sister created the stone tables and seating, Princess Aquamarine provided the drinking water, Emer's growing the fruits and vegetables, then Princess Peridot found a pig who'd eaten shards of—er, suffice it to say he was on the brink of death, anyway. If we had the power to make dough, then we'd have a full meal."

Lights, stone, water, plants, and animals. "They gained the power to influence these in their dreams?" Dia pondered aloud. She found Rindle at a table with Ranae and recalled the transmutations of her own dream. A scripture whispered through Dia's mind like a memory of the many times she helped pass out food with her sisters at the Veriae temple.

She quoted, "Seeing the need of the people, the Word of Materials spoke and turned stone to bread."

"What was that?" Caden asked.

Rather than answer him, she considered the impossibility yet insane probabilities of an experiment. Sliding her hand across the back of a stone chair, she whispered, "Become bread."

Starting from the trail left by her fingers, the stone began to transform. Marin gaped. Caden's eyes couldn't be big enough to witness, as his hands couldn't be fast enough to record the miracle before them.

Within the minute, the stone chair became a statue of bread.

"Whoa." A young man holding hands with Pearl skipped over to the edible chair and broke off a piece of the back. The crust crunched in his fingers, but the insides were fluffy and soft. He grinned at Pearl. "I'd offer you some, but I know how you feel about suspicious foods." Then he popped the piece into his mouth, chewed, and swallowed. "Looks like I'm the first man to eat a chair. And it was delicious! How did you do that?"

Dia blinked, still a little unsure herself, but as she spoke, the words came naturally and felt like truth. "You all have powers of the Words that created the world. I transmuted objects into gold. That's the power of changing materials."

"Still," Mica said, taking another bite of chair. This time, Pearl accepted a piece. "It's brilliant."

Marin, oddly, groaned and slid her face into her palm. "Then we truly are blasphemy in the flesh."

Before Dia could ask for clarification, a new voice called her name. Upon finding the speaker, Dia blushed with embarrassment.

"Prince Stanford. You were captured by the golden curse?"

He rubbed the side of his head. "Yes. Is what they say true? A whole century has past?"

Dia gave him a sad smile. "It seems so. It felt like only a few months, but… I don't know the affairs of your kingdom anymore. If it's anything like mine, a lot has changed."

The Urbanuz Prince gulped and nodded. "Yet, somehow, we were preserved. Is Ame with you?"

Dia turned to Emer who shook her head. "No. She must have left with Garnet and the others before the curse took over."

Stanford nodded. "She told me that she was leaving for Levamen with Topaz. Is that where you're all headed?"

"After we check on Sapphire, yes."

"Sapphire… Ame's little sister." He nodded again, as if reassuring himself of his memories. Then, with a determined head bounce, he met Dia's eyes. "I want to go with you to find Ame."

Dia smiled, hopeful. If true love broke their curses… "She might be waiting for you."

Epilogue

TANZI

"They did what?" Queen Tanzanite shouted at her magic mirror. From the other side of the glass, Chieftess Olga of New Remizio didn't shrink before the queen's anger, but responded with her own fury.

"Everyone from Old Remizio is awake! I have no idea how they did it! They must have used witchcraft and dark sorcery. I tried playing the part you said— to gain their confidence, but they were some of my rudest guests. I treated them with my best delicacies, and half of them barely even ate! They might have planned to attack me all along, as they were prepared to meet my guards after your command to kill them. Then, they used sorcery to build walls of ice and stone to block my men."

"Sorcery?" Though that possibility didn't bode well, it did explain the strange curses that surrounded and protected their bodies all these years. After her huntsman's first attempts against her sisters, he'd returned with excuses about plants acting oddly to protect them. Was this the cause?

"Yes, Your Majesty. They built walls of ice and stone in a matter of seconds. They even made a great shadow to hide from my soldiers and somehow trespassed into the golden city without being turned. Then, as I said, they broke the curse on the golden city. It must be sorcery. I expect your huntsman knows more, as he seemed to succeed where I failed."

"My huntsman?" Tanzanite hadn't heard anything from Chase for the past week, but she expected his silence came from the shame of not yet completing his duties.

"Yes. He came and went with their company. Your Majesty is wise and cunning, as always. As soon as I recognized the traitors for their true identities, I understood your clever ploy to have your huntsman join them to learn their plans and secrets. If Your Majesty wishes to use me or my people to exploit their hidden weaknesses, you need only to say the word."

The queen clenched her jaw to restrain her surprise and confusion. She'd ordered Chase to kill them, not spy on them. Did he think himself incapable of killing them without studying them first? He was a hunter, after all, a man who studied his prey to anticipate their habits and reactions before he struck.

The Queen of Rezhina stood tall before the chieftess. "Yes, you may be assured that the traitors will be dealt with. Keep your concerns focused on recruiting and training the army. If the golden city has truly awoken, then you may find yourself with a surplus of people from across the past century. Huiess has always been a land of warriors, and I expect you to recruit them. The ogres have broken their treaty, and since their royalty has abandoned them, the northern kingdoms need our aid."

Olga smiled darkly. "They will find themselves in debt to us. I can think of more than a few ways they can repay Your Majesty's kindness."

Tanzanite bit back her smile. She liked the way Olga thought, but she couldn't be sure that no one else was watching or listening to their conversation. "We march as humanitarians, not as conquerors. Though our soldiers will be rightfully rewarded for serving their duty."

The chieftess bowed. "Serving Your Majesty is reward enough."

"Then that is all I need from you. For now."

With final respects, the queen closed their communications, then commanded her mirror. "Locate Chase Bahr."

The mirror reflected a scene centered on her huntsman. He sat at a wooden table covered with a banquet. The queen didn't recognize his surroundings. His face was turned as if listening to someone.

"Mirror, widen your view."

The focus stepped back, revealing Chase's dining companions as Opal of Ormio and a large man. Tanzanite squinted at the man. Take away the beard and a couple of years, and he could be Chase's twin. Was this the older brother he mentioned? Opal said something inaudible that made Chase laugh and Tanzanite grind her teeth.

"Open communications with Chase Bahr." She waited a second for the mirror to work its magic, then forced herself to wear a knowing smile. She purred, "Huntsssman."

Chase's smile froze, and his eyes widened. "Excuse me," he muttered to his companions and left the table. Walking down the long aisle between banquet tables, he murmured, "Your Majesty?"

"Who else would it be?"

"Forgive me, I cannot speak openly—"

"Chase?" another voice called out to him from beyond the mirror's sight.

Chase waved to the unseen speaker. "I'm going to check on the horses."

"Good idea. Do you want Dot to go with you?"

"Naw, it's fine. She can stay to enjoy her sister's reunion." He stepped away, nodding to a few others as he passed through the large doorway of the great hall. The wide angle revealed the sand-carved walls and flooring of mosaic tiles. The queen had only glimpsed Old Remizio at night while dealing with Dia, but its palace seemed perfectly preserved by its golden

364

days. A long-forgotten piece of nostalgia wanted to visit and explore the city from the past.

Alone in the corridors, Chase whispered, "Forgive me, Your Highness, for my silence."

"Surely, you have a good reason that does not add a 'T' to 'reason.'"

"No," he said, urgently. "Never. My loyalties are to you, but I have gained the trust of your enemies. I've seen what they can do and have learned their fears."

Queen Tanzanite smiled. She wouldn't let her huntsman escape without punishment, but for the moment, she'd accept his information.

"Tell me everything."

End of Book Four

Acknowledgements

Oddly enough, when I first began exploring this series, I started in *Dreaming Beauty* then jumped right to this one. I think it's no small coincidence that I had finished my first draft (for the final time) of *Don't Marry the Cursed* (with its multiple Grimms retellings) in the same month I felt inspired in Dia's retelling of "The Miller's Daughter," by Brothers Grimm. This book was a quarter written before I even started on *Fairest and the Frog,* but unfortunately, it didn't age well. Almost all that had been written needed to be re-written. Then, it ended up as my longest.

A huge thanks goes to Julie Carpenter for helping with the developmental edit. With almost four years between starting and finishing the first draft of this book, it had a lot of continuity errors that she helped to check and sort.

Also, massive thanks go to my Alpha Readers, Robyn Aimee and Jim Doran, with their insightful comments to make the stories more believable. I've said it before, and I'll say it again; authors make the best readers, and I'll happily promote their loveable books.

Despite the time constraints, my Beta Readers still gave me their best feedback. Thank you, Ami Jacobs,

Bettilee Hunt, and Colleen Dowda! Your comments give me the confidence to publish.

For my last edit of proofreads, I give thanks to Enchanted Quill Press. Thanks for putting my commas where they belong without breaking my bank.

As for my third Alpha Reader and ever-supporting husband, thank you, Michael, for your love and encouragement to write every day. I couldn't do this without you.

Finally, I thank God, my Eternal Father. Every time I meet a goal and deadline is a testament to me that He hears and answers prayers.

About the Author

C Rae D'Arc has been involved in every stage of a book's life. As a writer, editor, retailer, reader, and reviewer, she has worked four part-time jobs at once. Thankfully, one of them actually paid her. She received her Bachelors in English from Brigham Young University, where she studied ASL, British and American literature, folklore, Shakespeare, and West European fairy tales. She now lives in the Tri-Cities of Washington with her husband and Aussie dog.

PS. To save you from hiccups, D'Arc only has one syllable.

www.craedarc.com
www.facebook.com/c.rae.darc
www.instagram.com/craedarc